ALSO BY GENE DESROCHERS

Dark Paradise
Sweet Paradise
The West Indian Manner

PRAISE FOR *CRIME PARADISE*

"Crime Paradise is the latest entry in the Boise Montague series by talented author, Gene Desrochers. Charged with multiple murders, the intrepid private investigator faces his greatest professional and personal challenges as he fights for his life. Agendas abound. Filled with heart-stopping tension and an array of characters who could flummox a platoon of saints, this murder mystery bounces from St. Thomas, Virgin Islands to Los Angeles as we follow Boise's quest to prove his innocence. Ultimately, he must confront the complexity of his own past, not simply the pasts of three murdered innocents. The Caribbean Noir roller coaster ride continues for Boise Montague in Crime Paradise, book three of his compelling series."
--Laura Taylor - 6-Time Romantic Times Award Winner

"After a wild night, Boise Montague is accused of a murder he didn't commit…or did he? Gene Desrochers once again scores with this compulsively readable tale which takes the reader from the sands of St. Thomas to the streets of Los Angeles and beyond as Boise runs from his past, but cannot hide."
--R. D. Kardon, award-winning author of *The Flygirl Trilogy*

"As finely crafted a mystery as they come! *Crime Paradise* takes the reader on a ride through the gritty backroads and underbelly of what most statesiders consider paradise. Gene Desrochers' intimate knowledge of the real Virgin Islands and their people make this the most authentic novel series I've ever read, for both the physical settings and the culture. This third book is the capstone, thus far, with even more action, red herrings, and "oh my gosh" moments as Boise's choices put him in greater danger than ever before. An excellent read, and highly recommended!"
--Thomas M. Wing, author of *Against All Enemies*

CRIME PARADISE

GENE DESROCHERS

Crime Paradise
First Edition

For information, address Acorn Publishing, LLC, 3943 Irvine Blvd. Ste. 218, Irvine, CA 92602

Cover design by Damonza

www.acornpublishingllc.com

ISBN-13: 979-8-88528-072-3 (Hardcover)
ISBN-13: 979-8-88528-071-6 (Paperback)
Library of Congress Control Number: 2023911193

CHAPTER 1

A couple wandered into Bob's Store, where I'd been working to make extra cash. They selected a pair of matching two-dollar t-shirts from the large wooden bin fronting a wall of souvenirs adorned with "St. Thomas, Virgin Islands".

"See ya, Wendel," I yelled. "Heading out." I checked back on the couple. The husband was busy admiring his wife's tits as she held the t-shirt over her bikini top.

Wendel appeared from behind rows of boxes where he kept a table to examine his latest estate sales purchases. Tuffs of charcoal hair appeared all over his body and head like puffs of smoke expelling from pinpricks in his mottled brown skin. He sounded annoyed. "Leaving so soon, Boise? Thought I had you till five."

"Reggae concert, remember?"

He scratched his scraggly head and burped. The couple's perfect smiles faltered momentarily, then reappeared like a nasty case of the clap.

"Right, right. Don't get too plastered, dude. I need you tomorrow. I gotta head down to Sub Base for a delivery."

***

I hitched a ride in the back of a pickup headed east. From the cab, an old man and his wife smiled over their shoulders as I clambered into the truck bed. His arm draped over her shoulders.

Through the open rear window, I asked, "How long you two been married?"

"Forty-three years," the woman said, beaming.

As I jostled around, I tried to imagine my wife's smile. My wife's breasts. Both were getting harder to remember. It didn't matter. If she hadn't died, we'd be divorced. Either way, marriage was a Rube Goldberg Machine. Complicated. Pointless. Evelyn had been my first and last.

The couple dropped me off in front of the concert tent. "Have a blessed time at the show," the woman chimed. She had close-cropped hair and freckles like my mother.

Patrice had not wanted me to marry Evelyn. To her credit, my mother never said, "I warned you," even after we found out Evelyn had cheated. Maybe it was because my wife had been killed the same day.

Yarey patted me on the back.

"What you thinking about?" she asked over the boom of the band.

Nice girl. Fun. Uncomplicated. Not interested in marriage … I presumed. We met on my last case, bonding over common trauma. Bad fathers. Hers a little worse than mine … maybe.

Yarey hummed along to the music. Perfect pitch. She wasn't a lead singer though. But, she loved it and wanted being a singer, even if she wound up being a back-up, forever in the shadows. I didn't love anything the way she loved singing.

"Nothing. Just zoning out to the music."

2

She shot me a skeptical glance, then continued humming along until the song ended. People danced on clouds of smoke.

Evelyn and I smoked weed sometimes. She hadn't liked reggae, but she tolerated my music, supported my interest with a birthday concert each year. She preferred Celine Dion and Anita Baker. I should have known something wasn't right. My mother liked Celine, too.

On stage, Joseph "the Dreamer" released a shower of dreads from his lion-embroidered tam and frisbeed the hat into the crowd. A boy, perched on his father's shoulders, caught it. He propped the tam atop his raised fist, the lion's golden visage facing back at the stage. "The Dreamer" tramped around the stage, dreads flailing. The crowd roared.

A rapturous couple in front of me fondled and kissed, their tongues ravenous. I had probably never kissed Evelyn like that, or my marriage wouldn't have failed. Although, we didn't part until after death. No divorce.

On the next tune, I primal-screamed and punched the air with the rest of the crowd.

As Kismet Dream stretched deeper into their playlist, my face grew hot, the canvas tent stifling. The more they sang about peace, love, and switcha, the more agitated I got.

"Boise? Boise!"

I sucked my teeth. "What? This here a concert, not a conversation place," I said. "What it is now?"

Yarey backhanded me across my bare shoulder. A sting ran down my arm into my hand. "Ow!" I bellowed. "So hostile."

The woman next to me stopped dancing and fingered her nose ring. "You all right, boy?" She laughed. "Your woman too strong for ya?" She held a joint out to me, which I accepted with a puff and a contented sigh. It had been too long.

"Boise!" Yarey yelled.

"What?" The weed had done nothing to lighten my mood … yet. I offered the toke to Yarey.

"You know I don't want that shit. You're, like, ten-thousand miles away. What are you thinking about? You see what I was getting at?"

"What you mean? I-and-I right here wid you, sista." I handed the joint back to nose ring. "Dank's good."

"What are you doing? Why are you throwing the lingo?"

Fair question. I giggled. "Me don't know, Yarey. Dis me."

"Boise, you're not supposed to be smoking. I told you before we came that there would be temptation." Her jaw clenched. "I knew this was a bad idea. Knew it!" Her fist tightened like she wanted to choke the life out of something, or someone.

I wagged my finger. "Uh-uh. I ain't drinnnnnk," I said. "No liquor." She started to say something, then I continued, everything sounding silly and cool at the same time. "Or beer. Or wine."

The band filtered into the next tune, a cover of an obscure African artist I'd never heard. Shifting in and out of full awareness, the show ended without warning, much the way my chaotic life as I knew it would soon end. I couldn't even recall the coda.

Yarey was no where to be found. I couldn't bring myself to care much, but out of politeness, I texted her. While texting, I ignored a call from Southern California.

No reply. She ditched me. I muttered to myself indignantly as we all filed out of the enclosure, "It's called Alcoholics Anonymous. Da main word be 'alcoholics'."

Hard to believe Yarey was an island girl. Acting just like Evelyn. When times got hard, when the work of life intruded, they abandoned me. Evelyn died, but still, abandonment.

I floated to the dirt parking lot, standing next to a vacant parking spot where Yarey's car used to be. I hunched to inspect the dry, dirty sand. Violent tire tracks. The thought intruded, like an angry pimple: *I hate women.* Okay, not really, but they can be really annoying. Bossy. Needing to change things all the time. What was wrong with being the same some of the time? Seeing the same face in the mirror, the same liquor in my hands.

Dana was always trying to change me, too. Trying to make me a lesbian. I'm no lesbian.

Someone wolf-whistled in my direction.

The nose-ringed woman who had shared the toke leaned out of a rusted RAV-4 and invited me to go with her and friends to an unnamed beach. Three women. They probably wanted a guy to go along in case something needed fixing or start a fire. Using me, like they all do.

***

Twenty minutes later, a bonfire. More smoking. They had a boom box, silver plastic casing, like the Rastas carried hoisted on their shoulders, speakers against their ears, circa 1989. I hoisted the radio onto my shoulder and pranced a long-armed monkey dance, my legs churning in the dry sand. Calypso blared in my already tattered eardrums. The concert lasted over three hours. Now we were on a beach, invading everything with more musical noise. I dropped the box onto the sand. It teetered over, but kept on trucking.

All I really wanted was to listen to the ocean, so I drank. The Jamaican girl with the nose ring offered me an already popped can of Old Milwaukee. Who could resist the good stuff.

Up to that moment, I could have argued that I was still a sober alcoholic. In fact, I was prepared to argue it to the death with Yarey once I located her. Then I thought, screw it, if I'm gonna be guilty, might as well do the deed.

The last thing I remembered her saying was, "You oughta grow your hair out. You'd look more manly." She took my hat and propped it atop her head.

I've often wondered in the days and months that followed what might have happened if I'd resisted the urge to drink that beer. I swear, I only drank one. No one believed me.

I wouldn't have believed me either.

The last time I passed out, I got kidnapped. This time, the consequences would be more dire.

***

A buzzing torched me out of a drunken sleep. My ear lobe erupted in pain. I smacked at the sting. Head ringing. On the shimmering sand, next to a shell, a dead horsefly. Nasty bastard, painful as a bee. The smell of charred wood and something else. Copper and hibiscus. Mouth tasted like I'd chewed on a Goodyear.

Water lapped. The temperature soared. The sun beat on me like a frat-boy with a paddle. My shoulder ached. Had Yarey really hit me that hard?

I crawled to the water's edge, dunked my face, swallowed a mouthful of salty water and swished. The rubbery taste persisted.

When I touched the top of my head for my straw fedora, I only found damp hair. My unkempt, greasy, loathsome hair was more chic under a hat. I attempted to push-up myself out of the two-inch deep water. No dice. Aching shoulder, bad taste, exhaustion.

The ground trembled. A wave? I heaved my head a couple inches. Sand suctioned to my fledgling beard—really a sloppy growth borne of sloth. No wave. The subtle pounding continued, followed by shouts. A strong set of hands yanked me to my feet. I hovered on the edge of consciousness.

"Wha?" came my articulate interrogatory.

"Detective! Dis one ova here still kickin'!"

Splashing. Shoes smacking on the wet sand. Detective Leber's bulbous head blocked the sun. The smell of his aftershave washed over me. I tried to speak, and wound up hacking.

I rasped, "Hey, Leber. You come to dance around the bonfire, too?"

"Jesus, Boise?" Leber fanned his face. "When was the last time you used mouthwash?"

"What day is it?" I managed.

"The day after." As he said this, the person holding me swung me around. A massacre. Some kind of staged thing. Couldn't be real. So much congealed blood on mouths and throats and heads. Had to be corn syrup. Something ... In the distance, through my black echo tunnel, I faintly heard Leber recite Miranda warnings.

"Do you understand these rights as I have read them to you?" Leber looked up from a yellow index card reflecting on his Aviators. "Boise, I need you to answer 'yes' or 'no'."

"Me? No?"

"No?"

"I'm not ..." I fumbled for words. My nether regions felt drafty. Then a release. The officer squawked, dropping me like a sack of ripe mangos. Leber swore. My cheek hit the edge of a broken seashell.

"Boise, where are your pants?" Leber sounded like an annoyed school principal.

"It's so hairy," the guy behind me bellowed.

I tried to look up, but couldn't move my neck much. Warm urine bathed my thigh, then washed away with the next lapping wave. There wasn't much in this world more satisfying than a hot piss after a hard night.

"I get hot at night. I probably just, you know, kicked 'em off in my sleep. They by the fire?"

One of the officers said, "But you kept your shirt on?"

Leber muttered something to the officer, who grumbled and trudged off.

"Hey, Leber?"

"Boise, don't talk. He's getting your shorts."

A shout from behind me. I sensed a lot of activity around the bonfire area. I tried to push up, but the downward slope into the bay foiled my plans.

"Hey, Leber. You're pulling my third leg, right?"

"Boise, shut up. Don't talk, man. You remember those rights? That one about remaining silent. That's the kingfish. Just shut up. I don't think you did this, but man, there's a lot of physical evidence." He leaned down and whispered in my ear. "A lot. We can't even give you your shorts and we're gonna need your shirt, it's probably covered too, only darker, harder to tell."

I stared at him, the question plain on my face.

"Evidence. They're covered in blood." He paused for a swallow. "We're bagging and tagging them along with the three dead people here with you."

That's when my ass started to ache, and not in a good way. For the first time since being diagnosed, I prayed that my chronic colitis was to blame for the blood on my clothes.

CHAPTER 2

My butt cheeks clenched. This was about to get ugly. "I need a toilet!" I howled. "And my pills. They were in my shorts. I need the pills!"

Pistoning my legs, I pushed myself farther into the water, then positioned my feet under me. A younger officer whipped out his pistol and trained it on the only part of me above the water, my face. "Freeze, scumbag! Hands!" He watched too much television. My heart raced as I relieved myself.

"Man, put that gun away," Leber said, gesturing palms down. "Easy, man, easy."

The cop, who had crouched into a shooter's stance, straightened, a sheepish look on his face.

"Where do you think he's going, Jenkins? Man, give some boys a gun …" Leber clapped the cop on his back. The guy shrugged his hand away.

"You detectives, always got it worked out." Jenkins stalked up the beach toward the crime scene.

I followed his trajectory, and got a sober look at what all the fuss was about. Three bodies, splayed around the smoldering remains of the bonfire I'd danced around only hours before. Blood pooled around two of the women's heads, the sand black. The other one, the one who'd invited me here, looked like she might be sleeping, except her chest didn't move. My poor fedora, mashed down and torn at the corner, was perched atop her head, the nose ring glinting in the sunlight.

A forensics tech cradled a softball-sized rock in gloved hands.

"Detective!" the tech shouted. "We got it. There's sand."

Leber pointed at me. "Don't swim to Cuba." He headed up the beach.

A wave gently pummeled me. I stumbled, trying to catch my footing in the shallow water. A pair of small fish circled my legs, moving close then darting away.

Yarey was right, the concert had been a bad idea. I was about to lose a decent relationship, a rare bit of fortune in my life, over taking a hit, and partying with three women whose names I didn't even know. Correction: three dead women I didn't know. Funny how people you meet briefly can change everything, while others you've known for decades linger like pocket lint.

I shivered, but remained in the water. Freedom, open air, these were things I was about to lose for the coming hours, maybe a day. Certainly this misunderstanding would be cleared quickly once they found whatever loon did this.

Jenkins, his eyes fixed on me, said something to another cop while bumping his fists together. He then wagged his stubbly chin at Leber. The look on that cop's face meant only one thing: they were all convinced I had killed these women.

Leber strolled back down to the water's edge, a look of resignation on his face. He wanted to ask me things, but he also wanted me to have a lawyer first. Leber believed in me more than I believed in myself.

"Come out of there," he said.

I squatted lower in the water, tasting salt. My pathetic rebellion.

"You're not done?"

"Did you get my pills?"

"Shit," he muttered and went back up the beach.

Five minutes later he returned, a Ziploc bag of large orange pills in his gloved hand, forefinger to thumb. "These?"

The sooner I took them, the sooner the aching and urgency would cease. I almost asked for water, then thought better of it. Leber and I were tied together, but even friends (I'd like to think we were friends), who'd been through battle, had limits.

"I got a towel out of my car," Leber said, holding up the cheap kind of flowery beach towel parents bought for their kids at Target.

I trudged out of the water, lost my balance and tumbled, ass-up. Leber held one of the pills out after he tossed the towel to me. His face continued to register concern, even alarm.

The pill looked like a coconut. I knew if I put it in my mouth without water, I'd gag and vomit. As if reading my mind, Leber said firmly, without breaking our eye contact, "Boot!"

Jenkins flinched.

"Bottle of water from the back of my cruiser, stat!"

Jenkins, scoffed. His chest puffed out, hands on his utility belt, feet spread, ready for whatever little men act ready for. The side chatter from the other cops ceased. Even the forensic technician paused, hand hovering over an evidence bag. A dog owner who used to walk her husky past my place in Los Angeles flashed through my mind. Her hand hovered like that when she picked up the animal's poop.

You do not show the lead detective disrespect at a crime scene, especially in front of the prime suspect. Even I knew that. Leber crossed his arms over his chest. Leber's face remained serene, but stern. The cop, blinded by something long past, stood his ground.

"Hey, boot."

"The name's Jenkins," the cop said. "I don't like when you call me that. I'm two years out."

Leber said, "Well, boot, I haven't worked with you before, that makes you a boot to me. First case. You get me?"

"I've worked cases. I'm good to go."

"Not with me, you haven't."

"So what, I'm your friend's nursemaid?" He glanced at the other officers for support. He got nothing.

Leber grinned, bright white teeth, dark black sunglasses glimmering over distant eyes. The guy looked like a goddamn movie star. "Now you're getting the picture. See, I knew you could learn. Just think, the next case, I'll call someone else boot, that is unless you mess up on this one. Then, you keep being boot. It's like this: 'boot' is a state of mind. Like 'punk-ass ho.' I might call you a punk-ass ho sometime, but that doesn't mean you a prostitute. It could mean you a boot." Leber paused—let it sink like an anchor. "It could mean you a punk-ass ho 'cause you don't learn. A boot can learn. He's still learning. Part of learning is listening. What boots have in common, is what?"

Leber scanned the other cops standing at the perimeter, keeping the reporters and onlookers at bay. Only one cop wasn't watching him, wasn't riveted to every word the detective said. That cop watched the sheep.

My ass groaned, again. If Leber didn't get that water over here soon, I was gonna have to go back in. I didn't have the heart to interrupt his monologue.

"Hey, Isaac, tell the boot how it works."

"Well, boot," the beat cop monitoring the bystanders said cheerfully, "The way this works is, Detective Leber asks you to do something, pretty much anything, while we're at a crime scene he's in charge of, you do it."

"See, that's how we like things at the VIPD. Simple," Leber said.

"No," Jenkins intoned, his voice deadpan as his countenance.

The other cops all put their hands over their mouths to stifle laughter, surprise, or both.

"And Officer Isaac, what's the other part?" Isaac glanced at Leber. Leber pointed at Jenkins. "Not me. Tell the boot."

Isaac said something into his radio. "Detective, Regina wants you to call her right away."

"She'll wait," Leber said.

Leber liked the drama. I, on the other hand, needed that water. I attempted a stage whisper to my benefactor. "Hey, Leber! Can we skip the theatrics? I need …"

He waved me off. It wasn't about helping. Leber could get caught up making a point. My stomach gurgled.

Isaac shrugged. "Like Detective Leber said, at the VIPD, we like to keep things simple. And like I said, the rule's simple. Detective in charge, you do what he says."

Officer Jenkins' face looked like the eye of a hurricane. "I'm not doing what he says. I'm not getting some murderer water. I ain't doin' dat." Jenkins spat in the sand.

Isaac didn't wait for Leber to prompt him this time. "That's where the other half of the lesson comes in. One of Detective Leber's cardinal rules: just because something is simple, doesn't mean it's easy."

With that statement, all joviality disappeared from Leber's face. He stalked over to Jenkins, who flinched as Leber shot past the lanky man, to the back of his unmarked detective car.

Leber kept a cooler full of bottled water on ice at all times. He brought one to me and I swallowed my pill. Next, he pitched cool bottles of water to every officer on duty, including Jenkins. He placed one next to each forensic tech on the scene, careful not to disturb the evidence. The heat had mounted, and now at almost eleven in the morning it felt like one-hundred in the shade. Everyone held their water bottles and stood tall. Leber turned, raised his bottle and said, "Here we make our vow, to find the people responsible, to bring knowledge to those who have none, to bring peace to those who have none, to bring justice to those who have none."

With this pronouncement, every cop twisted the plastic cap off his bottle and chugged. The sound of cracking plastic resounded as everyone sucked their bottles dry. Everyone, except Officer Shane Jenkins, who did not uncork the dripping bottle. He watched as the rest enjoyed cool water and the comradery of a shared cause recognized.

Leber held up his bottle. "Boot, would you be so kind as to collect the empties? There's a bag in the back of my cruiser for recycling."

Jenkins moved toward the car to fetch the garbage bag. A scowl crossed his face as each of the other police people tossed their empty into the opaque bag. He got to Leber last. Leber didn't look at the lanky man. He didn't need to. The battle of wills had been won.

As diverting as this police drama was, I had a much bigger problem: going into a holding cell wearing only a flowered towel. In the distance I could make out a green rock of land. The edges of my vision blurred, I wiped the sleep from my eyes. A triple-homicide.

If Evelyn were here now, she could have represented me in this matter. Evelyn wasn't a defense attorney, but I had no doubts about her ability to get me off. What would she have suggested I do at this moment to aid my defense?

Much as I enjoyed looking out at the sea, I needed to learn whatever I could about the murders I'd supposedly committed the night before. Things like freedom and happy marriages vanished when you weren't paying attention. It was time to examine the blood, study the wounds.

I inched closer to the carnage while gripping the towel to keep it from falling. Three women splayed around the dying embers of the bonfire, small eddies of smoke dancing in the clear air. Techs mopped their brows, the beat cops chatted as if handling security at a Frenchtown baseball game.

Congealed blood on the sand resembled misshapen pebbles, like those designer rocks people used in front of their homes to landscape in wealthy suburban neighborhoods. Neatly placed stones surrounded the bonfire.

My legs buckled--a side effect of the colitis flare. Sweat dripped off my nose as I knee-walked up the beach, my head bent with the exertion. My scalp bumped on someone's knee. Below me, black, patent leather shoes, a white scuff mark and some grains of sand littering the otherwise immaculate surface.

"Where you think you're going?"

I squinted up. "Wanted to get out of the wet sand."

"Uh-huh. Looks to me like you're looking to mess with the crime scene." Jenkins plucked my half-full water bottle from my hands. I had been enjoying the coolness against my stomach as I moved. "Did you want some more water?"

"Thank you, Officer."

He bent at the knees, his face next to mine. His pockmarked skin covered in a sheen of sweat, his officer's cap, shielding nearly black eyes.

"It's Jenkins, The Second," he said. "You remember reporting on my father? Them investigating him on account of your flappin' lips? You oughta learn to mind your own bee's wax."

I'd reported on a police officer who pummeled a vagrant, probably a veteran, on the day I arrived in St. Thomas nearly eight months ago. An officer named Wayne Jenkins.

Thirst seized my throat like a hangman's noose. The pill had gone down, but hadn't really begun its work yet. I was dehydrated from boozing, smoking, and defecating. My mouth still tasted of rubber. Jenkins uncapped the bottle. He offered it back before snatching it away and dumping it onto the sand.

"I'll handle this," came Leber's voice from behind Jenkins. "You ready for transport, Boise?"

Jenkins crumpled the plastic bottle next to my ear. In my hungover state, it was deafening as a carnival parade.

Leber pulled me to my feet. "Boise, this is serious. This is Wembley Stadium, not Virgin Islands bush league. You gettin' me?" He held his hand up, like a crossing guard, as I started to reply. "Keep your pie-hole shut. Don't talk to anyone besides your lawyer. Whoever you call once back at the station, should be your lawyer. I'm sending Jenkins back with you."

Exhaustion hung on me, like too-large clothing. I wanted to protest the decision. Leber read my face.

"I know you and he aren't best friends, but I need him out of here. He's distracting. I'd send someone else, but I need all my guys. The natives are restless. Victims first. We don't take care of them and their families, we're all dead meat."

The crowd had grown. Didn't people have work? Didn't they have to sleep? My eyes drooped. Leber smacked my cheek.

"Stay alert, man. This is the bigs." He moved closer. "I don't think you did it, but everyone else here sees a lay up that a four-year-old could make. They're about closing cases. This," he jerked his thumb over his shoulder, "this demands a swift resolution. Go with Jenkins and, hey, man, keep your pie-hole shut! No idle chit-chat in the car, no talking to fellow inmates. Understand?"

I started to speak and he slapped his gloved palm over my mouth. He repeated his question. "Do you understand?"

I nodded. His starlight teeth appeared momentarily like lightning, then vanished again. "Good boy."

***

The cruiser jostled along, the back seat smelling like wet dog and urine. Jenkins drove badly, taking turns too sharply and flashing his lights whenever a car pulled in front of us. The drivers pulled aside and each time we passed them, he glared out the window as if to say, "I'm watching you."

I didn't really know Wayne Jenkins. Despite being a private detective, I'd had minimal interaction with local cops. I knew Leber and his partner Barnes, who for some reason hadn't been at the crime scene, and a few others I'd briefly encountered. My last couple cases had been divorce stuff, catching spouses cheating, helping find information on hidden money. It's what I'd done for the law firm in Los Angeles. I knew the ropes. That mindless stuff paid the rent.

The police steered clear of domestic cases, unless there was violence, and even then, if they could get away with it, they deferred. If called, they played games, tricked or coerced greener cops who didn't know better into answering the call, which resulted in poor handling of a tense, unpredictable situation. Consequently, cops and I were strangers, which was how I liked it. I'd never been a cop and my brief stint in the military confirmed my status as a non-joiner.

"Hey, murderer." Jenkins' eyes bored into me from the cloudy rearview mirror. "You like killing women? Defenseless women?"

"They aren't defenseless," I grumbled. The pill had improved things, but I still felt nauseous and hungry. Jenkins' head looked like a giant cheeseburger, blood dripping off it. The blood wasn't the good watery kind after the meat's cooked. It was dark red, thick like mayonnaise, dripping in globs onto his uniform. The hamburger rotated, the lettuce flopped when he spoke.

"They aren't defenseless. That's da truth. Women are el diablo. They suck the life out of you." The hamburger eyed me in the rearview. "Tell me what it felt like."

The thick blood dried up, the lettuce shriveled, and the bread turned to flour. The black eyes appeared again. My stomach groaned.

"Slow down, will you?" I muttered, eyes shut, little amoebas swimming on the back of my eyelids.

"Tell me what it felt like. Come on, murderer. Tell me. They had it coming, right?"

Did this guy ever shut up? I opened my eyes. We passed a Kentucky Fried Chicken, the rotating bucket didn't rotate and someone or something had punched a hole in the side. Inside the broken bucket, a bare light bulb glowed through the crack like a tiny sun. The smell of fried chicken and biscuits wafted out of the open front door of the striped building.

"I need to eat," I said half-heartedly. "I'd like a drink. A Coke."

"What was it like? What did you feel? I'm here for you."

Jenkins. The name was so innocuous, like a middle school English teacher. The guy's tone scared me. The wonder in his voice, like he longed to know all the details.

"Nothing," I said.

"You didn't feel anything? Nothing? So what, you kill for no reason?"

"I didn't kill anyone," I shot back.

"Sure, sure, that's what you're supposed to say, but you can tell me. I'm here for you." The words matched the voice like a poorly dubbed video. My guard sagged. I knew I was making mistakes, saying things, but I hadn't killed those women. I knew it. Even blacked out, lost time, I didn't do anything like that, especially not after listening to reggae. Sure, I wasn't too happy with the women in my life, but ... I shook my head, trying to clear the flour.

This dude driving was anything but "here for me." Some people become cops for the thrill of being close to criminals, others for the opportunity to hurt people. Officer Jenkins struck me as one of the latter, like his dear old dad.

"Come on, man. I'm sorry for calling you 'murderer' earlier. I know you don't want to go to jail. I get that. I mean, it's not murder if they asked for it. They deserved it, right? You can tell me what happened, though. I'm here for you."

I couldn't resist. "You know what you sound like?" I muttered under my breath through the grating separating the back of the police car from the front.

"What you say?" he asked.

"I said, do you know what you sound like? You ever get those calls selling you a loan? You ever talk to one of those callers?"

Out the window, brick and stone buildings passed, along with cinder block, and the occasional wooden frame home, between six-foot blades of razor grass. This couldn't be real. No way this was real. I fell off the wagon for one measly night. I could get back on anytime. My stomach rumbled.

"Hey, can we stop for a burger or chicken fry? What about that place?"

His dark eyes didn't leave the road. I suppose we weren't friends anymore, his longing to help me out of my predicament gone. His cold call had gone cold. Jenkins wanted to make a name for himself by appealing to my need to be heard. I was beneath him. A means to an end that had worn out its usefulness.

"You think your precious ass hurts now. Wait till we take away your pills and you eat the delicious dog-shit cooking for the next six months, awaiting trial. I plan to visit, make sure the chef gives you extra shit in your shingle."

"How thoughtful of you," I said. I tried to laugh off his lousy analysis of my situation. Six months? Impossible. The guffaw died on my lips. I was in handcuffs, in the back of a police car. They had a murder weapon and bloody clothes. Me, the only survivor at the scene of a triple-deader.

I glanced down at the towel around my waist. No one was taking me home to get fresh clothes. My shorts were evidence. I knew I hadn't done this. Maybe Leber even knew it in his heart. None of that mattered. My feelings of innocence and Leber's intuition weren't admissible.

On the other hand, bloody shorts, fingerprints, weapons, bodies, my presence at the scene, lack of an alternative theory of the case, these things, they were solid as cinderblock. I'd always been on the side of right, never accused of anything more than overindulgence. Leber was right, I'd been called up to the big leagues, standing at the plate without a bat.

I shut my eyes. They salt-stung. I was going to jail for murder. Money. Trials were costly. I couldn't afford a defense attorney or bail. No way. I could barely pay for my room and my office. Six months 'til trial. No way to work. At best, if I was acquitted, I'd be homeless and broke. Best case scenario. Homeless and broke. Worst case. I didn't want to think about that.

Yes, I knew I hadn't done this. I knew it. I couldn't remember everything, but I knew I hadn't done this.

No more drinking, Boise. That's it. Off the hot sauce. Bad things.

It never used to be this bad. Drinking was like a mildly dysfunctional hobby, like gambling and losing a hundred bucks once a year. I'd sometimes wind up in a humorous incident involving nudity.

No one would be stupid enough to murder three women and then pass out at the scene wearing no pants. No jury would believe this level of stupidity. They'd see how dumb this was. When I testified they'd see I wasn't a total moron, and they'd vote to acquit me on all charges. Right?

CHAPTER 3

Three goddamn days later, I was still incarcerated. Three goddamn days. Thanksgiving in jail. There's something that'll make mama proud. Someone in the Alexander A. Farrelly Criminal Justice Complex had to have beer. The territory should provide a drink to the incarcerated awaiting trial on a major holiday. It was the humane thing.

They served us canned turkey, mashed potatoes from a box, and those plastic baggies of milk public school kids get--the kind with the straw you jabbed through the plastic. We had a choice of chocolate or plain. I treated myself to chocolate.

My one phone call, the night I was arrested, was to Dana Goode of the formerly red hair. Ever hear of a redhead dying her hair black? All the other women want red hair. Men want to have sex with redheads, something exotic about it. Not Dana. First off, Dana didn't care what or who men wanted to have sex with, and second ... what was I saying? Oh, yes, I called Dana. Left a message. Nothing happened. Truly unlike Dana. They refused to give me another call.

The inmate guard on duty the night of Thanksgiving took unkindly to working while everyone else ate good food at home. He'd brought a plate of home cooking from his mother.

"Dey making me work 'cause I have the least funkin' seniority. The warden says if I want to be one of dem, gotta pay me dues like all dem. On Thanksgiving, me family does dis dance."

The guard demonstrated the dance, counting out the steps from outside our jail cells. Six of us were being held in the section awaiting trial. He demanded that each of us dance with him, duplicating his family tradition. Most everyone in there awaited trial on drug charges or burglary. When I walked by, the other inmates simply stared at me with a mixture of reverence and disgust. Sure, they were criminals, but they hadn't been stupid enough to get caught for killing someone.

"Dat still ain't right! Do it again, killer." The guard laughed when he called me killer. He didn't seem afraid of me. I couldn't blame him. I didn't ooze "killer", "fighter", or even "mildly intimidating."

When he finished laughing, the humor vanished from his face. "Now, I show you again. One, two, t'ree, four, back, slide, front, drop, up, and den shake da shoulders like dis. Your fat Samoan ass handle that?"

"I'm not Samoan."

"Shut up, killer. Dance." He had this twittering laugh that didn't match his large pecs and bulging biceps. The guy could dance. Evelyn tried to get me into dancing. My feet wouldn't cooperate.

"Jesus Christ! What wrong wid you? Samoans can't dance?"

I stared at the filthy floor of my cell, wondering what kinds of fluids had been spilled or ejaculated there over the years. Dana left a message with my jailors, who seemed less than thrilled with her threats of a journalistic exposé if they didn't give me the message. She was on assignment in Venezuela and would be back next week. After waiting in line for two hours yesterday, I phoned Walter Pickering, her boss at *The Virgin Islands Daily News*. They couldn't figure out where my cell phone was as I'd deactivated the location app, but Dana had checked my voicemail remotely and discovered I'd missed out on three new client inquiries.

I hadn't received a call for a new case in nearly a month. Get incarcerated and people wanted to hire me, the same way women became interested the minute I got married. When I'd been single, getting a date had been as likely as me swimming from St. Thomas to Cuba.

"Hey! Try again, killer." This time he didn't twitter.

"Can I do it without the music this time? Just trying the steps?"

He sighed, his arms thrown skyward. "I done tell you. You got to work wid da music, da man. I don't play dat no music crap." He glanced at his watch, a watch that was far nicer than it should have been. Not for the first time, I wondered if I could bribe my way out, then I realized I'd need money to do that.

"We've heard this song at least fifty times today."

"Dat's right. When you do dis right, we only have to hear it tonight when I on da phone. I got to show you dancing to my children's an' me wife."

"I'm sorry, but I don't want to do this," I said without much determination. "Can I stop ..."

"No!"

He drew his weapon and trained it on me. A gasp came from one of the other inmates.

"I done tell you to dance. Now, you will dance. No more talkin'. Music."

The inmate in the cell next to me had been put in charge of music on a dented compact-disc player.

"Why can't he do the dance?" I asked, while simultaneously wondering if the disc-player had been dented when the guard bashed it over another inmate's skull because he couldn't dance right.

Colors flashed before my eyes. The switcha-sharer from the concert, the dead one on the beach, her eyes swelled large in my mind, moving toward me violently, the accusations of the damned directed at my mortal soul. The woman, who Leber had informed me was named Felicia Nichols, wore a purple flower. It nestled snugly behind her ear, a small reminder of impermanent beauty. I'd wanted to ask her what kind it was, but couldn't recall ever finding out. Even in death, and missing a petal, the wilting flower had made Felicia prettier … elegant.

When Jenkins had led me away, the flower hung loosely, caught in a strand of Felicia's hair, some sand strewn across her sunken, brown cheek by a digging red and black insect. The remaining petals creased and browned in the tropical heat.

"Don't be a moron," the guard said. "It's much funnier watching a squat Samoan try to dance than watching him."

My fellow prisoner glared at me, then gummed at his shriveled lips, his spider-web hair sticking up off his head like bolts of pathetic lightening. I didn't agree. That guy might be pretty fun to watch dance.

The guard tapped his watch, cued the deejay, and we continued. After three more hours, where I gamely tried, based on the expectation of a decent helping of the guard's turkey dinner, I transformed into a dancer suitable for his purposes.

He set up his cell phone on a wooden stool outside my jail cell. The stool had the abused look of elementary school desks. The guard squatted like a baseball catcher between the phone and my cell door. The keys on his belt loop hung within reach. But what was I going to do? Escape. And go where? Be a hunted man for the rest of my life? I knew one person who could help me if necessary. I had no real family ties, which at once made me pathetic, and extremely difficult to pin down.

The guard's screen glowed. A girl of about twelve, a toddler boy, and a rotund woman with shiny cheeks, squeezed into the phone's narrow frame. In the background iron pots dangled from a rack above a white stove.

"Hola, senors and senoras!"

The family laughed in unison, and the twelve-year-old girl clapped her hands in anticipation. The guard introduced me as prisoner number forty-two thirty-one. The twelve-year-old had a manner about her, a sparkle in her eyes, like that of someone who attended the funerals of people she didn't know.

"For tonight's entertainment, we have a multiplex killer! That's right, not every day we have one of these here at the CJC. They left him here with me for the holiday, and he's ripe for fun times!"

The family nodded. The girl bounced up and down, barely able to maintain her seat. Her hands had a red glow.

"Da-dee! Da-dee! Da-dee!" she chanted. "Da-dee! Da-dee! Da-dee! I love you so much. You make Thanksgiving so much better!"

The guard rubbed his eyes and rocked back and forth in his black boots. "Okay, okay, enough of this," the guard intoned. "We ready to rock?"

Everyone bounced. The snout of a dog rose out of the bottom of the screen, sniffed, and disappeared, then bounded up into view again.

"Dat is Jo-Jo. He likes dancing, too. Take your position." My captor grinned. The only things missing were his top hat and whip.

"Do I have to do this?" I grumbled.

The music started, the beat rolling out of the cell next door, my fellow prisoner tapping his toe. Humiliation rolled across me in waves, my face hot, my limbs heavy. I was no performer. I sat in the back of the classroom, I never raised my hand, I did not volunteer for political office, although I would gladly have done any of those things before dancing in front of a family of strangers at the insistence of someone with a gun on his belt. The guard muted the Facetime call after telling his family, "Just gotta give me dancer some last minute encouragement. He so eager and nervous, I'll put him at ease. One minute to curtain."

He turned to me, his face deadpan serious. "Do it now, or the next few months in here, and the rest of your life over at corrections, gonna be hell. Oh, and I recording dis for Jenkins. He say to remind you that he'd visit." He broke into a smile as tall as Crown Mountain. "Ready?"

The dance routine started tamely, with me marching forward three steps, taking one step back, then sliding to the left, followed by three steps back and one step forward then sliding to the right. I managed to get through four rounds, until a transition in the song where I had to hop, touch the low ceiling of the jail cell, clap my hands and spin. As I landed from the hop, I started into my clap and spin, but my foot slid on the rancid floor. My knee buckled. I yowled and collapsed.

The guard expressed his sympathy with a heartfelt, "What the fuck! Dat's not what we rehearsed!" His daughter burst into tears. The dog bounced in and out of the screen. Everyone else had the look of people drugged by tryptophan and dashed expectations.

Which is how I escaped from jail on Thanksgiving night, 2015.

CHAPTER 4

The hospital on St. Thomas was a tall white building that didn't look much different from the jail. I'd torn something, and had to go under for what the doctor called "minor surgery" to reattach a ligament or maybe it was a tendon.

"What did you do, young man?" the balding doctor asked, eyeing my handcuffed wrist.

"Dancing," I said.

He glanced over at the door to my room where a cop stood guard, if you considered surfing the internet on your phone, standing guard.

"I take it you're not a good dancer? Do you understand your predicament?" His speech had a lovely lilt.

I held up my wrist and the handcuff jangled against the metal side of the bed's safety bar. "Hard to ignore." The cop took brief notice of our conversation, then returned to scrolling. His radio buzzed. Something indecipherable filtered out, followed by feedback.

The doctor tapped the dressing on my knee. "This is the size of a coconut. You did a number twisting like that." The knee throbbed gently despite the painkillers. "Do you think you can refrain from dancing for six to eight weeks subsequent to surgery and rehab?"

I nodded somberly. The doctor leaned over and pulled at the dressing, examining something underneath. He whispered, "What are you in for? You have such a baby face, it's hard to imagine you in prison. Do you know jiu-jitsu?"

"I'm not supposed to talk about it," I said.

He clicked his tongue and stood back up to his full height. "I love true crime stories. Is yours a true crime story? I suppose every time you get handcuffs put on, it's a true crime story." He backed away and our eyes met like two actors on stage rehearsing lines. "Am I right?"

His glasses had fogged up. He removed them. His stare intensified, as if removing the glasses unleashed the full burden. He then said with false finality, "Just so, young man. Just so." He patted my leg. "You're going to be just fine. Am I right?"

I chuckled. "I'm glad someone thinks so."

He indicated the handcuffs. "I can't help you with the other thing. Do you wish to discuss it? Shall I promise a discount on your next procedure?"

Normally, these guys in hospitals were so overworked and rushed, there's no way they could stop for a chat. The doctor leaned in again, a wicked glint in his eyes. "Did you do it?"

It caught me off guard. The throbbing leg, the pre-surgery anxiety, the lack of alcohol. "No, I didn't do it," I huffed more loudly than intended.

The cop's head came up, the light from the phone shining off his oily skin. "What's happening over here?" He was young and had an American accent, but many islanders were good at masking with a standard American to put tourists at ease and improve employment opportunities. People who spoke the dialect were often assumed to be uneducated. "Doctor, are you treating …"

The doctor cut him off. "I'm consulting with my patient. If you must stand there and violate the doctor-patient confidentiality, I must request you to refrain from eavesdropping."

The cop's eyes fixed on the doctor a long moment, then returned to his phone. Maybe he was tweeting about guarding a murderer. Tweeting about the thing was usually more interesting than the thing.

"Sir," the doctor said more forcefully this time. The cop looked up. "Would you leave us, please?"

"Oh, I don't know. I'm supposed to have eyes on him at all times."

The doctor stood, hands in the pockets of his lab coat, his slightly stooped shoulders suggesting frailty, but the force of his voice firm as the bark of an ancient tree.

He took one step away from my bed and toward the officer, who had dropped his phone to his side. "Sir, I need you to leave us." He indicated the only window in the room. "This window leads to a seven-story drop. There is no escape. Do you believe I am plotting the escape of this, this hooligan?"

Confusion crossed the cop's face. He looked from me to the doctor and back. He sauntered over and tugged the handcuffs. He tested the strength of the safety bar, then looked out the window at the parking area below. "Mr. Montague, do not make me regret this." He gave the doctor a small military nod. "I'll be right out there. Be careful." He exited and shut the door.

The doctor broke into a toothy grin. "Well now, that was easier than I expected. So, you didn't do it?"

"Do we know each other?"

"I'm a colleague of Earl DeVere. Undoubtedly you remember Dr. DeVere?" He studied my face. "Of course you remember Dr.

DeVere. You ruined his career. You ruined his life. We went to uni together."

I didn't know what to say, but I was sick and tired of being accused of things I didn't do. "He did that on his own. I exposed his misdeeds."

"Just so. Just so. But really, is it such a crime to have a relationship with a woman, who less than two-hundred years ago would commonly have been married by her age?"

"I don't know. Is it such a crime to dog-fight or have slaves?"

"Touché." He paused, crossing to the window, looking down as if he were Napoleon observing the masses. "It would be a daring escape, I daresay. Worthy of a Bond novel." He turned back to me, his face masked by back-light. "Care to make the attempt?"

He seemed serious, and I started to answer. He broke into another toothy grin. His front teeth overlapped slightly. "I'm only having a go at you. Please, don't take my hypotheticals too seriously. I really am here to make sure you get the best treatment possible."

My knee throbbed, like a cat hissing at someone she didn't much like. I reached toward the dressing involuntarily.

"It looks like that hurts, even with all those painkillers. That's good. Although I mean to patch you up right as guardrail, it doesn't mean I won't enjoy seeing just a wee bit of suffering in the meantime."

"Why would a friend of Earl DeVere wish to help me?"

"Oh, I have my reasons." He put his glasses back on. The room seemed to cool. A nurse walked in and the doctor exited, humming.

"Who is that doctor?" I asked.

"He? He from Miami. He a fancy orthopedic surgeon. You special to get he."

An orderly wheeled me to the operating room. The anesthesiologist chatted with me, but had nothing to say about my doctor except that he was brilliant. I tried to press the matter. "Why would a doctor come from …" A deep feeling of great calm swelled through my arm, gathered in my brain. A symphony played one perfect note followed by a the deep *bong* of a bass drum.

"You going to feel a bit sleepy," she said. "Your knee gonna be blah, bleet, blooove, shill-streeeee."

I floated through the wall. Palms trees drifted across the parking lot on the hulls of upside down Boston Whalers, the outboard engines demolishing asphalt. On the side of one of the whalers, written in bold letters: "Ergo, Cecil."

CHAPTER 5

The shuffling of feet and the smell of fried fish brought me around. A nurse checked my IV. I shut my eyes again, the relaxed grogginess of the post-anesthesia hangover a much more pleasant tone than the alcoholic version. After my first knee surgery in 2000, I'd decided that an entrepreneurial anesthesiologist out there ought to go into being a drug dealer. There was simply nothing more intoxicating and peaceful. Nothing. Not even close.

I wanted a beer. Just a little jolt. A pint would suffice. I'd even drink American. Then, I recalled that alcohol had gotten me into this mess. Like, you had to fall off the wagon and crack your head on the hard earth to remind yourself why riding in the wagon was preferable. I'd stay in the wagon. The skeptic who lived inside my right ear laughed. I shot him the finger. "Screw you," I mumbled.

"'Scuse me?" the nurse stopped checking my IV as my eyes fluttered.

"Nothing. Sorry. Talking to someone else."

She looked at the housekeeper, bopping her head to music from her headphones.

"Can I see my doctor?" I croaked.

She handed me a plastic cup of water. "He ain't here."

I pushed up in my bed. My lower back ached. I tried to lift my arm to scratch my nose. It caught on the handcuffs. "Shit," I muttered. "Is he on a break? When's he coming back?"

"He ain't." She checked the clock on the wall. "I think he flight leavin' now for Miami."

My knee had been replaced by a softball.

"Did he come here just to treat me?"

The nurse pursed her lips, gave the IV bag a quick squeeze, then checked something on my monitor.

"You talk too much," someone said.

Miguela Salas, the attorney for my dead drug-dealing pal, Roger, filled the doorway. Her grey, nondescript business suit hugged her large hips. Her jowly face had the same humorless expression as always.

"Miguela. Freed any criminals lately?"

"Mr. Montague, I'm here to represent you, if you want me."

Miguela Salas did not show up in hospital rooms offering her services. She was the type of attorney that only those in the know knew about. She did not advertise on the back of buses. Her name wasn't in the yellow pages. Word of mouth, and only word of mouth, from those who had dough. Criminal defense tended to attract lawyers who probably figured if I'm going to defend the bad guys, I might as well get rich to buy truckloads of sleeping pills.

"Remind me, what's your hourly rate?"

"My defense rate on a murder case is a forty-thousand dollar retainer and six-hundred per hour."

I slurred some words, then spilled water on my gown as I tried to drink away the dryness in my throat. Miguela waited, expressionless eyes like shadows. Somehow, she always looked exactly the same: perfect makeup, perfect mascara, on plain, imperfect features.

I made faces, opening and closing my mouth, until it seemed my ability to speak returned. She stood, hands clutching the handle of her briefcase, her arms in a "v" in front of her hips.

"You remember where I live, Miguela?"

She nodded somberly. "You live in the West Indian Manner. It's close to my office."

"It's one room in the Manner. If I ever get out of this …" I paused, searching for the right word. "… situation, then I'll be lucky to have a place to live. I certainly won't have the money to pay for my room. I'm not working. I have about one-thousand in the bank."

"I'll work on the barter system."

"You mean I'll do investigative work for you in exchange for my defense?"

"How do you feel about getting married again?" she asked.

I blinked several times, trying to clear my head. "I'm sorry, a bit out of it. I thought you just asked me about getting married again."

"Do you remember us sitting on the steps outside my office, you showing me a photo of your wife, Evelyn?"

The woman had a good memory.

"You seemed to love her. Is love important to you? Would love be a deal-breaker?"

"Miguela, you are …" I wanted to say "strange," but opted for something more subtle. "… direct. Please get to the point."

"If you marry me, share your surname, I'll represent you free of charge for this trial."

It felt like I'd been slapped by an iguana's tail. The aching in my knee amped up two notches. I pressed the call button.

"We need privacy to discuss this," she said. I mashed the button repeatedly, the pain mounting as some kind of heat within the wrapping increased.

"Where is the nurse?" I muttered.

"Boise, we need to make a decision here. Do you …"

I held up my hand. "Stop right there. What's the matter with you?"

"We are discussing a mutually beneficial business arrangement. Based on my analysis, you would be getting the better part of the bargain, although mine is considerable. In short, the arrangement is commensurate with the compensation each of us receives in this transactional arrangement."

"Nurse! Nurse!" I pounded the button, but nothing happened. "Ah! What the hell's wrong with this button? Open the door, Miguela. I need the nurse, now!"

Miguela Salas propped open the door against her back and stood there, holding the expensive briefcase and wearing her boring suit. I yelled again. The nurse charged in, exclaiming, "What your problem is, Mr. Montague? I have other patients, and I just saw you."

"My leg, it hurts. It feels hot."

"Oh, that. Let me check." She prodded on my knee gently. "How that feel?"

"The same. Throbbing. It doesn't hurt more. But the heat."

"I don't know nothin' 'bout heat. Dat ain't nothing from knee surgery."

As she said this, heat blossomed in one of my elbows, rising to equal the heat in my knee.

"I'm sorry to be a bother, but can you take the dressing off? My knee is sweating. Feels like asphalt. At noon. On Main Street."

"I could put a fan on your knee, or an ice pack to cool it off."

"But this isn't anything? I'm imagining something happening to my knee?" I imagined, my knee as a red hot air balloon, expanding until I floated away dangling upside down.

"Sometimes, we have psychosomatic reactions."

I glanced over at Miguela. She maintained her unreadable expression, but for me, the expression said that this fool was nuts, there's nothing going on with his knee. Then I felt a sharp pinch as the nurse turned to leave for the ice pack.

"Ow!"

She turned back, her face registering open annoyance now. "What it is, mi son? You can't wait twenty second? Dis man your husband?"

Miguela again only stared at the nurse, who got the message quickly. "Okay, what it is?"

"I don't … ow! Feels like something biting me."

I slid my finger into the side of the dressing and felt something small and slightly elongated. I pushed hard on it and it seemed to pop. Then I slid my finger out. Crushed against my finger was a winged termite, white puss oozing from its rear end. They had come for me. Karma. I showed my finger to the nurse and breathed a sigh of relief.

She studied the insect. Her nose squinched. "Me don't like termites." Then she laughed. "Your knee taste like wood?"

The pain from the termite's nip lingered, but the heat dissipated.

"Just tell me, do I need to worry about infection?"

"From termite? Nah, mi son, you all right. I give you some topical ointment."

Miguela remained immobile throughout this minor drama. I wondered if there were termites in the operating room and about the general cleanliness of the hospital. Then again, if I complained further I might wind up back in my jail cell sooner. At least this room had mediocre ventilation and a television.

The nurse left. Miguela lingered like a dog awaiting her treat. I flicked on the television and found a classic sports station airing game one of the 1988 World Series.

"Do you want some time to think about my proposition?"

This woman wanted me to marry her. "Do I look like a

teenage girl from 1888?"

Miguela Salas didn't use sarcasm herself, but she wasn't stupid. "No."

"Then why are you asking me to marry you like I am?"

"Let me rephrase my proposition: I'd represent you as your criminal defense attorney and you'd marry me."

My knee had calmed. Earlier in the year I'd taken a baseball bat to a termite nest, a nest I believed would kill an avocado tree I was fond of. I destroyed the nest, then drenched the area with insecticide. I'd killed millions.

Lucy and Marge had shown mild gratitude, but in my opinion did not appreciate the beauty of the tree or how much ambiance it added to The Manner's front yard. For the next few weeks after bashing their home to smithereens, I'd imagined they had radar and had shared my description, scent, and taste with all the other termites on the island to locate and terrorize me.

"Yes, that's what I thought you said. I'm clear on the offer. Miguela, I'm not interested in marrying anyone. I'm not interested in marriage anymore. Besides, we hardly know each other."

"It's a business arrangement. I need a spouse. You seem acceptable."

"You don't know me."

"Can you pretend that we are a real couple?"

"Miguela, once more, I'm not interested in marriage. Please leave me alone now."

Miguela Salas lifted her briefcase and rested it on the edge of the bed. She popped the lid as a player on the television screen struck out.

She removed a business card and placed it on the table beside my bed. After she left, I studied the card. There was no name, it simply said "Attorney at Law" and a phone number.

What did I have to worry about? Everyone gets a public defender. Besides, I was innocent. The tissue I'd used to wipe off the termite fluttered to the linoleum floor as I dropped the card on the tray beside my bed, and reached for a cup of water. The brown spot that had been a termite minutes ago was no more than a discoloration on an insignificant scrap of tissue in a hospital room on an insignificant rock in the Atlantic Ocean. The brown splotch had as much right to this life as I did, but I was judge, jury, and executioner. There would be no trial for my heinous act.

I strained to snatch the tissue off the linoleum, but couldn't reach. My arm wasn't long enough.

CHAPTER 6

Four days later, I was back in lockup. On Saturday, Dana had bullied her way into my hospital room. The cop on the door shrugged at her, his calloused hand resting in a familiar manner on his pistol, the other hand twirling his baton. For a change he wasn't studying his phone.

"Walter threatened to make a stink in the paper about you not getting proper counsel or visitors. Is it true they held you without a phone call?" Dana paced like a caged tiger, dramatically waving her arms skyward. I managed a faint smile, flooded with relief at the sight of her disgust.

"Sure, but you know how this constitutional shit works. They say sorry, and the judge punishes law enforcement the way modern parents spank kids."

"Yeah, well, we threatened to report on it, which is why I suppose that gorgon at the door was ordered to let me visit. Who's your attorney?"

"I'm meeting my public defender on Monday."

"You don't sound convinced of his competence."

"I hear I'm his first murder case."

"Shocking that any public defender on this island has avoided having a defendant accused of murder. Did he get his license yesterday?"

*****

Thanksgiving does those accused of crimes no favors when it comes to hearings and a "speedy trial." The judge in my case was far more interested in gobbling turkey than my constitutional rights.

What tourists loved about the Virgins: the calm demeanor of locals, the laid-back way of life, the "limin' livin'." Unfortunately, that attitude permeated every crevice of the Virgin Islands' ethos. "In Sloth We Trust" should have been stenciled on the flag below the eagle.

In *The Count of Monte Cristo*, the Count eventually escaped. By the time he was deemed innocent, it was long past any doing on the part of those in charge of so-called justice. He had to do it himself. No one cared. Years passed. The slow erosion of the Count's soul could not be stemmed. Even freedom could not discharge the haunt of horrors inflicted upon him.

Mine was no *CMC* situation. No wise mentor priest resided in the adjoining cell itching to help me realize my potential as a member of the ruling class, then reveal the secret hiding place of a fortune that I could procure upon my timely escape.

As I recalled, the book was very thick, probably to duplicate the feeling of being incarcerated for over a decade. My big takeaway was that the bad parts of that story and my predicament had too much in common.

"Hey!" I hollered at my jailor. "Is there any way I can get a copy of *The Count of Monte Cristo*?"

A wooden box of books collected dust in the corner. He opened the gate, his gun in hand and waved me over to the box. I rummaged, coughing.

"Killer! Pick it up and bring da whole box in your cell. You ain't stayin' out here. Dis ain't no library."

I dragged the box into my pen, panting. My knee throbbed. The guard watched me intently while locking my cell and reholstering. He was one of those guys who couldn't leave you alone. He'd been given a warning by the warden, but he had an itch.

"Dat knee hurt? You know my daughter like your dancin'. She goin' want more."

A copy of *To Kill a Mockingbird*, a novel I'd never gotten around to reading, topped the stack. The rest were mostly trashy romance and popular fluff action genres. Those could be good for distraction reading to kill hours if the heavy stuff got too hard. Buried at the bottom, I unearthed a weathered hardback of *Crime and Punishment*. Pages had detached, causing them to stick out at varying angles. I took the book anyway; it might mirror some of my own thoughts at a time like this. Then again, it might just depress me, as Russian novels tended to do.

"Hey, you got a copy of the Constitution around here?" I asked.

The guard had returned to a world-weary desk, leafing through a file and typing on an ancient computer. He used the one finger method. The job involved so much paperwork, I wondered why typing hadn't become part of the curriculum for law enforcement personnel.

He squinted at the screen. I got the sense he heard me, but wanted to make it clear that he was too busy.

No specifics about the evidence findings they had were shared with me as yet, but I suspected it all pointed to me, or I wouldn't still be here. Leber, if he was to be believed, didn't buy any of it. He danced to his own beat. Detectives mostly wanted to close cases and move on, especially in a situation where more than one person was dead, on an island that wasn't used to triple homicides.

The phone rang and the guard picked up. After a couple uh-huhs and yeahs, I-got-its, he said, "All right, I bringin' he down."

He led me to an interrogation room, like the one I'd been in for my custodial interrogation the day of my arrest, except this room had no mirror. It served as a place specifically for prisoners to meet with their attorneys safely. The authorities probably listened anyway.

After forty minutes of staring at a smudge on the wall and delving into various existential thoughts about my choices and destiny, a short, stubbly man who reminded me of a tree in winter entered. His eyes dominated his face, ala Peter Lorre.

"Mister," he looked at a yellow legal pad that he carried in one hand. "Mon-tag-hue?"

"Mont-a-gue, like Romeo."

"High opinion of yourself?"

"Romeo was an asshole," I said, already disliking the guy. "I'm sorry, just edgy." He didn't seem to give a damn.

He fumbled with his coffee and the pad. Once seated and through with the introductions, Mr. Gill, explained that I should take a plea. He glanced at his pad again. A page of scrawl. "They have a lot, I mean a lot, of physical evidence. Blood, hair, fingerprints, the murder weapon. A rock." He tapped his pad with the back of his golden pen for emphasis. "Is it true that you were passed out with blood all over your pants?"

I nodded. "Except I wasn't wearing my pants."

"Oh gam. That is not good, mister. Not good. Why'd you do it?"

"You're my attorney, right?

"I'm Jack Gill. Your public defender."

"How many criminal trials have you worked?"

The guy wasn't a kid, but he wasn't past forty. Hard to read.

"Oh this is new to me. I've done a couple b and e's and one

assault. They all settled."

"You've never gone to trial?"

"You sound like you want to tell me what to do. Are you a lawyer?"

"No, but right now I wish I was." Dana had looked up some Con Law for me. "I'm promised a speedy trial. It's in the Constitution."

The man took out his cell phone, fired up the photo app, and checked his look. He patted his puffed hair. Through chapped lips, while shaking his head like this had been happening to him for thousands of years, he said, "You guys. You all think you want a trial. No one wants a trial. It takes months to get on the docket. The judges around here move slower than dial-up. Where you from?"

"What's it matter?"

"You're a statesider. You think things move around here? You think bureaucracy moves slow up there in New York or wherever you been? Ha! I can fix this right. Get you a better, faster deal."

"I didn't do this."

He patted his hair like a ninety-year-old woman who'd gotten a perm. "Yeah, yeah, that's the party line." Finally, he dropped the phone and made eye contact. "I've got other things going on. We really shouldn't drag this out, but you're the boss. I gotta do what you say."

"That's nice to hear." Then, the guy did something I could not abide. "Did you just roll your eyes?"

He shrugged. "Look, Bo-eye-see …"

"Boy-zee," I corrected. "What happened to Mr. Montague?"

"Sure, if you say so. Mr. Monta-goo. You're the boss. The head honcho. The moko jumbi. Tomorrow, we have the bail hearing and you have to enter a plea. What'll it be?"

I banged my forehead on the metal table. It reverberated. A guard yelled in without opening the door, "Hey, what's going on in there?"

My attorney hollered over his shoulder, "Nothing, Kenny. We're good." He sounded far more respectful of the guard than he did when speaking to me. "Don't do that. No loud noises. They don't like that."

"Sorry. You haven't listened to a word I've said. Besides, doesn't it concern you for our confidential meeting here that he heard when I banged my head?"

"Even if they hear, they can't use anything in court. Don't be so uptight." He raised his watch, a gold job you could bludgeon someone with. "I gotta run. So what's the plea?"

I rolled my eyes. "Not guilty!" I screamed it so his pal Kenny could hear, in case I needed a witness when this guy tried to enter a guilty plea. He was almost as impatient as Dana, who I wasn't about to hire to defend me either.

"All right. It's the way you want. You should do a deal. Not smart to not deal."

***

I called Dana.

"Jack Gill. Jack Gill." She typed in the name, the keys rattling on her over-used laptop. I waited. The pay phone receiver smelled like rancid lettuce. I pictured Dana's face, blank and distant, a cat tracking a bird. The prisoner waiting behind me tapped his foot.

"He's a schmuck," she said. "He was some kind of personal injury guy. There's stories about him pulling some shady stuff, but what can you do, big shortage of public defenders. Not sure why he's doing it 'cause there's no money there, and he's all about the bling."

"Yeah, I saw his watch. Thing would pay my rent for two years. Speaking of which, what did Lucy say?"

"She'll put your stuff in storage and only rent out your room on a short term basis till you get out."

"You tell her that's not looking too good?"

"Oh shut up, Jabuti. That's no kind of attitude. Did you do it? Never mind, don't answer that. They listen to these calls."

I wanted to hang up on her, but the call was collect, so continuing seemed a sweeter revenge.

"So, what if I get Annie involved?"

"No. No. I don't want anyone footing the bill for me. This is my mess, I'll clean."

"This is no time for your Proud Boise act. Next time, you know what you can do? Stay on the wagon."

"How did you know …" I immediately realized I'd been had. "Shit."

"First name 'Gullible', last name, 'Jabuti'. All that sobriety, out the window."

Annie and Dana had now been seeing each other for nearly a year, which for Dana was like being married. She didn't relish long term relationships. Not since her daughter had died. Dana had also been the one who got me into Alcoholics Anonymous.

"I'm sorry Dana. I really am. It's all the God-talk."

"Jesus, Boise. It's 'God as you understand him,' not any particular God."

"Things get tense, or hard, or not good, and I don't know." I picked at my lip. "I'm gonna go. Please, I don't want charity."

"Boise, it's not charity. It's a gift. Everyone can take a gift. We all need help sometimes."

"No, Dana. I don't. I don't deserve it and I don't want it. I'll figure this one out. You can stop rescuing me now."

I banged the receiver into the cradle. It slipped off and banged against the wall. "Hey! Keep it cool, inmate." Guard Kenny had either promoted or demoted me to "inmate" from "killer" and "murderer."

I returned to my cell, pouted for a while and thought more about the futility of marriage and alcohol. They didn't mix, yet somehow continued to rear their heads in a montage, like lions coming and going as they feasted on my depleted organs: the heart and the liver. This day marked the eight-month anniversary of my not-so-triumphant return to St. Thomas.

The problems I fled from in Los Angeles seemed microscopic in hindsight.

CHAPTER 7

My colitis flared early the next morning. The metal toilet somehow chilled my ass, despite the throbbing tropical heat. The toilet's not there because they give a damn about inmates, but because it saves them having to clean up any messes. Drunks get put in here nightly. Drunks throw up. Before climbing on the wagon months ago, I had thrown up in a car after my latest bender. That puke had saved my life.

The lights flicked on at six am as I squeezed out a bloody mess. I needed my pills. I let the opening guard, some new guy, know my predicament. He was a laconic sort.

"So."

"So, I'm sick. I get dehydrated. Lose blood when I … you know." I indicated the commode. "It's not pretty."

"And."

"And, well …" I had to mull it over a few minutes. I trundled back to the toilet. Colitis made me forget my other problems. It occupied my entire consciousness, the way real hunger made all other problems infantile. If this kept up all day, the long waits in the courtroom were going to be an issue for everyone around me. "Before I go to court, I need my meds. At least one hour before."

"Use the phone." His hand moved glacially toward the lock. I wondered how old he was. He had one of those faces that looked forty when they were twenty, looked forty when they were forty, and looked forty when they were sixty. His feet clomped as if he wore weighted boots.

Dana's edgy voice blurted as soon as the recorded voice connected us. "Boise, what is it, I have a deadline, but I plan to attend your hearing today. It's at ten, right?"

I explained the situation. Dana Goode did not spend a lot of time doing much besides working. Her hours were seven days, whenever and wherever she found enough conflict to make an interesting story.

"You sure Lucy will let me in?"

"Are you listening to the words coming out of my mouth?"

"You want your meds?"

"Sorry, sorry. I'm on edge. Lucy cleared out my room. You're the one who told me, remember?"

"I got it. She has your stuff somewhere, including the pills?"

"That's right. I need them before the hearing. By nine at the latest."

"I got it." Before I could ask her to bring an Egg McMuffin and hash browns, the connection cut. Always in a hurry.

Lurch escorted me back to my cell.

This guard was a lot quieter than Kenny, more centered, less controlling. Non-controlling, that's probably not the trait most sought after in prison guards.

"Hey, Mr. Guard?"

Lurch stood by the desk chair, slightly slouched, toes fanned outward. Everything about him chanted, *tired*. The man had had a long, hard life. I stared through the bars, while a Hobbes quote repeated in my mind: "Life is nasty, brutish, and short."

Despite my jailor's hardships, his eyes emitted a kind light. The soul behind them hoped for something decent.

"Yeah?"

"Where's the other guard, the one who's usually here?"

"Kenny doesn't work on Tuesdays."

"I like you better," I noted. He didn't respond. "What's your name?"

"Julian."

"Nice to meet you, Julian."

A snort came from the cell next to mine. It was the prisoner who had handled the music during my dance recital.

"Likewise." If Julian's voice were any lower it'd be in a coffin. "You can call me 'Frankie,' if you prefer."

"Frankie? Is that your middle name?"

"It's short for Frankenstein."

"Do the women swoon when you speak, Julian?"

The older man's eyes twinkled. I decided that Julian had passed the age of sixty long ago.

"Swoon?"

"Yeah, Julian. Go weak in the knees? From your voice."

His lips stretched and the twinkle brightened. "Yeah, could be I had some women who liked my speech in the day."

"That's what I thought."

Another scoff from the cell next door. Then a soft, but audible derisive along the lines of, "Kiss-ass."

And why wouldn't I kiss my guard's ass if the guy was decent? His hands held my life. He could brighten or darken my days and there wasn't much I could do about it, besides befriend the man. And so far, Julian, had no interest in making me dance like a monkey.

"What's with that other guard?" I asked cautiously.

He stared through me. I heard the guy in the bunk next door shift as if to get a better angle to hear the response.

"Kenny?" Julian wiped his forearm across his mouth and made a sucking sound, then exhaled a deep, troubled breath while looking past me at the painted cinder block wall. "Kenny is all right."

He turned away, so I settled back on my cot and perused *Crime and Punishment*, holding the book at an angle to keep the loose pages from tumbling out, while simultaneously thinking about *The Count of Monte Cristo*, struggling to remember the main character's name. The so-called hero of the story, had been about to marry a beautiful woman when they tossed him into the Chateau d'If. He imagined they were going to have some perfect life where he owned his own ship and became a wealthy merchant, while she remained by his side and loved him like a puppy dog.

The desk phone rang. Julian picked up, and after thirty seconds of listening, uttered two words in an elongated tone: "Alllllllll riiiiiiight." He stalked over to my cell and pulled out his keys. "You gonna behave?"

"Of course," I said, trying to sound as innocent as possible.

He opened the door and led me to a room. After twenty minutes, which I was beginning to surmise was fast for our prison system, Julian led Dana into the room. She wasn't a lawyer. No privilege applied here. A generic sign with a picture of a camera on it announced: "video-recording in progress."

"No touching," Julian said before leaving us alone.

I checked my look in the mirror.

"You look like hell on a bad day, but the diet's working," Dana announced.

I put my index finger to my lips, and pointed at the sign.

"Where are my pills?"

"They're inspecting them, then they'll give them to you once we finish in here. I also gave Lurch an Egg-McMuffin, hash browns, and a cup of o.j. for you."

"Oh, if I could kiss you."

"Please, no. You don't smell great. When did they last let you bathe?"

"I haven't felt much like it."

"You smell like that by choice? Okay." She held her hand up to her nose. "Glad my hands smell like plastic sheeting chemicals. How's your mighty public defender?"

I described our interaction.

"You told him 'no' I assume." Her head thrashed like an angry barracuda. "What a complete ass! We have to get … "

"Don't make me regret telling you about him. I told you already, I don't want any help. I'll figure this mess out. I'm not a story or a project."

"Sure thing, big-man on campus. You handle your stuff. I'm only here to help with pills and breakfast sandwiches. I got it." My stomach gurgled and something shifted. "Woah. You got molten rock in your midsection?"

My face cracked into a grin. "Damn you, Dana!"

"That was a good one, right?"

"As you can hear, I need to take my pills. Hopefully, the sandwich won't completely counteract their effectiveness."

I called for the guard.

Back in Shangri-La, I downed the pills and ate. The prisoner next door eyed my food, like a German Shepard waiting for table scraps.

"I love dem Egg-McMuffins," he said. "Love dem."

I had one bite left, plus half the hash-brown. "You want the rest?" I didn't think my gut could take any more abuse.

His face lit up. "Yeah, da man." He eagerly snatched it away. "Ketchup?"

I threw the bag with some napkins and packets of ketchup through the bars. Julian watched us, his large face a mask of tranquility. A transport guard entered and announced that it was time to drive the prisoners to court. I boarded the shuttle bus, shackles around both feet and hands, an orange onesie and dripping balls. All the windows on the bus were sealed shut except the driver's. The air conditioning only blew on the driver and his partner in the first seat.

The treatment of those awaiting trial did not imply "innocent until proven guilty." It was more like, "if you are in here, you are guilty, even if your trial has not taken place yet." I'd never given prison reform a great deal of thought before now.

***

At the courthouse, my attorney appeared at the last minute as I fingered a loose thread in the leg of my onesie. He did not apologize, or acknowledge me before we went in.

"How do you plead?" Judge Bugleson asked, the gap in her front teeth whistling when she said, 'plead.'

My attorney cleared his throat, and nudged me. I announced, "Not guilty."

Gill resisted rolling his eyes and had let me enter my own plea. Perhaps we could work together after all. The attorneys discussed my bail and Gill did not even dispute the quarter-of-a-million requested by the defense.

"I got another case over in room sixty-two. I'll draft some motions. Are you gonna make bail?"

"What do you think?" I said. "I'm a private investigator, not a hedge fund manager."

"Hey, man, you wanted this. I said to deal."

"I'm innocent."

"No, you are 'not guilty'. Remember that."

"What's that supposed to mean?"

He checked his gold watch. "I'll be in touch."

Before I could repeat "innocent," I was back on the bus.

CHAPTER 8

I phoned my so-called attorney twice over the following three days. No response. The weekend was nothing to look forward to anymore. The toothbrushes in this place sucked. They were the gratis version from Econo Lodge. They snapped if I pushed moderately, plus I had to shove my knuckles halfway into my mouth to reach the back where most of the tartar built up. The hygienist would not be happy if I failed to brush back there. The hygienist. What a joke. I wasn't getting out of here. Ever. My attorney wouldn't even return my calls. Finding a good attorney seemed almost as hard as finding a loyal spouse.

One option remained: accept a proposal from a woman I hardly knew. She had me bent over a barrel. I'd wager Miguela Salas knew I'd cave because she knew how lousy my public defender was.

I requested a new public defender. The court asked what was wrong with mine. I told them that he thought I should plead guilty. They didn't care and didn't have time for my whining.

Although I'd worked for a law firm as an investigator in L.A., I had no idea how to write a motion or any other legal documents. St. Thomas didn't have a very aggressive prisoner's rights group to assist me. Dana even reminded me that a case the ACLU won in 1994, to improve prison conditions, still wasn't being complied with.

When my attorney finally got back to me, three agonizing days later, he told me three things: my court date (two months from now), his displeasure that I had sought to have new counsel named ("I'm going out on a limb for you, buddy. I already told you what to do."), and that he still thought cutting a deal was the best scenario. I scoffed and banged the phone down so hard, Kenny threw me back in my cell.

"What happens next?" I asked ruefully. "You putting me in the stockade?"

"I can recommend solitary if I think you're a danger to yourself or others."

I'd asked my attorney to report on my treatment and how I'd injured my knee. "That'd be a mistake. Don't rock the boat till you get out." He laughed. "I mean if you get out. Don't want to be too optimistic. I make no promises."

It might have been the only good advice Gill gave me. The knee gradually improved, at times it felt better than before. I'd suffered a chronic knee injury in basic training in my early twenties. It got me out of serving, but I'd walked with a minor limp ever since. After the dancing injury, in exchange for the free surgery and physical therapy, the V.I. Department of Corrections demanded that I not sue. The story for now was that I'd suffered an accidental fall on the damp floor. I agreed because the physical therapy got me out of lockup twice a week. The therapy center only treated prisoners on certain days. They locked down the therapy office.

In the years since I'd last been treated by a physical therapist, techniques had improved dramatically. My leg already felt stronger than before, and the pain in the knee had gone from a constant five down to a two.

I'd gotten better treatment as a prisoner than I had from the military. Perhaps whatever I'd done to my knee gyrating for Kenny's sadistic family, had shifted something in the joint, which resulted in less pain, greater mobility, and with the strengthening exercises, more leverage and balance. I couldn't wait to try running, something I hadn't done much in years, except when running after or away from people I was investigating.

Alone in the cell at night with nothing except crickets and thoughts, a pain arose in my chest, a kind of pneumonia-pain. Although the cell was friendly to claustrophobes, being the classic open bar style, I often found nighttime increasingly terrifying. The prisoner in the next cell mumbled in the darkness. Every night the police would dump anywhere from two (Sunday – Thursday) to ten (Friday & Saturday) drunks into the drunk tank. Alcoholics sleep like gravity, and snort like steam locomotives.

Since being in here, I hadn't gotten much sleep at night. The schedule being less hectic than outside life, I dozed during the day, nodding off as I valiantly attempted to navigate the dark recesses of Fyodor Dostoevsky's psychological madness. Raskolnikov had done it, assuming anything in the book took place outside the confines of his harried mind.

Maybe I couldn't sleep because of the subject matter. I considered trading the Russian melodrama for some lighter fare. A few more books had been brought in by Julian. It turned out the large, slow man liked to read the epic poems that he'd failed to read when assigned in grade school. In his usual laconic style, he dropped the new box next to the other box of bad romance and brought over a copy of Milton's *Paradise Lost* as well as *For Colored Girls Who Have Considered Suicide When the Rainbow is Enuf.*

"This is good. Superior to what you're reading."

"You a fan of Milton?"

"Yes. I like Shange, too."

He returned to his spot beside the desk and stood, eyes straight ahead. I stacked the books next to my bunk and resumed *Crime*. I wasn't much on religious writings, but didn't want to offend Julian. I'd never heard of *For Colored Girls*.

After a while I stopped reading and dozing and asked, "Why do people call you Frankie? I mean, I get what it's short for, but …"

His eyes remained fixated straight ahead and his uniform cap sat awkwardly atop his large head. "'Cause I'm big." Despite being tucked in, Julian's shirt looked disheveled, his shoes bent at the toe like they were at least a size too large, and his pants puddled around his ankles.

Other than the grimy metal, mildly reflective mirror above my aluminum trough that passed for a sink, I hadn't seen much of myself lately. My hair itched and even after showering, my armpits stunk. The heat engulfed me. My back ached and itched. The only fan pointed directly at the desk, which explained why Julian always stood in the same spot. I envisioned the lightning rods sticking out either side of his neck.

"You know, Julian, as a point of dispute, Frankenstein was the doctor." Julian's expression made a miniscule alteration, a pebble tumbling off the face of a thousand-foot cliff. After our weekly talks, I'd slowly begun to recognize when words failed him, but his curiosity was aroused. "The reason they call you Frankie is because you are large, like the monster, not because of Dr. Frankenstein. You see what I'm getting at?"

"Maybe."

"They are not only callous, they're also ignorant of the actual story. You and the monster have humanity in common. Just maybe what you and the beast have in common is that those calling you that name are the actual monsters. I think that would be Shelly's position."

Julian studied me, the twinkle in his eyes shifting slowly as a constellation. I had my own motivations for being kind, as my days with him were the only ones I looked forward to anymore.

"If anything, I'd call you Ferdinand," I said.

"Julian'll do, Boise."

CHAPTER 9

My trial date had been pushed back to mid-March. My lawyer made no effort to get the date moved up or to meet with me. My messages went unanswered. Ignoring your client could land a lawyer in disciplinary hot water. It didn't help me in my current predicament. Each day I grew more restless, more claustrophobic, more impatient.

Miguela Salas' offer sounded better and better.

Dana kept offering to have Annie pay. I was determined not to be at Dana's mercy. Dana asked to visit a week from Friday. To break up the monotony, I agreed.

***

"I'm checking into your case." I started to protest, but Dana held up her hand. "It's not for you. It's for the paper. This is a triple-homicide and Walter wants coverage. We've reported on the case already and on the evidence against you. We're being unbiased per the reporter's code, but I think I'm convincing him it's all bullshit. You and he have a love-hate thing going, but you need us and we need you. I want to go over what you remember from that night again."

I stared at myself in the two-way mirror while recounting the concert, the beach, the girls, the drinking. My hands trembled. Deep, brown sacks hung beneath my drooping eyes. My throat stung from the harsh food.

"Goddamit, Boise. Your fucking habits! Uhhhh! What's your problem?"

"I'm sorry. I know I suck. What about the journalistic objectivity you mentioned?"

"You look like shit. Let me get you out." When I closed my eyes, about to doze off, she nudged me with her foot. "Look, you've been indicted and a trial date set, then pushed. Is there anyone who can help you get out of this hole?" She squinted at me. "Are you enjoying laying around in your cell?"

"Have you checked my phone messages?" I asked.

Dana rarely showed any kind of remorse for her behavior. "Jabuti, I have a deadline. What am I checking your messages for anyway? Can't you do that? Once I finish this story, your story will have my full attention, unless something more interesting comes along." She waited almost two seconds before punching me in the arm. "That was a joke. You know, a joke?"

Through a small crack in the door, like a scene from a horror movie, Guard Kenny poked his head in. "No touching." We sat wordlessly until he sucked his teeth, then shut the door.

"They have some antiquated notion that we should still call everyone collect from the pay phone on the wall between the cells. Very limited communication options."

Dana shook her head, her dyed black hair showered her cheeks from beneath the ever-present Carnegie Melon baseball cap. "Fucking pigs," she whispered under her breath. "Sometimes

I just think the whole thing sucks. I keep writing about this shit and it just keeps going. Innocent until proven guilty. Ha!"

"I'm in trouble. I'm concerned about losing everything. So far, I'm getting by because most of the people in here did the stuff they did while on drugs or drunk. People are edgy, but somehow less violent, so far. Did you let the landlord know that I'm good for the rent for my office? Can you pay my cell phone bill? I want the account active, even if my phone's missing. It's locked and off. No one can use it. You asked what you could do. These are the things I need."

"Sure thing, captain, my captain. What's the latest with the actual trial and hearings, etcetera?"

"My attorney … never mind." I had kept Miguela Salas' business card inside my pillow case. Marriage number two looked more and more like an option—maybe my only option. "I'll handle that part of it. Just get my messages and write them down and bring 'em to me. Can you do that?"

"Sure thing." No one wanted to do the little things.

I squinted at a shadow on the wall. "Hey, you ever get freaked out by the night? Like darkness? Ever since we got thrown into that long, dark shed …"

Her answer was quick. "Nope."

Dana had my password to check my messages.

As she got up, I said, "One more thing. Can you check to see if any knockout agents cause you to taste rubber?"

***

Kenny rousted me at seven a.m. I hadn't slept more than two hours.

"Rise and shine, killer."

I gingerly planted my feet on the floor and groaned. Although my knee felt stronger, the physical therapist had warned that one wrong move could set me back. I had made decent progress in

60

one month.

"Come on, come on. How you could kill anyone moving dat slow?" He opened the cell and yanked me out. "You stink! Ya pig. Go shower."

The shower resembled a kill room in a bad horror film. Little hard dots dotted the soles of my feet. I had one pair of prison issued cloth shoes. I hated wearing wet shoes, so I dealt with the slimy floor and the itching.

"No one cares," Kenny said when I complained. "We can't be spending taxpayer dollars on the likes of you. Shower quick and get your rass back out here. You work on da dancin'?"

I glared at him, screwing my eyes down to slits. He knocked me to the floor and kicked me in the ribs, a solid strike. Prison was good for losing weight. I managed a couple hundred crunches per day. There wasn't much else to do. Even so, I doubled-over sucking air like I had a plastic bag over my face.

"Shut up, bitch!" My towel and soap had skittered across the floor when he knocked me down. "I sick of your shit. You keep talkin' to that bitch reporter. You best not be saying not'ing 'bout me." I managed a thumbs-up. My knee throbbed, but nothing like the pain in my ribs. I crawled under the showerhead, stretched up and turned on the faucet. Cold water doused me. Despite the heat, I shivered.

Dana complained when I staggered into our meet twisted like a question mark. "I've been in here for nearly an hour. What gives, Boise?"

I hunched into the seat. The room stunk of bleach and chemicals. I longed to lay against a coconut palm at Lindberg Bay and doze off, watching a happy couple stroll along the sand at sunset.

"Sorry. Really sorry," I grunted, still breathing shallowly.

"What's up with you?" she asked. "You look constipated. You taking your pills?"

"Yeah."

Kenny poked his head in again. "Hey, Kill, er, Montague, remember I monitoring dis discussion." He closed the door. I stared a long time at the usual scuff mark on the wall.

"You gonna tell me …" she stared at the bruises on my arms. I tried to cover them, but there were too many.

"I'm taking my pills." I inhaled and straightened my spine slightly. "Got some gas. No big deal. Why are you here so early? One of my few pleasures these days is sleep."

"I have bad news, but I'm not sure I should tell you."

"That's not like you, Dana. You love giving bad news." I regretted saying it. "I'm sorry. That wasn't what I wanted to say."

"Yes, it was. It's fine. I have a thick skin, and you're going through something. Something you did to yourself because you can't control yourself, but nonetheless, I get it." She hesitated. "Boise, this is bad. You had a lot of messages. Some about the rent and bills and such. Most were about your mother."

I waited. I'd left my mother behind in Los Angeles. She was a big part of the reason I'd come back to St. Thomas. She hated the island, so it was one of the few places I could go without her following me.

"What does she want?"

"Your mother's in jail. She was arrested for killing Evelyn."

CHAPTER 10

My ribs ached. Kenny ventured into my cell hours later as I lay there keening from the pain in my mid-section on my atom-thin mattress. The rusty metal bed frame creaked. I had never been good at resisting the shame of pain, or more accurately, acting like I was above it all.

"Shut up or I'll do it again, ya little twat."

"It hurts, man," I groaned. "You probably broke my rib."

"Please, fool! I held back. Right?" He directed the "right?" to Antoine, the poor bastard in the next cell. After weeks of being next to each other, I figured out Antoine was accused of attempted murder. He'd been awaiting trial for over six months. Nice enough guy when sober. Put some rum in him--watch out.

Antoine said, "Yeah, he didn't kick you dat hard."

"How would you know?" I shot back between moans.

Antoine grunted. "He kick me."

Kenny stalked over to Antoine's cell, his baton drawn. He beat Antoine, returned to my cell, grabbed my hand, and tried to wrap it around the baton. When I pulled my hand away, he elbowed me in the face. My nose filled with fluid and my eyes glazed. I laid face down for ten minutes. Someone yanked me up, threw water in my face, then two guards I'd never seen before dragged me into a black hole.

***

I counted nine meals before they released me. My eyes burned from the onslaught of light. I kept them closed or squinted for hours after my release. In solitary, I was fed bad beans soaked in clumps of lard, and rotting vegetables. The stale bread nearly cracked my teeth. I dreamt about hamburgers. In this place, burgers might as well only exist on the moon.

Kenny had broken Antoine's arm and his lip needed stitches. One eye was nearly swollen shut. The bruising around his face was probably nothing compared to what was under his coveralls. Antoine winced every time he shifted, but managed a more stoic attitude than I did. I tried to apologize, but he avoided eye contact and pretended not to hear me. So much for McMuffin camaraderie.

Jack Gill finally met with me. I told him what happened, about my need to get out to help my mother. The man sat back from the table while scribbling on the yellow legal pad propped on his knees. Between notes, he kept the tip of the pen pointed down, gripped in his hand for easy stabbing. Miguela Salas flashed through my mind, her chipmunk cheeks filling with air, her lips mouthing, "Marry me."

"Look, Boise, sounds like you don't fall far from the tree. Your whole family has issues, problems, etcetera. What are you going to do? Fly to Cali?"

Some brownish-green stringy thing had caught in my teeth. I

picked at it. "I need floss."

"Stay with me here. We've got hella-nothing. You have no alibi because the cops found you at the scene. There were four people there on a deserted beach at night. Three are dead. You were covered in blood. The rock has your prints on it in the blood of two victims. The other one was strangled. The only teensy positive is that they don't have your prints on her neck, so there's a six-percent chance you'll only go down for two counts of murder, and a ninety-four percent chance the jury'll just hat-trick you to keep things simple." He paused for dramatic effect. I wanted to hit him with a hockey stick and wipe the all-knowing smirk off his face. "Do you see the problem? I know you say you didn't do this. How the hell do you think I can win this case? Do I look like I walk on water?"

"Was the blood on my clothes my blood?"

He squinted at me, his mouth ajar. "What the hell, man? You cut yourself shaving that morning? What the hell kinda question is that? The blood belonged to the dead chicks, not you!"

I slumped. He was right. I was going to prison for murder. Three counts of second degree murder, or in my attorney's more colorful language, depraved heart murder.

"I deserve a pat on the back. I convinced them that you did not plan this. You lost it. Can you believe it? They won't get you for first degree. They have no evidence that you planned the murders, no 'laying in wait.' There is no connection between these girls and you, that the police found. You ought to be sucking on my cock for that."

"Gross," I said, knowing it would fall on deaf ears. He liked to praise himself by saying I should grant him some sexual favor.

"I'd settle for a settlement. See what I did there?" He flipped through his legal pad. "I really think you should reconsider. Their offer remains open. One life sentence. Not bad considering you killed three people. Like an Amazon sale."

Who says things like that? "For the fiftieth time, I'm not interested. I didn't ..."

"We cannot prove that! Do you understand?"

"I'm testifying."

"Yeah, I know. Also, we have another problem you've created. Why did you beat up your cellmate?"

"He's not my cellmate, and I didn't beat anyone up."

This guy, who called himself my lawyer, who was in fact my lawyer, rubbed the bridge of his nose like he was dealing with a child and couldn't convince that child to eat his green beans. "Look here, Mr. Montague, you do not seem to understand the situation." He showed me photos of the dead women. Finally, I was getting a look at actual evidence. "You see this? You see the gruesomeness?" He shuddered. "That's what a jury is hella going to see. Three young-ish ladies, covered in blood, strangled, head wounds, matted hair. This isn't some long-distance shooting. The jury will want blood. Your blood! We cannot go before a jury with this!" He smacked the photos with his open palm.

"Move your hand please and move the photos closer so I can pick them up." My hands were cuffed to the table. They had decided that I was too violent to ever be out of cuffs when in a room with someone.

The photos depicted a battlefield. My mentor, Detective Henry Bateup, always said to study crime scene photos like *The Bible*. "Look and look and look. Stare and stare and stare. Study and study and study. Then, take a break, eat a sandwich, and do it again. Take a wander. Then, do it again. Every photo has hidden messages, but you have to pearl dive for days, and days, and days. Each time you return, you are different. Your eyes are different. You will pull different pearls."

"Can I have these photos? Will they let me?"

My lawyer deflated. "Why? What the hell are you gonna do with them?"

"Can I have these photos? Yes or no."

He threw up his hands then rubbed the bridge of his nose again. "I have duplicates."

"You know, you're not supposed to give your client such a hard time about assisting with the case."

"I'm here to represent you. To get you the best deal I can. If you feel that's over-zealous, it's for your own good."

"Like a car salesman?"

He nodded slowly. "I'd sell Aston Martins. I am here to deal. You have some old-fashioned notion about justice. This isn't about that. This is about getting someone for three murders. You are it."

I chuffed like a bull ready to charge. "That's enough. I have to deal with being framed not once, but twice."

He checked his cell phone, tapped the screen and held it to his ear. "Perfect," he muttered, then stood, buttoned the lower button on his jacket and shot his cuffs, as if he'd just given a speech on how to beat the real estate market.

"When you are ready to discuss this like a man, you call my office. We are going to trial it appears, since my profession does not permit me to override the wishes of my client. We have n-o-t-h-i-n-g. No thing! You have no alibi. You have no evidence of any kind showing you didn't do this."

"I also have no motive. I didn't know these women. I smoked a joint and took a ride to hang out at the beach. I passed out. Didn't realize that might be punishable by life."

My attorney studied me. "Life imprisonment would be the sweetheart deal I can get under the best conditions. The prosecutor's talking death penalty." He waggled his cell phone at me. "Just got the message. Special circumstances."

I contemplated the end of my life. From somewhere inside the jail, a metal pan banged and water ran.

"The Virgin Islands has the death penalty?" I asked finally.

"There is no death penalty law. In 1978 there was a referendum where the residents voted three options. They voted to abolish in all cases. That said, it was nothing binding, just an opinion vote."

"Doesn't a state need a death penalty law to have the death penalty?"

"This is why you need to listen to me."

"You haven't been very forthcoming or clear with my options," I shot back. "We should have more of these conversations where you explain why I should deal, instead of you treating me like a moron."

"I'm an expert on defending criminals. It's what I do." He spat on the floor. "Instead, I have to put up with this shit. You killed three people. You have to live with that. It's not my fault you can't keep your shit together."

My stomach gurgled. I needed another pill. I'd forgotten to take it this morning.

"So what? I'm dead if I don't deal. You've given up? I still don't understand. Is the death penalty the default rule in this country now?"

"Federal law allows for the death penalty, you MORON!"

"Federal? I thought you had to violate a federal law or do something outside this jurisdiction."

"The women you killed were visiting. They're not from here. They are going after you, saying you killed someone from out-of-state. Interstate Commerce. It doesn't matter. They may or may not succeed." He bit his lip before proceeding with his diatribe. "People want blood. Three innocent women were murdered. You are the only person who could have done it." He rubbed his nose some more and for a moment looked like he was a human being instead of a boss ordering an employee to mop the floor. "You may not mind dying, but I'm not much for losing death penalty cases. It is not good for business."

"Where were the victims from?" I asked in exasperation.

"Los Angeles and Jamaica."

Chapter 11

Ever try getting anything accomplished on Sunday? It's a goddamn nightmare in the best of places, like Los Angeles, where there are fewer religious fanatics. Even secular people think of Sunday as a day of rest.

I called Dana. She didn't answer. I tried to say something after the beep. Who knows, maybe something recorded.

They make you wait thirty minutes between each call, even if no one else is waiting, but Sunday, everyone wants to call someone. Since meeting with my illustrious lawyer the day before, I'd begun considering marriage more seriously.

"Till death do you part. In sickness and in health. For rich or poor." Forever plans. The death penalty was also forever. Life in prison was, well, for life. What was that saying--"It's not a life sentence." If only that were true. Dana had forced Gill to send over my entire case file. I'd spent the night reviewing everything in it. The victims were all nice young women with histories that suggested they were going to lead productive lives.

"Hey killer." My buddy Kenny had reverted to calling me "killer" on good days and "murderer" on bad ones. I wasn't a big man, and it grated because he didn't seem scared of me. "You got a visitor." He dragged me out of my cell. He sneered in my ear as we walked to the visiting area. "I ain't scared of you, but some of the newer inmates, are. You can thank me later."

When someone other than my lawyer visited, I saw them in a common area. You had to whisper. The open cells, the nightmare screams of the sleepless guilty, eating in a room full of violent people who sometimes snatched your food. I'd experienced a few close calls, but I kept my head down and my arms wrapped around my tray like an animal fighting for every scrap. For some reason, I still had my own cell.

Today, they stuck me in a private room. Kenny cuffed me to the table and left. Fifteen minutes later, Leber entered. I nodded politely.

"You not speaking to me?" he asked.

I scratched at the surface of the table, then said, "Do you still believe in me?"

"You look worse than the dead palm in my front yard."

"Then we agree. Are you looking for him?"

"Dana said I should come talk some sense into you. You're refusing help with your representation. You got that public defender. What's his name?"

"Gill. Something Gill. Can't remember."

Even in this fluorescent lighted room, Leber kept his sunglasses on. His teeth glowed when he grinned in disbelief. "You don't know your lawyer's name? Your life's in this man's hands, man."

"I should probably have him here while I'm speaking to a cop."

"That reminds me, sign this."

"What's it say?" I was too exhausted to read it.

"I can't use anything from this meeting in court. It's safe." I signed the paper. He pocketed it. "I'm here to recommend you get another attorney. Also, I heard about your mother. Very sorry, but you need to stay focused on this."

"Believe me, I'm focused."

"Why did you beat up that prisoner?"

"Pleading the fifth."

"So, you didn't do that either?"

People who seemed normal and adjusted did horrible things all the time. A man like Leber knew this.

"Boise, you might try trusting me. I told you that I believe you didn't do this, however, I have to testify in court to facts. You were at the scene. You were covered in blood. The blood of two of the victims, as you should already know." He stared at me, like a man watching his old dog being taken into the back room by the vet. "Give me something."

"You want to help me? Really?"

"I can't take on helping you like it's my job. I still have a caseload, but I'm happy to do anything reasonable ..." He glanced up. "... to get the right person."

"The girl who hailed me into her car after the concert. She's from L.A."

"We called her parents out there."

"I lived in L.A. before moving back here. Doesn't that seem weird? People from L.A. normally don't come here much. Hawaii is the island Californians visit."

Leber adjusted his sunglasses and rubbed his cleanly shaven scalp. The man somehow always looked like he'd just stepped out of the shower in his white button-down and slacks. Islanders were a casual group. Not Leber. He and Pickering looked like they'd be more at home on Wall Street. I wondered if Leber was itching for a transfer to one of the more prestigious assignments stateside.

"The woman was originally from Jamaica. Her parents are Jamaican and American. Not strange for her to visit the Caribbean."

Marriage crossed my mind again. Miguela Salas' stoic demeanor, pouty lips and chubby cheeks would never appeal to me. Then again, I'd known people who married for citizenship.

"Always check your coincidences."

"Look who's telling people what to do. Boise, we've had adventures. If I recall correctly, our last adventure was due to you passing out."

"I've been thinking about that. Something's not right. I only remember having one drink the night these three women were murdered. One. I know I haven't been drinking for a little while, but I'm not that lightweight. Also, my mouth tasted like rubber."

"We ran a tox-screen on all of you. Nothing out of the ordinary for people partying. Nothing that would knock you out. Your blood-alcohol level was low for someone who passed out, I'll give you that."

"Boy, for someone who says he wants to help, and believes I'm innocent, you sure don't act like it."

"You have to give me something real. I need some way to refute overwhelming evidence."

"Check out Felicia Nichols' connection to L.A. What else can we go on? If I'm going to find who's responsible, that's the place to start."

"None of the victims are from here. The other two are from Jamaica. She's currently from L.A. You got anyone out there who can check her out?"

"Anything else you care to share? Anything?" I begged. I snapped my fingers, "Oh, what about my phone? Did you find it?"

"No phone. Two of the girls, the ones who live in Jamaica, Ronica and Jill, the way they were killed was … different, I mean different from how Felicia was killed."

Gill said the other two, Jill and Ronica, were stoned to death and Felicia strangled, but I wanted it from Leber. "Remind me."

"Felicia's kill was more …" he considered, his brow knitting,

"… emotional. Strangulation. The others, more violent. They were also more …" Leber rubbed his scalp. "They were more … arranged."

"You mean laid out or something?"

"Yeah, farther away, like maybe they were necessary, but not intended. Then set up next to each other. There were drag marks in the sand."

"Leber, how do you feel about marriage?"

"Fine."

"Do you think you should reserve marriage for love?"

"Boise, sometimes your attention deficit is exhausting. It has never occurred to me to marry for a purpose other than love."

CHAPTER 12

The following day I attended another hearing. The father and mother of Felicia Nichols had the look of a pair of kids lost in a toy store. Mrs. Nichols' chin jutted out like a rock on the face of a cliff. On her face as she looked through me was a passionate distaste mixed with wonder, that a man, an actual human, existing in the same courtroom, had done this awful thing.

I had only given cursory thought to the victims over the past couple weeks. Initially, the women's dead faces haunted me, as if I should have been able to do something about the murders. As if, had I maintained sobriety, things could have gone differently. Maybe I'd be dead, instead.

During these weeks, I'd often wished for death.

Mr. Nichols' manner was more subdued. His dark face had pain, yes, but also strangely, compassion. It was as if he pitied me, but more than that, he wanted to save me from the guilt. Was that kind of informational neutrality even possible?

When I thought about those courtrooms and transport buses, moving murderers around, it floored me that no one blew them up. That no one killed everyone on board just to get to the man who'd shattered their lives. I suppose it happened, but one didn't hear about it much.

I tried not to look at the parents. They did not deserve to have to deal with the eyes of the person they thought strangled their Felicia. I couldn't resist. "I didn't hurt your daughter!" I shouted.

The judge's eyes darted from his conversation with the bailiff and leveled on me. "Counsel, quiet your client."

"I will help you find who did this," I went on, unheeded by the rebuke. "I will help you find justice!"

The father's arm tightened around his wife and the mother blinked rapidly, her chiseled chin thrust to the lights above. The judge banged her gavel. "Counsel! One more outburst from your client, and I'll hold both of you in contempt!"

My lawyer yanked me into my seat, speaking fast in a tone of annoyance and embarrassment. The guy liked looking and acting cool. I had no use for cool anymore.

"I didn't hurt those girls," I shouted at him.

The bailiff rumbled over, grabbed me by the arm and escorted me back out the way he'd brought me in. Kenny had his feet propped on a table, skimming *The Daily News*. Both feet dropped to the floor.

"Hold him!" the bailiff demanded.

The bailiff re-entered the courtroom.

Kenny shoved me into a seat, my chains rattling. "What you do?"

Going to jail sucked, but seeing the parents brought home another reality. I had realized, over the months since I'd moved back to St. Thomas, that what I craved were the who and why. Were I convicted, those people would have no justice. The case closed, everyone would move on. Falsely.

Sure, I wanted out. Out of the system, the self-pity, the whole goddamn mess of my addiction. Out to go see my mother and possibly help her.

The strongest feeling came when I saw that couple, trying to hold on to neutrality, trying to cling to their fleshy existence, but finding it impossible. Their life would continue in a downward spiral as their place together and their places apart would never be solid again. Naming the evil that killed Felicia might keep them from spinning off into space. After all, they were married. They were held together by that thing I no longer believed in.

Someone slapped me across the face. "I say, what you do?"

Kenny's usual look of hatred had morphed into indignation. "They said they're ready to let you come back into the courtroom, if you're ready to keep your mouth shut."

I pictured that mother's upturned, rain-splattered chin. The way the ugly fluorescent light thinned her cheeks. The sinew, stringy in her neck. The father's attempt to remain in peace by dissociating. Like me, they must have contemplated the sweet kiss of death. They were already floating away. If one of them drifted into space, both of them would be forever lost in a vortex.

The judge chided me. "Are you going to behave like this at trial?"

I remained silent, which angered her. The only person present who didn't seem to despise me was the stenographer, who stared straight ahead, between the Star-Spangled Banner and the Virgin Islands' flag. I tuned in to the tapping of her keys and lived in my own world.

Eventually, after being pressed, I answered one question with a solitary, "Yes, ma'am." This pleased the judge. Then I said, "Judge?"

"What is it, Mr. Montague?"

"I'd like new counsel."

Jack Gill rubbed his nose.

"Who?" the judge asked.

"Sorry, Your Honor. Her name's Miguela Salas." A calm overtook me. What of vows? I should be grateful that someone, anyone, wanted to marry me.

"Your trial is less than two months away. Why did you wait so long to request new counsel?"

"I wasn't ready for matrimony yet," I said.

The judge shook her head, then said, "Does the prosecution have anything to add?"

"No, Your Honor. If the defendant wants another lawyer, the territory has no issue."

The judge's assistant came out of her chambers and whispered in the judge's ear.

"Fine, fine. I'm hungry, and everyone could use a break from this circus. Before we adjourn, Mr. Montague, I will not tolerate further outbursts. You are entitled to be in court for hearings and your trial, however, I cannot have the kind of chaos exhibited here today. Will you behave moving forward, or do I have to muzzle you like a wayward pit bull?"

"Yes, ma'am," I said. At the time, I meant it, but I also knew that the person I was becoming in that jail was not someone whose behavior I knew anything about.

***

God, was I stupid. Henry. Henry Bateup. He could check this girl out for me in L.A. Henry taught me much of what I knew about investigation. The most important thing Henry taught me was to take every little item of interest and dig into it till I hit bedrock.

I was in a state of shock for the first several weeks of my incarceration. Helplessness. Disbelief. Total belief. I couldn't stop reading *Crime and Punishment*. Dostoyevsky lived those years in Siberia, coming moments from execution. Those bleak moments he shared across decades, thousands of miles, in a different language, made me realize that even in prison, my version of freedom wasn't the worst. The phone worked. I knew people. I knew how to investigate. I could accept help without sacrificing my ideals.

I whispered, "Talk is cheap," to myself as I stood in line for the pay phone. Henry would have been my next call, but I no longer had his number committed to memory. So, I called Miguela Salas. She said she'd come over right away. My colitis swirled. While waiting, I swallowed an extra pill and fretted about money.

Chapter 13

An announcement from Kenny interrupted me trying to read through the screaming and stench. "Today we have some music coming your way. A live band that I found offered to play for you convicts."

Two guards led us out of our cells and down the hall to a room where a four-person steel drum band had set up and softly practiced acoustic music. As I entered, Kenny patted me on the back. "I hope you enjoy the music, Montague."

The band played. We all reclined. The men in here awaited trial. Everyone maintained their innocence. The system prevented most innocent men from being charged, but no system guaranteed justice for all. Henry had once insisted that no matter how well the system operated, or how much of a statistical anomaly a wrongful conviction was, to that less than one-percent who got convicted of something they didn't do, the system was an abomination. I tried to enjoy. I bobbed my head to the rhythm. For moments I forgot, but the feelings of hopelessness that nested in my heart would not fly away.

Movement.

A burly prisoner rose from his seat, plowing through the chairs, charging at the musicians, who scattered like ants. The barrel-chested man seized one of the steel drums, hefted it over his head, then pivoted toward Kenny. Folding chairs tumbled as my fellow prisoners and I cleared the area. One guy in the back cried out, "Do it! Yeah, mother-fucka, smash his ass!" One of the musicians, a slight man with an oval face, stumbled over another drum. It crashed to the floor with a *gong*. Kenny cowered in the giant's shadow, his hands raised to cover his quivering head.

A shot rang out. The drum held by the prisoner clattered to the floor. The rim crumpled. The prisoner tumbled. Blood gushed. Julian held the smoking gun in his oversized hands.

Silence and sulfur. Kenny dropped his hands and rose out of his cower. His scared eyes darted at our staring faces, then he lifted his baton and beat the body of the giant as tears streamed and obscenities flowed. No one moved. After the welter of blows, Kenny stood tall and commanded in a shrill voice, "Every one of you motherfuckers get on the fucking floor!"

Every available officer and staff member rushed in and ushered us back to our jail cells. Kenny kneed me in the stomach just to be sure I wouldn't try anything, then shoved me face first into my cell. I stumbled, grateful for the safety of the four walls.

Later that night, a rumor spread that Pepa, the giant, hadn't been given his meds the day before. He should have been in an asylum. Now, he lay in a coma. I hoped that Pepa's actions would lead to Kenny's suspension or dismissal.

Hearings for the questionable actions of guards were quick, and hardly any evidence presented. There simply weren't enough guards for all the prisoners, so the Virgin Islands Bureau of Corrections couldn't afford to suspend, much less fire, anyone, no matter how questionable their actions.

CHAPTER 14

Two days prior, Jack Gill had expressed disgust with my decision. He scoffed, "You're gonna regret this. You should have listened to me," then, adjusted his collar and greased his nose. "I got more important people to keep out of prison. Guess I'll read about your poor decision-making in the paper after your conviction." Christmas was now two days away, and getting rid of that clown was an early present.

Miguela Salas had kept Roger, my drug-dealing buddy, out of prison for years, and he'd actually been guilty of his crimes. Certainly she could handle my innocence. She arrived late and greeted me with an excuse that didn't sound like an excuse because she never seemed to care whether you cared about the excuse. "That other lawyer was hard to track down, but I got him to sign off. He thinks you should settle and take a life sentence. He thinks you're guilty."

"I'm aware," I said. "What do you think?"

"I do not concern myself with such picayune issues. My job is to represent you to the best of my ability. That representation begins when we get married. I have rings." She showed me two plain gold wedding bands. "Try this one on. I guessed your size. They said I could return it."

It fit. "Now, what?" I asked.

"I've arranged for us to get married today, at the courthouse. The corrections authorities will escort you over there. We'll get married. I'll file for my name change. Then we begin preparation for trial. There's some discovery Mr. Gill failed to request properly that I will immediately seek. I'll work through the holidays, and be in touch as things progress."

"Any chance of bail?"

"In a triple homicide there is no chance of bail, generally."

"What about me, specifically?"

"Innocent face. That helps at trial, but it does not get accused murderers out on bail very often. Additionally, the press would have a field day if any judge granted you bail at this juncture, even if you are best buddies with the editor at *The Daily News*."

***

We got married. I said the right things in the right places. Julian acted as our witness. I had little pride left, but I wasn't inviting anyone I knew to witness me marrying someone out of desperation.

When the justice of the peace stepped out, I whispered to Miguela, "Remind me again why we're doing this?"

"You cannot afford me." Miguela studied the non-descript room's wood paneling. Her hands hung loosely at her sides, her shoulders slumped slightly to the right as if that arm weighed more.

"I mean, why are you doing it?"

"Are you satisfied with this arrangement?"

"It's just odd is all, this kind of bargain. Are you an American citizen? 'Cause I've had friends try that, and they got caught."

The justice returned. We signed the paperwork. After we completed the bureaucratic mumbo-jumbo, we filled out a change of name form. Miguela elected to change her name from Salas to Montague.

"You're taking my name? Why? Why would you do that?"

"Women take men's names when they marry. It is normal behavior."

Julian announced that we were done, but that I was entitled to a conjugal visit with my new wife the next day.

"Um …" I muttered, dumbfounded.

"Like a honeymoon, only faster," he said. "We even got a honeymoon suite for you love birds."

"Yes, I will be there tomorrow for our conjugal visit, Honey," Miguela announced and pecked me on the lips.

I stared at my new wedding band. A constant reminder that I was now married for a second time and that it should last forever. That was almost as long as the prison sentence I faced.

I removed the ring. Miguela's brow furrowed. "What are you doing?"

"The wedding ring is a nice touch. Really. But in there, having jewelry, not the wisest move. Hold on to it for me when I get released?"

Miguela studied me, suspicion clouding her features. "Yes, that is true. It's for the best."

***

They called, "Time," ending my shower. I generally showered quickly, but today, my wedding day, I just couldn't get the water hot enough, or scrub hard enough.

How had I gotten here? Drinking. Drinking and passing out. How easily desperation took up residence. From desperation came irrational behavior. One did things one never thought one would do before the noose tightened and the air vanished. My mother must be going through her own version of hell in her jail cell. Patrice was a strong person; a lot stronger than me. She had wanted me to be a pulmonologist. She had an unnatural fear of a punctured lung. Miguela was my iron lung now. My last chance at breathing.

Back in my cell, a letter, more accurately a printed email, from Henry Bateup rested atop my bunk. The prison read everything sent, so Henry knew better than to reveal anything except basic concern and a reminder. Despite the four-thousand mile gap, Henry kept teaching.

> Hello Boise,
>
> I'm not much for computers, but they help. This letter should reach you much faster than if I mailed it. I'm not going to waste time bemoaning your situation. Although you don't deserve this, some part of everything that happens results from our deeds. Search your heart for what you may do differently in the future. Maybe nothing. We are who we are, after all, and we'll do what we're destined to do. Life is here to teach you something about yourself and about itself. Learn it, but don't let that lesson defeat you.
>
> That's all I'll say on the matter. Good luck, and if you need me to come down, let me know. Dana is my kind of lady, direct and no-nonsense. She's a good one to have on your side. Don't alienate her. Remember, you count. We all count.
>
> Best,
>
> Henry

> P.S. – Keep studying the evidence,
> especially the crime scene photos. I know
> it's borbing but you've been given the gift
> of time. Ha! Silver lining of being in jail.
> Looking into things here.

I couldn't even muster a chuckle at his "borbing" typo. The marriage haunted me through the night. Some light always permeated my cell from the yard outside. Jails have lots of lights. I crouched in the corner, enjoying the pain in my knee while I lifted the crime scene photos into the diffuse light. I'd been staring at the snapshots for weeks. I stared at them some more, spiraling from the center like a nautilus shell. The shapes etched into the sand around the bodies. The way their hair fell. The size of the wounds. The blood. The calm faces.

I selected photos of Felicia, her features obscured by mascara and long lashes. Close-ups of her mottled neck. Her face like a half-deflated balloon. I felt closest to and most responsible for her. She'd invited me to that beach. I blamed her, and wished she were here to share the blame. She'd put the switcha in my hand. She'd given me the beer by the light of the bonfire. She'd hijacked my time with Yarey.

There's only so much a daughter can overlook in a man who did what I did to Yarey's father. She overreacted to something minor because she wanted out. Needed out. Couldn't reconcile being with me.

Had I done this? Some kind of sleep-killing? I felt certain that if I hadn't been there, this wouldn't have happened. My presence was crucial to the killer, whether that killer was me or someone else. Why was I wasting my time staring at these photos? Because Henry said so. Henry wasn't God. He didn't have all the answers. He didn't know what had happened here.

I let the stack of stills drop to the filthy floor. They scattered, laid out in the semi-darkness like skulls, the whitish sand matching the stained gray stone.

I wanted a fucking drink, imagined it gushing from a spigot, shepherding me to a world without loss. My head drifted in the Caribbean Sea. Fish floated by. Above, the faint sound of a motor as a boat puttered across the far-away surface dimpled and hidden by the silence of the deep. Above the water, palm trees grew from the Boston Whalers.

Screaming from the entrance where guards ushered new prisoners into lockup startled me out of my half-slumber. A drunken fool, kicking at the cops as they shoved him into the drunk tank, shouted something about his mother and a cop's mother being friends. My chin hung off the edge of my flat mattress, amid the not-so-faint smell of urine.

Julian had procured my wallet photo of Evelyn from my belongings and I'd taped it to the wall above the cot. The gray paint behind the photo bubbled. Somehow, this morning, it had spiraled to the floor. Her glowing face had alighted atop a crime scene photo of Felicia. Evelyn's picture had landed directly on top of Felicia's face, making it look like the body belonged to Evelyn.

The t-shirt Felicia wore that night was something Evelyn might have worn, although Evelyn would have chosen a more feminine style. I shuffled the photographs around on the floor and pulled out the photos of Felicia. I separated the ones of her naked body in the coroner's and focused on the ones from the actual crime scene.

The black, oversized shirt, knotted in the lower left corner, admonished the reader to "SAVE THE WETLANDS" and showed a white heron soaring above leafy bushes sprouting out of a marsh. My wallet photo showed Evelyn on the beach, wearing sparkling red lip-gloss, her black hair billowing as if at a photoshoot. In the background, the famous Santa Monica Pier Ferris wheel was frozen, mid-rotation, someone at the top, their hands flung to the sky. She squinted in the brilliant Southern California sun.

How many people wore wetland-themed shirts? Furthermore,

how many were from Los Angeles? I had been studying these photos for weeks, seeing the imprints in the sand. The blood, the rock. The head wounds on Ronica and Jill that covered their dead eyes. The expression on Felicia's face, unblemished except the faint mottling. Her life flashed before my eyes in fictional snippets. Yet, the huge written letters and image on the shirt she wore, which took up the center of many of the photographs, had slipped past, like a shark in shallow waters. The nautilus shell had failed me.

I asked the guard if I could meet with Leber. Miguela Salas would not like me cavorting with the enemy. Henry wouldn't like it either. But Leber had my back. Leber made an appearance, and whenever someone from the police department met with me, the wait to get out of my cell shortened dramatically.

"What is it, Boise?" Leber grumbled.

"You find a jumbi in your Cheerios this morning?" I asked, trying to lighten his mood.

"I'm trying my damnedest to hold on to my conviction that you didn't kill these women, but that's getting harder. We cannot find anything linking anyone else to this thing."

"What about footprints or tire tracks?"

"Yeah, there's lots of tire tracks. So what? Tire tracks don't come with a timestamp. We can't track every tire that went skinny dipping."

"Footprints?"

"In dry sand? Come on, Boise. I spoke to your pal at *The News*. She's vouching for you. You guys a thing?"

"Okay, look, Leber. If I were good for this, would I be meeting with you?"

"Does your lawyer know about this? Sign this. If I have to testify about this conversation ..."

I snatched the paper and signed it. Boilerplate on me agreeing that I waived my right to silence and asked for the meet.

"Happy?" My voice elevated two octaves. "Is it your job to catch the bad guy or put someone away?"

The door popped open and the guard poked his head in. He addressed Leber. "Everything all right in here?"

"We're fine," we said in unison. The guard raised his eyebrows, then closed the door, muttering something about just doing his job.

"I know this is stressful, trying to do the right thing when everything points at the wrong thing."

"Boise, man, we are talking about physical evidence here. You were there. You're the only one alive on a beach with three dead bodies. There is nothing obvious about your innocence."

"I am innocent! I didn't do this." It felt good to say it. I was ninety percent sure it was true.

"Then give me something."

"You've got nothing? Really, nothing?"

Leber leaned in. "I'm not one to shoot a flame thrower into your mouth and say it's hot sauce. I have friends in Jamaica. They've checked." He licked his thumb and flipped a page on his note pad. "One of the girls with the bashed head, Ronica Mathews, had a friend from school who got in with a bad crowd. That person evidently asked Ronica to help her get out of that world."

"Drugs?"

"Just like Roger," Leber said solemnly. "This dude who Ronica's friend dated, I like him for an alternative to you. I'm calling in a favor over there to have a buddy check him out."

"And?"

"Nothing so far. Somewhere along the way Ronica started dating him and maybe he got a bit obsessed. Guy says he was home by himself that night, so no alibi, but still."

"The gang could have connections here. Just because he didn't do it himself ..."

"I know how this works. I'll run it aground, trust me."

I trusted him, but wished I had a Jamaican contact of my own. "You have a photo? Are you showing his photo around here to see if anyone at the concert saw this guy?"

"Yeah, I have a photo. A mug shot."

I didn't recognize him, but I wasn't paying much attention to the other concertgoers, especially after hitting the switcha. The name below his photo said, Simon Gaines.

"Well, shit, Leber, that sounds like a lead."

"You better hope. The other one, Jill, was a girl scout. Literally. She spent her time working for the Girl Scouts as an assistant to the head of the organization, then on weekends would volunteer helping the girls get their merit badges or whatever they call them in girl scout lingo. She hardly dated. On Sundays, she went to church. The pastor over there at the Lutheran Church said she was considering the clergy."

"Wow. Okay. What about the third one?" They had allowed me to bring my file. I dropped three photos of her on the table between us. "Felicia."

"Felicia Nichols," Leber said reverently.

"Right, Felicia Nichols."

"What's the point of these photos, man. I've seen them. I'm the lead detective."

"Sorry, I didn't mean to imply you weren't doing your job," I said, although part of me felt like no one was doing their job. "But you are probably the only person on the government side who hasn't already locked me up and thrown away the key."

"It's worse than that, Boise. The governor wants to make an example. He likes you for the first execution in the Virgin Islands since the U.S. took control. Your light-ish skin and the heinous nature of the murders also make you politically popular for his agenda."

Fear and calm both fought in my chest. My breathing elevated as stars circled on the edge of my vision. A cold beer sure would be nice.

"Look, man, I tried to convince them to send me to Jamaica since that's the connection between the three vics, but no doing. They won't waste more than a phone call on this. They got iron-clad physical evidence. The prosecutor has a home-run and the governor loves you for it, too. It's all so easy. The VIPD has a terrible percentage of homicides solved. Terrible. And we have an overcrowded prison system. With you, they get three-in-one."

"Is this supposed to cheer me up?"

"You get married?" he asked jokingly. I didn't laugh. "Your lawyer can sleep with you if you're married or the relationship started before representation."

"Can we get back to this?" I jabbed my finger on the photo creating three smudges on the t-shirt Felicia wore. "You see this shirt? It's interesting. Have you followed up on this?"

"No. It's a t-shirt." He squinted through his sunglasses. "What's the wetlands?"

"Wetlands are places where the ocean and fresh water meet."

"How do you know so much?"

"On the coast between Santa Monica and El Segundo, there's a place … it's a stopping point for migratory birds, among other things. Land developers would love to drain them and build condos. There's some enviro organizations, who fight the developers and have managed to save a portion. It's ongoing. See the heron?" Leber nodded at me. "The heron's one of the birds that hang out there."

Leber leaned back and studied the clock on the wall. His phone buzzed. He pulled it off his belt and studied the screen.

"Gotta go, so wrap it up, Boise. I want to help, but I have other cases."

"Look, my wife, Evelyn, she was an integral part of one of these conservation groups. She and another guy ran the thing. I need you to check into this. You're the only one they'll listen to. Maybe there's something. This wetlands thing."

"And what, you think that someone out in L.A. killed Felicia because of her non-profit dealings?"

I tugged on my chains and they rattled. "Leber, what are the odds that someone here died and might have known my wife in L.A.?"

"Known your wife? Because she's a savior of the wetlands?"

"Yes. That world isn't very big. There's only a few organizations doing this. Felicia could have known my wife."

He sighed. "Or she bought this shirt online or at a thrift store for two bucks because she thought it looked cool." He paused, then said, "When did your wife pass?"

"One year and nine months ago."

Leber fingered the photo, rotating it in a circle then moving the three photos of Felicia around like a street hustler. "Then again, probably this Felicia and your wife never met. Probably she didn't get into this saving the wildlife thing till after your wife passed." His phone vibrated. "Look, I can try some phone calls, but …"

"Leber, you gotta go out there. I'd go, but …" I held up my hands.

"You think I don't want to?" Leber said. He kept his eyes down on Felicia's photos. Now his phone actually rang. He kept the conversation brief, then hung up.

"I really gotta go," he said as he pushed away from the table.

"Leber, I need you to go out there. You're the one who might convince them to check further on this angle."

"I can't. We don't have resources like that. We don't have the manpower."

"So that's it? I get the electri-fried because it's not in the budget? Is that what being a detective around here is?"

Leber's breathing dropped to an inaudible level as he faced the wall, hands on hips. "We have too many homicides, robberies, drug dealers, prostitutes, and not enough detectives or funds to catch 'em all. What do you want me to tell you?"

"I want you to help me. I didn't want to bring up our last adventure."

"What about it? You mean where I saved your ass?"

"I think we saved each others' asses, Leber. Isn't there some code after you save a life?"

"Oh please. This is St. Thomas. Beaches and rum, not feudal Japan. No codes."

"So, you're satisfied with that? If this was you, I'd do whatever it took and you know it. Maybe you ought to consider the good you could do without those constraints."

Leber turned suddenly and got in my face. "I'm a cop, Boise! A detective on the force. I do what's necessary, but I work for the territory. We can't all go around getting wasted and passing out and expecting everyone else to clean up their messes!"

He backed away. I wiped a bit of spittle off my face and called for the guard.

Chapter 15

Things would shut down for the 2015 Christmas holiday at noon, not that I'd be celebrating the birth of baby Jesus much. Felicia's photo haunted me the night before, her face shown both hard and innocent in death. An ashen tone covered her skin. Her hair clung to the sand like one of those starfish with the long, slender arms.

There was no word from Henry, but I trusted that he would pursue the avenue I'd provided. Henry was swamped with responsibilities between his three kids from two ex-wives, his alimony and child support bills kept him working for whomever would pay, including law firms. He had to prioritize money over enabling a destitute friend.

Henry's hobbies included serial monogamy. Engaged for the fourth time, the man picked the same kind of woman every time: a jealous-type who wanted him to give up his one true love to prove his love for her. One didn't give him relationship advice. Almost anything else was fair game. I hoped that his current mate would give him the freedom to pursue my leads and still give proper attention to the paying gigs he already had in the pipeline.

Once a week, the information technology staff at the jailhouse reviewed and printed out emails if you agreed to give them unfettered access to your email account. Dana had created a "prison email" account in my name that I didn't mind the corrections bureau having access to. We called it BoisesPrisonMail, with the idea that when my release date arrived, I'd have the symbolic pleasure of deleting the account.

Printed emails arrived on my floor, dropped through the bars like trash. One page had gotten wet from water that had splashed from my sink while brushing my teeth for the second time today. Jail provided more time for personal hygiene. Whenever sitting around my cell, I generally had floss wrapped around my finger, running it absentmindedly through my teeth. I brushed four times a day. They allowed Dana to bring me extra toothpaste and floss. I'd taught Antoine, the guy in the cell next to me, how to floss. He did it regularly. He grinned and said, "Me feel da difference!"

The printer sucked. Many of the words on the pages overlapped and smudged or printed too lightly. After thumbing through the junk mail, including a marriage proposal from some lunatic, I found an email from Henry sent days earlier.

> Boise,
>
> How you doing? I found a Felicia who worked out here for a coffee shop in Mar Vista, called Coffee MV, as assistant manager. The owner said she was a good worker, but complained frequently about wanting to make a better living. She was going to school down at LA Trade Tech in the evenings to get a certificate as a lab tech. Teachers say she wanted to work in a fertility clinic. So far, nothing as far as the

> wetlands angle. I'm scarce on time, but I
> know this is a priority (duh!), but your
> dumb old cop buddy also has a lot to do
> for the wedding and you know the support
> issues. I'm going to check that angle next,
> but needed to get basic background first.
> Hang in there.
> H.

The email didn't give me much to go on. I needed more information on Felicia and her cohorts. Working at a coffee shop and attending a tech school in downtown Los Angeles. I mulled that over for a while, then dialed Henry.

He didn't answer and the phone disconnected. I tugged a piece of floss off the roll and continued to mull over the scraps of information I had on Felicia. I considered her life, the people who would miss her and wonder why she had never returned to the places she frequented, like the coffee house, and her classes. I envisioned her serving coffee and studying, all the things she'd never do again.

The other women could be important. Hopefully, the guy who followed Ronica would prove fruitful. Felicia was the catalyst for the trip to St. Thomas. To get more metaphysical, neither Ronica or Jill's photos struck a nerve, assuming my investigative instincts had any value.

We needed to head to the mess hall. My appetite had died along with my presumption of innocence. The food here upset my colitis every time I ate. I took three pills a day, but my insides refused to settle. I'd thinned out to well below my fighting weight. I should be doing push-ups and hitting the rusty weights when out in the yard, but I only had the energy to read and lay around staring at photos of dead women, while masticating on how far down the sinkhole my life had plummeted.

My mind cued on a line I'd once read or heard: "You can't go back to a place you never left." All the choices I'd made in my thirty-odd years had led me here. Married for a second time to a woman I'd never seen naked. Pining for a wife who'd cheated on me before being murdered. Even if I got out of this jail cell, my life wasn't stuffed with hibiscus petals. The long shadows of my choices had driven me back to the place I thought of as home, but it hadn't been much of a homecoming. My close friend, Roger, had turned into a murdered drug dealer, and I hadn't been much help to his son, Elias.

"Hey, Boise." Julian slouched outside my cell, his hang-dog look even more hang-dog than usual.

"Hey, Julian. You all right?" I asked.

"The Pirates traded one of my favorite players. They don't spend no money. This owner's cheaper than me sister husband."

"That's what you're upset about? Really?"

Julian sighed. "And you."

"Me?"

"Yeah. I been around a lot of bad people, dem. You know? Criminal types. You don't be right. You don't belong."

"T'anks, my friend. I'm not sure you belong here, either."

Julian led me down the hallway toward a non-descript meeting room that reminded me of a by-the-hour hotel room. He'd stopped cuffing me. "Hey, man, maybe you ought to cuff me. What if your boss finds out? Don't you have cameras here?" I fingered the floss in my pocket.

"No cameras. Dey always broke," he muttered. He still made me walk in front and his hand rested lightly on the handle of his baton. I guess he didn't trust me entirely. I didn't blame him.

"Sorry, Julian, but why am I here?"

"Visitor. He on your list."

Julian locked me in the room after cuffing me to the table, then returned a few minutes later with a handsome young man.

"I'll be damned. Elias." I moved to hug him, but the cuffs

caught.

Julian's eyes narrowed. "You know there ain't no touching."

Other than the guards shoving me around from behind and grabbing my shoulder, I'd had no touch. Julian left and Elias scraped the old wooden school chair into place across from me. On the surface of the table, someone had scraped an anatomical heart inside a circle. In another spot on the table was an ejaculating penis with gigantic hairy testicles. Surprisingly realistic art.

Elias sucked a concerted breath. He looked at the testicles, but didn't see them. I stared at the blond-black hair on the crown of his head. We'd had many difficulties, but had patched things up, although I hadn't been in touch. A thought entered my mind, sneaky as a splinter.

"You didn't call me," he said softly, sneaking a glance. "I don't rate a call?"

It was my turn to look down and mutter in the direction of the testicles, "Sorry."

"Sorry?"

I pulled my eyes up to see disappointment tinged with anger. I couldn't stop disappointing Elias any more than I could stop drinking. I wanted to be a stable figure in his life. Before I said the words, I regretted them. "You're probably better off without me around."

I could hear my mother saying, "Grow up, you wimp. Be a man, like your father."

Elias smacked his hand on the table. "I'm studying pre-law and I work for a lawyer. I could help you, you know?"

I jerked backwards. "Sorry." The thought, again like a splinter. It couldn't be, but there it was. Paranoia had set in.

"Is it because I'm younger? You got some complex about me helping you? You didn't mind coming into my life and figuring out what happened to pops, but now ... Why do I keep doing this?" The last question was a conversation with himself. "Your rass could rot in here." A fan kicked on somewhere, probably the exhaust in the kitchen where they constantly burned food. "What are you gonna do? Are you mounting a defense? Do you need our help?"

"I have an attorney. She's good. I'm good."

He scoffed and scratched his short hair. "Who?"

I was suddenly very conscious of my Adam's apple bobbing as I swallowed some spit that had gathered under my tongue. Everything felt stuck inside my mouth. I wanted to floss. Finally, I said, "Miguela." *We're supposed to have a conjugal visit today*, I thought apprehensively. Should I tell Miguela about the splinter?

Elias leaned back, let out an Axel Foley laugh, and clapped his hands together. "Miguela! You on a first name basis? How can you afford her? Did you start dealing? 'Cause last I checked, dealers were her specialty." When I didn't respond, he said, "So what? She throwing you pro bono for old times' sake?"

"I'm paying her, but it's … an exchange."

He clapped again and let out a more controlled laugh like a professor who just heard that his student lost the spelling bee on a three-letter word. "I don't even wanna know what that means. Okay, yeah, I do."

"Can't tell you."

"You gotta."

"No, I don't. Is there anything else, esquire?" I smiled while saying the last word, although I felt anything but happy about the arrangement.

"I saw you, night before. Kismet Dream. It was a good show. I saw you with that girl, then I saw you leaving the lot with some others. They the ones who bought it?"

Probably my imagination or me putting my own spin on his features, like that exercise where you listened to the same noise hundreds of times, and after a while started to hear different phrases despite the noise itself never changing. I couldn't get the thought out. It was ridiculous, but this whole situation was ridiculous. Elias believed I'd abandoned him. Abandonment made people lash out.

"Yeah," I said. "They were the ones. Why didn't you come say, 'Hey.'"

"Same reason I wasn't gonna come here. Same reason as last time we met at the college. I feel like I'm always doin' the chasing and you runnin' like Usain."

"I'm sorry, Elias. It's not like that. I'm just busy. Trying to keep my head above water. You were there, at the concert on that Sunday night?"

"That's what I already told you."

"That seems like something you should have told me sooner. Did you talk to the cops?"

He rubbed the scar on his forehead. "I didn't see nothin'," he spat. "You think me, the son of a murdered drug dealer, makes a habit of hanging out with cops? Volunteering information? You think my dad and Phil didn't taught me better than that?"

"Did you see …"

"See, that's how it always is with Boise Montague. Always comes back to what everyone can do to help you out another mess. I'm done. You come correct and we can talk, but I ain't playing that game. 'Sides, I didn't see nothing."

"Fine," I said. "Don't you have studying to do?"

Elias shot one last comment as the guard led me back to Shangri-La. "Merry Christmas, Boise."

CHAPTER 16

As promised, the guard put me in a room with Miguela Salas for a conjugal visit at four-thirty in the afternoon. I wasn't feeling very romantic. I'd just watched another prisoner pull out his penis and slap it against the bars of his cell while yelling to be serviced at a female guard. He'd disappeared a few minutes later.

"Miguela, we don't have to consummate this deal. I'm sorry, but ..."

"We aren't consummating anything, Mr. Montague. But, we will say we consummated if asked. In past times, kings and queens had to consummate in front of a witness to make the marriage valid." She pushed her fingers through her short, curly hair and messed it around and made a moaning noise. "Come on, play along." She banged a fist against the wall, removed a shoe and flung it against the door, then howled, "Yesssss!"

I grunted a couple times and kicked my chair half-heartedly. This seemed to satisfy her.

"Are we done?"

"Yes, I hear the first time goes quickly."

She patted down her hair again, but it remained moderately disheveled. She pulled her shirt slightly off kilter.

"You hear?" I asked. "You've never …"

"We must retain appearances. Now, while I have you here, please sign these documents."

"What is this?"

"Pro bono hours. I'm not much for pro bono work. Also, I need to complete the name change forms. That's what these are for."

I signed.

"You know Roger's son, Elias?" I asked.

"I know who he is. Works for Attorney Patrick Roberts down by the university. Are you two still in touch?"

"He came by earlier today."

"You were friends with his father. Nothing wrong with that."

"He's quite angry with me. I'm not good at staying in touch with him. Maybe he sees me as a big brother."

"You and Roger Black were about the same age. He looks up to you."

"His father was a criminal."

"I'm not at liberty to discuss my client's criminal history."

"Do you think Elias is capable of murder?"

She watched me a while. "You mean, do I think Elias would kill three women and frame you? Why would he do such a thing?"

"I dunno. I'm not a good friend."

"Mr. Montague, that is a leap."

"He has crime in his genes!"

She banged on the door and left. As Julian led me back, he commented, "Beautiful woman. She your lady?"

"Yeah. Yeah. I suppose."

CHAPTER 17

Christmas Day 2015. In here not much changed, except for a string of lights high up in the dining hall, above the mess area, the joy of those green and red lights drowned by the slapping sound of man-made meat being slopped onto our plates. The eggs tasted as bad as the rations they fed us at basic training. They certainly hadn't come out of a shell this morning. Big, disgusting plastic bags of yellow stuff. It beat the usual gruel they called oatmeal.

I sat in my spot at the front, closest to the exit, near the guards. They walked us out to the "yard" to supposedly get a little exercise. Winter featured seventy-five degree evenings and eighty degree days. Downright chilly by Virgin Islands' standards. I didn't remember very much in the way of seventy degree weather growing up, but childhood memories are fickle things. I managed light walks with my crutch around a dusty field the size of a tennis court. Dirt kicked up, my knee aching gently. Three guards to ten inmates. Kenny rejoined for the overtime holiday pay. He scowled at me as the sun slipped behind a harmless white cloud.

I plopped onto the grass and positioned myself to admire the speckled sky. Lindberg Bay had a coconut tree I sometimes fell asleep on, its contour fit my body like a hammock. Here in the withered prison yard, imaginary palms waved in the gentle breeze.

A jarring kick to my ribs. "Get da hell up, killer!" Kenny's angry face replaced the palm fronds. "Why I have to come get you all the time? Everyone else goin' in. We done call you. What you looking at?"

I pushed up on my elbows. "I've asked you to stop calling me that."

"What you say to me, killer?"

He'd already set me on a path without a solution. The man he'd attacked, Antoine, had vanished, and I was accused of assault. It would be my word, someone everyone thought killed three innocent women, against a guard. What else could he do to me?

"I said stop calling me that!" It came out more forcefully than I'd intended, but felt good. It was my Christmas gift to myself.

Kenny pulled his baton off its loop. "Pick up your crutch." A flash of him standing in his living room in front of the mirror, perfecting the maneuver the way a magician might practice sleight of hand. Before I could roll away, he dropped a knee onto my chest. My arms splayed. He rammed the handle into my navel, knocking the wind out of me. I crumpled and rolled in the dirt as he peppered my back with kicks and baton strikes. Things cracked. He screamed, his cries of rage swirled in the speckled sky. One kick struck the back of my head.

***

The same hospital room. Everything ached. Calm, neutral voices from the hospital P.A. system drifted through the open door. I tried to speak. Too dry. Blinking hurt and the back of my head throbbed. The handcuff clanked against the bedframe as I reached to touch my face. The only thing that didn't seem to have suffered further damage was my knee.

The nurse agreed to turn on a football game. I dozed in and out. She explained my situation. Three broken ribs and some severe bruising. My torso was wrapped, and I'd been given a strong dose of painkillers.

Dana strolled in and plopped into a plastic seat next to my bed. "Wake up, Boise." My eyes fluttered.

"Eyes hurt. Light," I croaked.

"Hey, buddy. Turn off the lights."

The same phone-studying guard leaned against the door, acting like he wasn't listening. He did nothing. When Dana was next to the guard, she looked directly at him and said, "These fuckers. That's it, no more mister nice reporter." She flicked off the lights. The guard eyed her, the glow of the phone giving him an ominous look.

"Don't look at me like that. Yeah, I'm talking about you fuckers." The guard came to an attention stance and dropped the phone to his side. Dana stepped back, but her words reflected her inability to take cues when a matter became dangerous. "Don't get all bully-ie with me, pal. My boss knows where I am. I also have mace in here." Her hand had disappeared inside her giant Kenyan purse.

The guard said, "Mace is illegal."

"Oh, he speaks. It's pepper spray. It'll still hurt like a bitch."

At this, the guard shook his head and dropped his attention back to his phone as if to say, "You're not worth my time."

"Merry Christmas," I grunted. My whole torso ached when I spoke.

"Who did this? Was it that asshole guard? The one you said beat up the other inmate?" She touched my cheek tenderly. I flinched. "Motherfuckers … That's it, right? That's it?"

I wrote down what had to be done on all fronts, from the outside, while Dana did something on her laptop. We needed to find out the status of my mother's case. Henry needed to get something on Felicia's connection to the wetlands. The other women, Jill and Ronica, had no discernable connections to anything in my life. They were friends of Felicia from Jamaica. They didn't reside in Los Angeles. Nothing in their photos brought any new avenues to mind.

I needed to see my emails and snail mail. Dana agreed that she could swing by The Manner and pick up my mail, then request that the jail send printouts of my emails over to my hospital room.

"Do they usually do that for prisoners?" Dana asked. "Like, is it standard?"

They didn't go out of their way for incarcerated people, ever. The idea was that Dana's presence, as my emissary, broadcast an implicit threat: *Give this Montague joker what he wants or this story will be out sooner than you'd like.*

***

They stalled Dana as long as they could, but a couple days later she brought my various mails to the hospital. I was in the bathroom peeing when she entered. The guard stood by the bathroom door looking at his cell phone and listening to my urine hit the water. I washed my hands, flossed, and brushed.

Once I got onto whoever framed me, my life might be in more danger than it already was being inside a cage surrounded by a bunch of violent criminals, and Kenny. I was a broke private dick on an island smaller than most counties. One small citizen with virtually no family. I slid back into a chair and the guard cuffed me to the bed. My arm kept falling asleep as I held it in some odd position trying to find comfort. I propped my bad leg on the edge of the bed. My voice felt better after a few days of sleep and hot tea with honey, a luxury afforded me only because the nurse insisted.

The nurse smiled as she checked the bathroom and my chart. More oral pain meds. It wasn't as good as a drink, but it edged off the took. I had a way with caregivers. I'd married Evelyn after she took care of me, and look how well that turned out. My caregiver had Hulk Hogan's build and Oprah Winfrey's sassy attitude. She tugged on the chain.

"Why you need to trap dis man to da bed?"

The guard remained fixated on his phone.

"Dis younger generation so rude," she said loud enough for the cop to hear. Even this didn't elicit a response. "You da same Boise Montague, who find out what Doctor DeVere was up to?"

Dana's face lit up. "You're a celebrity.

The nurse put her hands on both of her cheeks and wiggled her bottom around like she'd just won the lottery. "Oh, gam! I can't wait to tell da others. You is he. I tell dem you was he, but they ain't believe me. Oh, gam. I read about it in da paper. Hey, you know what happen to he?"

I grinned, which hurt.

Dana shook her head. "I take it you weren't close?"

"Dat man so full he-self." She moved closer and whispered to me, "I gonna bring you some banana bread, mañana. But, no, but seriously, you know what happen to Dr. DeVere?"

Dana removed her cap, ruffled her hair, then tucked it back under, adjusting it till she had it just right. "The good doctor got involved with some unsavory folks. We never figured where he went. You hear anything?"

I shook my head. Speaking hurt, but I couldn't resist. "Do you crush the bananas yourself?"

"Yeah, da man. And I use da figs."

I shot her a thumbs up.

After the nurse left, Dana asked, "Figs? Figs in banana bread?"

"Fig bananas. The small ones."

"Don't eat bananas."

I gave her an incredulous look. "They're manna." Somehow, the more I spoke, the less it hurt.

"Whatever. Listen, I got stuff for you. Let's try to get some actual work done so you can stop being chained to a bed and getting your ass kicked."

A bouquet of flowers had appeared in the center of the white pressboard table outside my bathroom. The bulbous red vase held local blossoms that I rarely saw during my years in California.

"Honey, you shouldn't have," I said.

"Annie sent them. She likes to pick flowers out of the garden and send them with me to injured private detectives."

"Lucky me," I said, admiring the assortment and wondering how a romantic like Annie put up with a pragmatist like Dana.

She pulled out a stack of my emails and some unopened mail. Together we rummaged. Dana's focus on a task once started always impressed me. She skimmed each sheet and discarded anything worthless. I explained what to look for, mainly emails from Henry or anything personal on the off chance someone else (no idea who) came forward to offer assistance.

"How many marriage proposals do you get per week?" Dana asked. "Jesus. These people are nuts."

"Women love bad boys," I muttered, then cursed at a paper cut.

"It's not just women, two of them are men, and one goes by 'they'."

"Dana, the marriage proposals are not only irrelevant, I'm unavailable."

"Oh yeah, Yarey. How is the lunatic's daughter?"

"She hasn't spoken to me or answered my calls since this thing started."

"Poor girl has had her fill of run-ins with law enforcement for one lifetime."

Dana fetched floss. While I threaded my teeth, we scanned

the emails from Henry. The first gave little additional information about Felicia's connection to the Ballona Wetlands. Henry claimed that when he went by to interview the people there, the place was locked up tight. He had excuses about how busy he was with another investigation. I asked Dana to send him an email asking why he couldn't go more often, or find out how to reach the executive director or someone in charge of personnel.

"Send Henry an email to check it out again and drop Evelyn's name as needed."

She started to type, then stopped, pinching her lip. "We oughta wait till we go through all the emails before getting on Henry's case." She put the laptop aside and rummaged through the papers some more. She flipped a sheet out of the stack. "This looks like something."

She handed it to me and continued through the stack. The woman was a bloodhound. "Do you ever get tired of being right?"

Henry had made the connection. Felicia volunteered at the same organization Evelyn worked for, BWPP. It was iffy whether Felicia had been there long enough to have ever met Evelyn. Despite Evelyn's deep involvement with BWPP, I'd rarely set foot inside the place.

Reading the email reminded me of another thing I had asked Henry to do. After finishing my pile of mail and emails, all junk, plus two more marriage proposals, and a sexual liaison request that included a penis shot from some guy in St. Croix, I asked Dana if she had anything else in her pile from Henry.

Dana had already switched back to the computer. "Nothing else," she said between keystrokes. "Hold on, I gotta answer a question from Walter about a source on this other thing."

Always another thing.

"You seem busier than before," I muttered. She made a face. "Sorry, but it's true. Do you sleep? When did you last go out with Annie?"

"We stay in a lot. She's really bothered by what's happened to you and that you won't let her help. They tightened the budget at *The News*. I have to write two more stories per week, and they changed our health insurance. Never mind. It's boring."

When her fingers stopped flashing across the keys, I asked her to find out what was going on with my mother's trial, by emailing Denise St. John, an uptight lawyer who, once upon a time, enjoyed having martinis on Fridays with Evelyn and I. A ferocious divorce attorney, she was the only one who didn't look down her nose at firm investigators, like me.

Dana composed a separate email to Henry asking about my mother, again

"Okay, that's it for now. Annie is worried about you and so am I. I'm going to try getting Walter to put more heat on the Bureau of Corrections to keep you in a safer environment."

I shrugged my resignation. "Do whatever you want."

"Jeez, don't rush to hug me or anything."

"Dana, you aren't the best listener. I told you I can handle this. Besides," I held up my manacled arm. "Can't hug, and my whole back aches like arches."

"That was before. Things have accelerated. You've been in the hospital twice. This isn't your forte."

"Give me my pills, will ya?"

I stared at the bouquet. Dana asked what I was thinking about.

"Can you wait a little longer here, and call Leber to see if he can join us? Did you bring the book?"

She rummaged in her bag and pulled out a worn copy of *Crime and Punishment*. "Not sure this is the most soothing reading in your predicament."

I'd managed six pages of the book once I'd found where I'd left off in the jailhouse copy. Raskolnikov wandered the streets after alienating his mother and sister who he claimed to miss so much.

"Goode," Leber said, nodding at Dana and crossing his arms inside the doorway. A file dangled over his forearm. "What do you want?"

"I wouldn't likely ask to see you," Dana replied.

Dana had reported on allegations of police misconduct against Leber, of which he was later acquitted. It wasn't her fault. Pickering assigned the case, she reported what she'd found out from the people at internal affairs and other reliable sources. Leber knew it, but knowing didn't eliminate the tension.

He shifted his sunglasses to me. "Yeah, I'm here. What's up?"

"You have an up-close photo of that flower that Felicia Nichols had behind her ear?"

"No. Why?"

"Just not like any flower I've ever seen. Looks extraordinary."

"Boise, stop wasting my time." He made a swirling motion with his index finger. "The point."

"I only remember having one beer." Dana and Leber watched me. She looked skeptical, he impatient. "Why would I have blacked out after one beer?"

"Because you don't remember right what you drank," Leber said in a clipped tone. "Happens all the time. You know how many drunks claim to only have had one? Almost as many as convicts who claim they're innocent."

"Hey," I said. "Easy with the 'd' word."

Dana and Leber exchanged a look. They both had lots of experience with alcoholics. Everyone who'd spent any longer than a couple of years in St. Thomas realized that drinking was the primary pastime.

"I brought the photo of the vic from the crime scene. It's the best I could do. You can see the flower here. What's the big? It's decoration. Women like flowers, although this one's seen better days."

He was right. The five-petaled lavender flower showed signs of wilt. There appeared to be no stamen, but on closer inspection I spotted a couple bits of yellow-orange fuzz in the center.

"The stamen is missing," I observed.

"Flowers lose parts when worn as jewelry. It's not their primary function," Dana responded.

That's when Miguela Salas appeared in the doorway followed by my good-natured nurse. "Not supposed to have this many visitors at once," she said. "But I make an exception for you." She winked at me. "Try and be quick."

She left. The guard didn't seem to care, probably because Leber was there.

"She seems taken with you," Dana said.

"Hello, Miguela. Do you know Dana Goode and Detective Leber?"

Miguela brushed past them. "I need you to sign some documents."

She pulled out four sheets of paper from her ever-present briefcase.

"What are these?" I asked.

She glared at me. "Are you saying you want me to speak in front of these people?" We hadn't even shut the door. "My advice is that no third-parties be present or you'll waive privilege."

Leber nodded and stepped out. Dana followed. The guard stepped out as well and shut the door.

"Happy?" I said.

She splayed out the documents. "Your release documents. I convinced the judge to release you pending trial. I filed an emergency hearing after your ..." She squinted and pursed her chubby lips. "... thrashing. The prosecutor objected, but not vehemently."

I reviewed the papers. One showed that I had agreed to accept bail and would forfeit the money if I failed to appear on the appointed trial date.

"Who put up bail?" I asked.

"I don't know. A benefactor. About an hour after I got them to agree to this lower amount. Tall pale woman, waist-length blonde hair of Scandinavian origin."

Annie. Even the people who dated Dana couldn't stay out of my business. I thought about not signing, then a shooting pain rippled through my mid-section.

"I thought murder suspects didn't get bail?"

"Your situation and the press may have altered the equation from its usual course, as well as having an attorney as good as me."

I signed. An unexpected wave of relief flooded through me. "So, what now?"

"You cannot leave the island."

"What?"

"You are confined to St. Thomas. You'll surrender your passport and you'll be given a temporary I.D. card that allows you to drive, but not to travel."

"What about those ankle things?"

"We're in the Virgin Islands."

"And when?"

"The hospital insists you get out tomorrow. You go back to jail for processing, then probably out the same or next day."

"Happy New Year," I said.

"Do you have any new information that will help with your defense? This case is going to be tough unless the police make a mistake on the DNA or with the evidence. So far, there's nothing."

I lowered my voice. "Hey, we got married. You sure you aren't expecting a conjugal visit?"

"Rest assured, I'm aware of what you have given as payment for my assistance. I will grant you my undivided attention in this matter."

She packed the papers into her briefcase, stood, and turned to leave, her back ramrod straight as a foot soldier at inspection. I had to figure out a way to get to L.A. That would be two Christmas gifts. I probably only deserved one.

CHAPTER 18

Over the weekend, Silent Marge had stopped by to wave hello. When she heard about my impending release, she hurried back to inform Lucy, who swung by on Sunday bearing flowers, and to tell me that my old room would be ready and waiting with all my things back in place.

"What things?" I asked.

"Your cards and your booze dat be hidin' under da mattress, boy. Don't t'ink we ain't seen dat. We ain't tell your reporter friend. She would not like dat! You practice?"

"They wouldn't give me any cards in here. What was I going to do with them, slit someone's throat?" As I said it, I realized that was probably exactly why they didn't allow playing cards. The flowers brought me around again to my conundrum. "Hey, Lucy, you know anything about herbs and flowers and knockout agents?"

She knitted her brow and studied me as if I'd asked if she had iguana dung on the Manner's menu.

"Never mind."

"No, never mind. What you mean? You mean like voodoo or somet'ing? Like people who can mix herbs and know what all dem plants do?"

I sat up, wincing. "Exactly."

"You hurt still?"

I moaned, sliding down the pillow, the white sheets bunching.

"Do you know anyone?" I asked again as she got closer, trying to help me adjust.

"No, me ain't know people like dat."

One final option remained, and now that I would be free, I could pursue it. There had been a guy out east who helped my father with back issues, a kind of medicine man, who seemed to perform miracles with his fingers and local plants, but I'd never known the man's name or exactly where he lived. The guy seemed ancient even then. I'd be shocked if he were still alive after more than twenty years. I didn't live in that world, and none of the people I commiserated with lived there, either. My father did it out of desperation, not any genuine belief in natural remedies. I'd hear him and my mother arguing about spending the money on this quack, but my dad would tell her to get off it, his arms outstretched. "I haven't been able to do this in two goddamn weeks."

"It's because you fell off the bar stool, not because you have a bad back!" she'd yell back. "It's psychosomatic."

"Bahhh! What do you know?" Then he'd head out the door for The Normandie to argue with his fellow patrons. Ah, the good old days. One of those guys still sat on the same bar stool.

***

The next day at ten, Dana picked me up. The jail looked less treacherous from the outside. I hoped I'd never see the inside of such a place again.

She had no time to hang out or assist, but she did take me by Little Switzerland to thank Annie. Annie waved me off in her elegant, long-fingered manner, commenting that I'd do the same for her if it ever came to that.

"I doubt you'd pass out on the beach with three strangers," I said.

"You would be surprised what I did in my youth. We all make mistakes. You look good despite your ordeal." Her vague Danish accent gave her words a delicate elegance that matched her fingers.

We headed back into the heat on Dronningens Gade among the milling tourists.

"Listen, I gotta get back to the newsroom. You wanna come, check on your cantaloupe door?"

"I haven't lost my office yet?"

"Not yet."

"Don't tell me …" I said, gesturing back inside the famous jewelry store owned by Annie's family.

"Oh, God, no, Annie didn't do that. We got a collection together and did a drive on our website. You might have to do some investigative work for a few people in the future, but we collected enough to keep you current. For some reason, people on this island know, and even like you."

"And some want to kill or frame me for murder," I retorted.

"That's true. I've seen it first hand."

"Take me to The Normandie."

Dana had started to back out of her parking space behind the store and slammed on the brakes of the dusty Sentra.

"You expect me to take you to a bar! You've been out for less than two hours."

"I'm not gonna drink," I said. "I'm gonna eat and talk."

She glared at me for a while before a car honked. Dana shot the guy the finger as she whipped the wheel around and we sped down the small street. We didn't speak till we arrived in Frenchtown.

As I got out, she said, "You need a shower and fresh clothes."

I sniffed my armpit. "I need a new hat."

"What happened to your hat?"

I wanted to say something witty, but didn't have the heart. "It's … just gone."

I slammed the door and gave the roof one hard rap before she sped away, a piece of gravel kicking onto my jeans. An old Camaro with a pink Bondo door rumbled past, blasting reggae. The first reggae I'd heard since that night.

It felt like five years had passed. I had the bruises to prove it.

The crickets in the semi-darkness, the slow crawl of the sunbeam across my cell floor from the lone window. Reading and thinking. Now, limited freedom. Could I get off-island? Get all the way to California? Would I bother for my mother? For myself? Henry wasn't getting anywhere fast.

The Normandie's brown and white tile floor showed wear, but not as much as one would have expected. I'd been coming here since I was a toddler, maybe longer. The floor had never changed in my thirty-three years. Irene stood behind the bar, hands on hips like a gunslinger. She didn't let anyone sneak up on her, ever.

A wide man who smelled of leather and sweat eased out the door and slithered around me. The bar dog lay asleep next to his water bowl.

"Oh gam, look what da cat drag in," Irene declared, picking up an empty beer glass and wiping off the ring of water. "Dis seat still warm."

"Sorry, Irene. Is it okay if I sit there?" I indicated a stool near the end of the bar, next to my father's old drinking companion.

She raised her eyebrows, flipped the formerly white towel onto her shoulder and followed me the length.

"Guinness?" she asked, grabbing a glass and starting to pour from a tap.

"No!" I said quickly. "Not today. Uh, club soda."

Raised eyebrows again. "Well, well, da planets must be out of alignment, mi son." The fountain gun gurgled. "Lime?"

"Please."

She looked me up and down. "You lose weight. And wha' happen here?" She indicated my face and the brace on my knee.

"Yeah, prison diet. Food goes in and comes right back out."

"You so crude. Yeah, we hear 'bout dat. You killin' people again? Dat why your face all mess up?"

She wasn't going to let it go. "Prison guard's billy club had an affinity for me."

"Ha, ha!" Norman slapped the bar at Irene's quip or my response, not sure which. "Terry Montague's boy, back again, makin' the family proud."

The man's breath, a combination of foot cheese and skunky beer, could have drowned a tiger shark. I tried to speak while holding my breath.

"That's funny, Irene. Very funny. I didn't kill anyone." I turned around and a couple sitting at a table near the vacant piano left.

"You always were good for business," Irene said.

"You remember when Terry got put in the clinker? Apples and trees, baby, apples and trees." Norman was a kid holding a magnifying glass up to the sun. I was the ant.

"You burn me up," I said, trying to control my anger. It wasn't happening. "Didn't I ask you to lay off my old man last time we spoke?"

"Bah! What do I care about Terry. That old asshole abandoned me here all those years ago. Never even sent a postcard. No call. Nothing. He went and got fancy, I reckon."

"You're angry he skipped town and didn't stay in touch?"

Norman's eyes welled, watery and red. He blubbered, "Yeah, maybe. Thought he and I were friends. I don't got a lot of 'em." Wow. Norman hadn't stopped razzing me about my father since I'd returned.

Irene studied Norman, then switched her gaze to me. "Why you in me establishment if you ain't want a drink?"

"Old times' sake." I shrugged. "Food?"

"Burger, bloody," she said and walked toward the kitchen without waiting for a reply.

"Do I get a choice of cheese?" I yelled after her. She shot me the middle finger over her shoulder. "Okay, Swiss it is."

Norman's comb-over hung loosely as he leaned into his Irish whiskey. The man had seen better days and I couldn't fathom why a man of his vintage clung to pretending he wasn't bald. Then again, I'd never had a lack of hair, therefore hadn't struggled with that particular brand of vanity.

Audible drops plunked into his whiskey. "Does it taste better with salt, Norman?" I asked, patting his shoulder. Beneath his shirt I felt hard bone and loose skin. The man had always subsisted on whiskey and nuts, mostly whiskey, and I couldn't figure how he hadn't contracted cirrhosis. Norman muttered something into his glass between tear-plunks.

"What?"

His head rose slightly, a dirty waterfall dribbled down his cheeks. "Why am I still here?"

"In this bar?"

He micro-shook his head, as if this question was one of the great mysteries of the universe that could only be answered by a higher power.

"Everyone else." He gazed past me at the vacant barstools. "All the others, all those people I called friends. Gone. Moved on. One by one. In the great beyond. Why am I still here?"

It's not for lack of trying.

"Maybe to help me?" I said, glancing over my shoulder, hoping I'd have a couple minutes before Irene rejoined. The ice in his glass clanked around as he downed the remaining whiskey. His mouth flexed, his lips forming two horizontal hills around his gums, then reformed to normal, then flexed, then normal, then flexed, then normal. His eyes blinking and red. The deep lines betrayed a life of hard labor and harder drinking.

The blandness of my club soda made me want to cry, too. Being here was not a good idea. All the labels, the smells, reminding me of who I really was and where I belonged. I envisioned a gutter with brackish water running downhill. Norman and I had more in common than I'd like to admit, the biggest difference being the amount of time gravity had had its way. And, although I drank my share, no bars could claim I was a significant portion of their bottom line.

Norman dabbed at his eyes while I studied the Guinness tap. "I have a question for you. You knew my father well, right?"

"Terry and I were like brothers," he blubbered. The sunlight coming through the front door and around the edges of the wooden slats came and went as clouds rolled across the sky. It smelled of rain and that dirty rancid flavor that invaded all drinking establishments past a certain age. Irene yelled something at the cook. The cook yelled back. Sitting on the inside of this bar, we could have been in any city or town, anywhere in the world.

"You heard about what happened to me?"

"Course I heard. I'm not living under a reef," he moaned. "I probably should take one of my pills, but not supposed to take with alcohol."

I pushed my drink over. "Here, have mine."

He studied the club soda like it was cyanide. "That's fine, I'll wait for Irene."

I pulled the plastic cup of soda back and took another sip. I reached over the bar, stole another lime wedge, pinched the juice into my cup. A drop of lime juice spiked my eye. I splashed some club soda on my face and blinked. "You remember Terry having a bad back?"

"Why're you callin' him 'Terry'? He's your father. Show some respect."

I wanted to ask him where that respect had been for the last half-year he'd spent telling me that my father could go fuck himself every time I came in here.

He tugged a dirty handkerchief out of his sagging back pocket and dabbed his stained cheeks. His skin looked so fragile, I thought it might rip. I pressed my question. "You remember he had a medicine man type he used to go see when his back went wrong?"

"Medicine man? Like hocus-pocus in the jungle? Your father wasn't some dumb-ass with no education. He coulda done better than that bitch he married, too."

I had been looking toward the kitchen/pool hall area for Irene, thinking how she still made my head spin. Something about the way she walked. I was nothing but Terry's little boy to her, always would be. Suddenly, Norman's words registered, I spun around, my stool tipping as I lost my balance, having to jump away as it clattered to the floor. I knocked over the club soda in an effort not to tumble. Irene returned and plopped the basket down.

Norman reared back, cackling. "Careful with that knee!"

"What you doin'? You break it, you buy it," she scolded.

"I'm not gonna break anything, babysitter."

She smiled. "You wish I was still your babysitter. What happen? Norman, you say somet'ing about Patrice?"

Norman slapped his thigh and kept laughing like some caricature from a bad western.

Irene wiped up my spilled drink and filled a new plastic cup. She propped a fresh lime on the lip. "One day, someone goin' knock you off dat chair and crack your skull on me nice tile. You'll have to pay if you crack da floor and dis style ain't easy to find."

I reset the stool. "You don't say shit like that about a man's mother!"

He waved her off. "I'm just messing with you. Sometimes, when Irene leaves, I like to see people's reaction. I'm bored. We usually bet and bait."

"Oh, so it's a test?" I asked, finally resuming my seat, but inching farther away from Norman. "You want to lose what teeth you have left?"

He took a sip of the new glass of whiskey Irene set in front of him and smacked his lips in a self-satisfied way. "I'm just fucking with you. But seriously, do you like Patrice? I think she ruined Terry's life." He waved his hand dismissively. "Ah, who cares? You had a question."

"Man, I can speak ill about my mother. You cannot."

Irene leaned down to wash a glass in the sink below the bar. "What question? About Terry?"

For a few moments I steamed. Norman chuckled softly. Fucking asshole. I drank some club soda as the anger drained out of my ears.

I didn't want Irene involved, but it seemed inevitable. "Terry, my dad, used to go see this medicine man. Out in the country. You remember that?" Both had known my father, but it seemed more likely that Norman would know about this.

They exchanged a look, then back to me. Irene asked, "Why you want to know about that?"

"I'm trying to find out about local plants and if one in particular was used as an anesthetic or a sedative."

"This medicine man," Norman said slowly. "That's all you want from him is help with your case? Are you gonna need him as a witness for your trial?"

Irene's eyes fixated on me. They seemed to know what I was talking about.

"Uh, well, not sure. I'm hoping it won't go to trial if he can help me."

"Can I talk to you?" Irene waved Norman to the other end of the bar. "You, eat your food before it get cold. Don't want da blood congealin' and dem fries goin' get soggy. How you payin'?"

From the cramped walls of prison to the narrow halls of penury. "Put it on my tab?" I said sheepishly.

She sucked her teeth. "Dis one on me. Your last supper."

Norman moved slowly, his knees always slightly bent and his back hunched. He rested his palm on each bar stool all the way down as if checking for stability. One stool wobbled on uneven legs.

The burger was moist and the bun soft, but I chewed without gusto, chasing it with the club soda. I started daydreaming about my bed at The Manner, imagining what a silent night might be like. Imagining that I could hear the soothing sounds of the crickets, instead of men screaming and guards pacing or watching television. In jail, things never settled. The lights never went out. Roaches had scurried over my back in the night, the spiny legs like needles.

I finished my burger and wiped. How long did it take to discuss whether they could tell me about this guy? "Hey, what's up? Over here trying to stay out of prison, and I'm out of club soda."

The bar dog rose and lapped at his water, then plopped down. I stole over to pet him. He'd been clipped by a car as a pup and had always had a twitch. Smelled like he'd rolled in some old lettuce.

"Hey, we need to bathe Spaz," I commented in Irene's direction. She pretended not to hear me. "He smells. You got fleas. Poor boy." I rubbed his golden head. He thumped his bushy tail, the edge of it smacking the water dish and thrashing liquid about. Outside, a light drizzle dampened the world.

"All right!" Irene said to Norman loudly. "It's not national security." She waved me over.

"We'll call them and see if they're willing to see Terry

Montague's boy after-'n all these years." Norman grinned, his lips stretched into white hills once more.

His dental hygiene made me shudder.

"When will ..." I started to ask.

Irene cut me off. "I'll call them. Dey not into seeing people dey doesn't know, but dey might make an exception for Terry. Don't get your hopes high." She sauntered back behind the bar and picked up an ancient cordless phone that looked like it had been used to brain some wayward drunks.

Norman sipped his whiskey and I picked at lettuce in my teeth while considering my next move if this didn't pan out. I kept telling myself that Elias wouldn't do such a thing, but growing up with a drug dealer for a father ...

Irene hung up. "Dey see you. Tonight. Midnight."

"Midnight?" I echoed. "They?"

"Dey feel safer at that hour. Dey believes in spirits and da wheel of fortune dictated by da orbits." She pointed up at the ceiling. "Also, I have to drive you out dere blindfold. Dat is you blind, not me. I been dere before."

I laughed. She didn't. I looked at Norman. He sipped his whiskey, his hand quivering. The glass clinked against his brown teeth.

"The last time someone took me somewhere like that, I nearly wound up with an arrow through my chest," I muttered.

"I'll be there at eleven," Irene said.

"I'm going too," Norman chimed in.

Great, I thought. *Two drunks and a crush driving to see a medicine man. What could possibly go wrong?*

CHAPTER 19

"We don't trust you," Irene said.

"Oh, you're supposed to trust me?" I responded.

She rolled her eyes and indicated the yawing mouth of the trunk. "Tied and blindfold in da backseat, or trunk?" She held up a length of clothesline wrapped in cellophane.

The Manner loomed over us, the big red-and-wood sign swung lazily in the breeze. We loitered behind her car, under a star-studded sky, in a damp pothole the size of the Puerto Rican Trench. She read the disbelief on my face. "Listen, Boise, you fidget a lot. You sniff your hands, play with something in your pocket." At this last comment, she lifted an eyebrow. "You no good at behavin', even when you was a child. If you hadn't showered, dere be no choice, but you smell better, so I give ya options."

I punted the surface of the muddy water in the pothole. "Irene, I won't touch the blindfold. I won't peek. Promise." I stopped fingering the floss in my pocket and held both hands at my sides.

She glanced at Norman, who shook his head. He smelled like he'd been drinking non-stop since I last saw him hours ago.

I gestured at Norman. "He's the picture of discretion?"

"Norman know from long time. We done know. No new people knowin'. It for your own good." She tapped her foot. "Trunk or hands?"

"Might as well be back in the clinker," I grumbled as I crawled into the trunk. She blindfolded me. "Can't I put the blindfold on when I climb out, like when we get there? How are you gonna know I'm even wearing it?"

"We need his phone," Norman chimed in.

"Wow. You can barely walk the length of the bar without falling over, but you can …"

Irene cut me off. "Em-hmm. Phone. And turn she off."

"This is bullshit," I said, handing the powered off phone over, amazed that these two had thought of the navigation system.

"Shut up," Irene demanded. "I had to get me modda to come ova and babysit for dis, so no lip. Make sure you have da blindfold on before you get out, real careful. Dey don't mess."

"Fine, fine. Can I have a light?"

She pulled a small Maglight out of the webbing on the side. "If you open da trunk before we get dere, I turnin' 'round? Check?"

My breath rasped, the sound magnified by the enclosed space. The car jostled along, the potholes and hairpin turns thrashing me about, until I pounded on the back of the rear seat and yelled for her to drive more carefully. It didn't get better.

A piece of gravel jabbed my hip. I attempted to adjust and push it out of the way and eventually succeeded. Sweat beaded my forehead. The mingled smells of exhaust and rubber made me faintly nauseous, the way I often felt around my mother.

I'd misbehaved drunkenly with Irene in the recent past, and for a time, she had taken to ignoring me, or actively disparaging me. We'd made up, as people who are connected by alcohol invariably do, because if you exist on a small island bound by drunkenness, you have to forgive or you'll have no friends.

We jerked to a stop, the brake lights providing some illumination before going dark. Crickets and the small rustle of leaves. The secret spot where the medicine man lived must have been out country at the far end of the east side, because it had taken nearly half-an-hour of continuous driving.

A rap on the metal lid. "Your blindfold secure?" Irene asked from outside as the key entered the lock. I'd forgotten and it had fallen under me. "Aye?"

"Gimme a minute," I said. "Trying to find it."

She sucked her teeth. "You see! Wonder why we don't trust you?"

I fished it out and secured it. "Got it."

"Make sure it covering everyt'ing. No peeking."

"It's secure. I'm blind."

As I got out, I winced at the pain in my knee. It stiffened in the cramped trunk. My ribs and back ached, the bruises still evident. Fantasies of beating the hell out of Kenny constantly ran through my head.

"Little help," I said, stretching out my hand for Irene's shoulder. Instead, I felt Norman's loose skin. "Come on Irene, you're having a drunk guy lead a blind man?"

"I got you," she said, taking my other hand. "What's with your knee?"

"Dancing injury. You didn't know you're required to dance for your dinner in jail?"

I jerked when she leaned her hip into my ribs for leverage. "I don't want to know. Were you drinking?"

We ascended a set of creaky stairs. I held a railing on one side, as the stairs were too narrow for the three of us to stand side-by-side. Norman grunted with the effort and, even in the outdoors, his fetid breath assaulted my nose. A door opened and we entered a sauna of a room scented with incense and sage.

"Whoa!" I exclaimed involuntarily.

Irene elbowed me in the ribs.

I winced.

"Quiet. He sensitive to noise."

A strange voice filled the room like smoke. "Dis Montague's boy?"

"Yes," Irene replied softly, her voice tinged with reverence. "He seeks your knowledge."

"Payment," the voice said. "He has nothing."

Irene sucked her teeth, then whisper-hissed in my ear, "You ain't bring no money?"

"Remove blindfold," the voice said.

My eyes adjusted to a small room cramped with mostly wooden furniture of no particular persuasion. In the center, a simple concrete dais covered with brass incense holders and a bowl of smoldering sage. A bathroom in the corner glowed with a stained-glass night light, otherwise candles provided the only illumination. The medicine person drifted back and forward like an apparition. They occupied a gliding rocking chair.

The person's eyes looked clouded by cataracts. "You've noticed my eyes." They stopped rocking and waited in the forward position, like someone leaning forward in anticipation of a punchline. When I said nothing, they continued, "Babaz, tell he, he could answer."

Irene relayed the message. My lips froze. As I attempted to speak, I burst into a coughing fit.

"Yesssss. Clear dem demons. Let dem go. No fight. Let dem devils flee your ribs, flee your knee, flee your soul."

When I finally stopped and managed to swallow and breathe out the excruciating pain in my ribs, I muttered, "How did you …?"

"I observe," they stated.

I wondered what a person with clouded eyes could observe. They had named my two injuries without touching me. What else did this person know? Although they had a man's timbre, their appearance implied no discernible gender.

"You take da word 'observe' too limited. Too limited. Your fadda, Terry Montague. He open he mind to da possibles." Their skin had the sheen of a nineteen-year-old, yet seemed ancient. Despite their broken English, their speech had a regalness. "Step forward, young detective."

I glanced at Irene and Norman, who both shrugged. I stepped forward within arm's length of the smoking incense and sage. My knee let out an audible *pop!*

"Ah, your knee announce she presence. Bring she here."

As I approached, something in the corner behind them moved, and I realized a shadow there was actually another person.

"Ahhh!" I screamed, breaking the mounting tension in the cramped room. "What is that?"

"Me assistant," said the medicine person.

Upon closer inspection, the candle-lit eyes belonged to a bushy-haired boy of ten or eleven.

"What do I call you?" I whispered, all the while watching the boy, who moved in a eerily purposeful manner, edging only the tip of his form into the candlelight. His skin had the sinewy pink of healed burns.

They folded their hands in front of their face, then said, "I don't use name. Call me 'U' if you want label." The pain in my ribs flared. I needed to lay down. "Come, sit." He indicated a hard wooden chair. I crumpled onto the chair although the hard surface provided little comfort. "You have no money," he said. It wasn't a question. "You loss everything. Dis is good. You owe a favor, but I help you."

"Everyone calls you 'they'," I said.

"Everyone should be 'they'," U responded. "I have lived t'ree lives in one body. After each journey I different. I not da same. You will not be da same after dis."

The intensity of the fragrance from the incense holders increased. I glanced over my shoulder at Irene. She made no move and nothing changed to encourage or discourage my course. Somehow, my chair had wound up right in front of U. My father was not renowned for his judge of character, so there was no reason I should trust this man. The boy in the corner resumed being a mannequin. He looked like he'd just returned from surfing, wearing only dusty board shorts.

"Didn't Irene tell you, I've only come to ask a question."

"She tell me, but you here for more." U blinked. Their eyes were like the sun breaking through a morning mist. "You married."

"I was. My wife passed," I said. I resisted the urge to glance around to see if everyone was paying attention. "Can we do this without the audience?"

U nodded. Everyone left. The boy scurried out of the corner, stuck his tongue at me, then darted under Irene's arm into the warm, starry night.

"Do not play wid me, boy," U said, his pretense of being a gentle old soul vanishing. "You married that new *woman*." He said woman as if it were a curse.

"Do you have a problem with women?"

"I have a problem with t'ings out of dis world. Out time. Her motives be selfish and you getting selfish payment, so da bargain, while uneven, give you somet'ing. You here because of she. If you don't get here, you like da lost lamb."

"Miguela is my shepherd?"

"Aye. Listen to she, but keep sniffin'. She have she own ways. You not in any regular marriage. She need title."

"What about the flower? The round flower. Five connected petals. Purple, missing the stamen. Maybe the size of jasmine."

"I know she. Why for you?"

"I want to know for my case." They might have hailed directly from Africa. "I'm accused of murdering three women."

"You ain't murder no-body."

"Yes, I know that, but the police."

He shuddered. "Don't bring no police 'round me way."

"No, no, no," I said, with difficulty, shaking my head. "I would never …"

Smoke snaked out of the bowl. U's lips moved silently as if some unheard conversation took place, a conversation I had no part of. Their lips stilled, then they said, "Dat flower do what you ask. Very unique property. One petal. Only one." He held up a single finger and kept it between his eyes. "It heighten dis alcohol effect, but no trace. Powerful. Must be given wid alcohol."

"Beer?" He stared at me. "Okay, right, beer is alcohol. So, the flower would knock me out?"

"Total dark," he muttered. "You smell or taste rubba?"

"Yes, I smelled rubber." The flower had left a residue of rubber in the nose. Felicia handed me the beer, *already open*. Why would they drug me, then let someone murder them?

"Now, come. I must done wid dis job." He directed me to a wooden table. "Lay on back. Top of table."

He glided over, his robe trailing like a cape. My exhaustion returned, stronger, deeper. Sleep. Non-jail sleep. My knee ached, my mid-section throbbed. Despite the discomfort, sleep swept in like a wave.

***

I bathed a horse. A spot on the horse's front leg, in the top right, like gum, knotted into her hair. Using soap and a brush, I scrubbed and scrubbed, but the knot stuck. As I brushed and washed, it spread. The horse did not move, waiting for me to make the spot go away, its nostrils flared in the misty morning, little bits of moisture lobbing off in its heated breath. I scrubbed, my arms aching. I tried to examine it, pull on the gooey substance. The horse nipped at me. I returned to scrubbing, then darted my face closer to her leg, trying to see what the spot was made of, what caused it. The horse reared back and kicked me in the face.

CHAPTER 20

My hands jerked up. Irene studied me from across the room, her chair leaned against the door, her eyes half-closed. She had removed her boots and wiped a tattooed forearm across her forehead, the skin spreading beads of sweat into an even sheen. A single ceiling fan provided the only circulation. Slivers in the louvered windows let in little air. Outside nothing moved. Someone snored from one dark corner. Norman. The strange boy curled in a ball in his corner.

"Where's the medicine … person?" I asked Irene.

"Outside. He sleep in a hammock. He claim dat's he secret to long life. Sleep in da outside."

Her eyes slipped shut, fluttered open, then shut again. Irene was thin, like people around alcohol often are. I had once spotted a small butterfly tattoo on her upper left breast that tried to be red, but the color was mostly lost in her brown skin. That butterfly filled my mind, its wings expanding into elephant ears. I marveled as it rose out of her shirt and hovered in the air above her head like an apparition

I rubbed my matted hair and stretched. My knee felt good. I walked around the room and positioned myself next to Norman, who had obviously chosen the spot because the fan blew directly on him. His old-man, alcohol smell saturated the air.

I tested my knee further, trying some angles that usually caused discomfort. Nothing. I attempted a lunge between Norman and the dais. Still nothing. A squat. Nothing. What had they done to my knee? The tenderness in my ribs had dissipated as well. After a few hours of sleep, I felt ready to walk to Los Angeles.

"Lay back down," Irene muttered, eyes at half-mast. "I will punch you in da ribs you try an' come through here."

I couldn't remain cooped. "Let me out," I said. The boy's eyes opened. I could feel his animal stare. I pointed my tongue at him. "What are you looking at?"

The kid didn't move or speak. Little devil.

"Leave da kid alone. He not dat talkative."

"Living out here, no wonder. You in school, kid?" I said, stepping toward him.

"I wouldn't …" Before Irene could finish her warning he lunged at me, his teeth barred, his jaws snapping like a wild dog. I jumped back, banging into the dais. The metal bowl of sage ashes clattered to the floor. The kid retreated back to his corner, growling.

Norman started, letting out a vicious snort. "Who-sa!"

"Norman! Norman!" Irene said, rushing over to the elderly man and rubbing his shoulder, while still blocking my escape. "It's not'ing. It's okay. We still at U's place."

Norman collapsed back onto the floor. "Ah, my back. What's with the bangin'?"

"Boise's a klutz," Irene said. "Go back to sleep."

"No," I said, scooping ashes into the bowl. "I gotta get outta here, Irene. Get me back home."

"You need more rest. The treatment doesn't work as well." She checked her pocket watch. "You need to lay down for two more …"

"Sorry, but no. I want to go home. You aren't listening to me!" My need to leave had grown into a golem rising out of my chest, its arms spread, its heavy legs ready to run.

"Good God, mon. Hold on. Norman, don't let he out."

Norman grumbled, stood. Irene slipped out, he dropped into her chair blocking the door. "Norman, I can't stay in here any more. Man, I can't stay cooped. Let me out!" I moved toward the frail drunk whose eyes suddenly cleared.

"No." Norman spoke like an owner commanding a dog. "You aren't going out this door."

I moved toward him, but before I could grab his shoulders and pull him away, the boy leapt onto my back, tackling me to the floor. Norman plopped onto me and wrapped himself around my thighs, the boy around my ankles. The door opened and U entered, shoving the chair aside.

"Stop!" U said, their deep timbre boomed through the small enclosure. My elbow froze, mid-attempt to shove Norman off my back. "You will reinjure yourself!"

"Not myself," I said angrily. "Him!" I pointed my thumb over my shoulder at Norman. "Norman, this hurts! Get off me."

Norman grinned a denture-less grin. "You gonna behave, or keep acting the fool?"

"I'll behave. Just get off me!" Panic gripped me.

"Don't move," U said to Norman. "He not thinking clearly. Dis sometimes happen."

I clenched my teeth. I banged my fist on the floor and tried to move my legs, but the kid held strong.

"Can't feel my feet, kid. Let go!"

"You need to calm down," Irene said. "Nothing gonna

change in dis situation till you calm."

Norman's breathing had become labored with the effort. Irene grabbed one of my arms and twisted it behind my back as Norman rolled away.

"Ow!" I yelped.

U clapped. Irene grinned. "Self-defense class at my gym. Get the asshole on the ground face down then lock his arm, if he struggle, keep pushing till the shoulder dislocate." She shoved my arm farther up my back. I howled. "Want a new injury?"

"No!"

"Quit struggling. Dis for your own good."

"Ow! Okay. Okay. I'll stop."

"You cannot leave dis shack without blindfold."

"I saw the outside," I said.

I banged my free palm against the wooden floor. "Fine! Fine! I just can't be cooped."

U leaned into my field of view. "You behave now?"

"Yes, yes, I'll behave."

"I could put your knee back in a mess," U said.

"No, no."

Irene leaned in and whispered in my ear, but did not ease up on my arm. "You got a funny way of sayin' t'anks. Like peeing in da graveyard."

"Oh, sister, let it go already."

U nodded at Irene, and she released me. The kid and Norman let go, too. I rolled over and rubbed my feet.

"Damn kid," I said.

The kid retreated, hissing like a tea kettle. When he hit the wall, he slid to a seated position and stuck out his tongue, his eyes glistening in the early morning twilight.

"We practice wrestling," U said as if this explained everything. "The boy has ... mess-head, but we workin' on it. I understand he, he understand me. He no flee. He like physical exertion. Maybe you come wrestle with he again?"

"He's a little devil," I said. "You have a strong grip. I'll call you 'Snake'." I said. The kid's expression never wavered.

"Be grateful he ain't bite a chunk out your foot," U said.

I found my shoes and yanked them on. "Can we go? I'll wear the damn blindfold."

"How's your knee?" Irene asked.

"Perfect," I said.

U seemed satisfied with my sarcastic response. "Take dis when you already layin' in bed. You sleep for ten hours. Don't do not'ing today. Go home. Drink one liter of water. Take all of dis and sleep."

They led me to the car. I crumpled into the trunk without complaint. The small bottle of whatever U had made for me provided only one dose. The liquid had a terracotta tint and smelled like Bacon rum.

CHAPTER 21

I'd slept exactly ten hours. The yellow two-hundred thread count sheets at The Manner felt like two-thousand thread count satin in comparison to the jail's. My ribs ached. I hadn't moved at all. The smell of wet rubber flooded my nose.

I called Irene and left a message asking to speak to U. I brushed my teeth in the shared bathroom at the end of the hall. A fat tourist waddled in and made grunting sounds inside his stall. The hot water wasn't very hot. A hot shower was the single biggest thing I'd missed while incarcerated. If you got a hot shower, no matter what else happened that day, you had something to be grateful for. As I leaned against the wall, I was specifically grateful for a private stall with a shower curtain, and not being worried about some lunatic beating the crap out of me to bolster his reputation.

Although I had been put in the section of the jail for people not yet convicted, most people who were arrested were guilty.

They were career criminals. I was also in the "awaiting trial" section with the most violent people. My triple-homicide charge helped my cred. Even criminals steered clear of murderers. Alternatively, taking me out might have been attractive to some lunatic trying to make a name for himself.

I wanted to send that bastard, Kenny, a basket of mini-muffins for getting me released. Better yet, I wanted to release Snake into Kenny's home some night to bite ankles and hiss at his demented daughter.

On my new Miguela-phone, I rang Henry for a progress report. A message and a text. No response. Was he avoiding me? Up till now, the limitations of the prison payphone system provided ample reason for his not getting in touch. However, here in the real world, Henry rarely took more than fifteen minutes to return a text. Until now.

Next, I tried Dana. She didn't respond either, and I hadn't heard if she'd gotten in contact with Denise St. John. Strike two.

I searched the California Prison Database to see if I could send my mother a message. If I bought her a tablet, we could exchange phone calls and emails, otherwise it would take time to send and receive email. My energy shouldn't be spent on my mother. The woman rarely spoke to me, except to criticize my life choices. She had followed me to California, and she would have followed me here, except she despised St. Thomas. That was the point. She fought with Evelyn. She wanted me married, then when I got married, she wanted me to herself. Part of me hated her--part of me loved her.

I found a website where I could look up her inmate number. I had to buy "stamps" to send an email, then I had to buy these same "stamps" for her to send a return. It cost one stamp per page, but the inmate would receive the email within forty-eight hours and could respond immediately after review by prison staff. It was a hell of a lot better than the Virgin Islands system of waiting in line to use the pay phone and calling collect on the off-chance you'd get the person to answer when you finally got to the front of the line. I called Miguela Salas, figuring she'd answer at night. She never seemed to stop working.

"Yes," was her clipped greeting.

"Hello, honey," I said.

"Boise, I'm busy preparing your case. What?"

"I'm happy to hear my matrimonial payment is going to good use."

"Do not talk about that. I need you to come here tomorrow to sign some papers to finalize my name change and put me on your address."

"Okay. Why not tonight? I could come by and we could get plastered and do the nasty."

"That is no longer necessary. You are not a king. I am not a daughter from some royal family trying to join lineages. There is no requirement, and no one ever asks. You do not have to sleep with me." Once the history lesson ended, I heard papers shuffling.

"My mother is incarcerated in California. I may need assistance with it."

"I am not licensed in California."

"Still, I need some basic advice." Silence clogged the line. After a while I said, "Hello?"

"What?" Miguela asked. More shuffling of papers and the light tapping of keys.

"I need help with my mother."

"I see from the history you provided that her name is Patrice."

"Yes, yes, Patrice Montague." She said after my father died that she would change it back to Sampson. She hadn't.

"What do you want?"

"Can you find out exactly when she'll go to trial, or if she copped a plea?"

A long pause. Lights dotted downtown and the surrounding hillsides. People under the lights, playing out their self-important existences, oblivious to the trials of others, justice an afterthought. They existed outside the system.

I jumped, startled by Miguela suddenly speaking again. "She's charged with second-degree murder. Looks like the claim is she ran over Evelyn Montague with her car while the woman was riding a bike on the side of a road near the Ballona Wetlands in Los Angeles County. In summary, Patrice is accused of killing your deceased wife." With no emotion or inflection, she declared, "Family members often kill each other."

"Thanks for that, Miguela. I feel so much better." My cell phone felt like a fifteen kilo dumbbell. I dropped it on the bed as my head swam. My whole life was one big Houdini act. I was hiding, like a child, in the place I'd lived as a child.

I screamed, long and hard, then dry-heaved. The cell phone squawked from a great distance, muddled and indistinct. I snatched it up.

"Boise, I must go. See you tomorrow. Stop by anytime before one."

Pounding on the door. Lucy burst in. "Boise! What da hell wrong wid you?"

I fell on the bed. "I don't know. It wasn't news. I already knew, but somehow it hit home this time."

Lucy shook her head. "You cannot scream like you bein' stabbed to death. I done almost called da police and you wake one of dem people who pay da bills! Dey gonna put a bad review ..."

"Get out," I said. "I can't worry about tourists right now. Leave me be, Lucy."

Lucy looked like she'd been slapped. "You ungrateful wretch! I get dis room ready. I hold dis for you. I stand by you. Me and Marge. We treat you like family."

"You wouldn't like my family. You're being paid. You're always worried about money. You have a good life. You're married to someone you love. You and Marge, you have it so good."

"Boise, I gonna pretend you ain't say deez horror t'ings. I will expect an apology. We all got problems."

I stared down at the bed. "I need some fresh sheets."

"I ain't cleaning up any more of your messes. You sleep in dat bed. An' so help me, if you make a peep, I will kick your rass out fasta dan you could say muka-jumbi!" She slammed the door. Her muttered curses filtered down the hall as she stomped away.

I opened the door once her footfalls died away and watched Christina illuminated in a blade of light. Her bent knees and bony shoulders recalled Norman's frail physique. The painting should be called *Nora's World*. I'd even called it that in my thoughts over the years, until I tried to look it up online and couldn't find it. She just seemed more "Nora" than "Christina."

Had she married for love, money, or to escape? Her finger bore no ring, but I knew all the same. The arch of her back and the strands of gray spoke to the trajectory of her pain.

CHAPTER 22

A paper sign hung on the door of Island Bakery: "Happy New Year! – Closed at NOON today." The adjacent courthouse parking lot was deserted, except for a white compact with the word "security" stenciled on the door. I grabbed two cheese Danishes and two coffees to go.

I offered Miguela a Danish and coffee. "Don't drink coffee or eat cheese."

"It's not really cheese, per se." I set them on the floor next to my seat and slurped coffee. Files crammed the desk alongside her noise-canceling headphones. "You lied to me."

"I like to test my clients to see how stupid they are."

"And where do I fall on the stupid scale?"

"People are so wrapped in their predicament after arrest, they are useless to me in preparing a defense. You might be of some use."

"I slept on a wooden table most of last night," I said as if I'd been through the labors of Hercules. "Why'd I have to get out of my room early to come down here on New Year's Eve? You don't have hearings."

"It got you out."

"I need to get to California."

"You cannot leave the jurisdiction. Specifically," she paused to glimpse a file. "You cannot leave this island. They took your passport and gave you a temporary driver's license that's only good here and only good for driving. Airlines won't let you onto the plane with that identification."

"You don't understand," I said and showed her the email. "There must be some other way."

"Those ways are illegal. I'm an officer of the court. I cannot participate in illegal activity. You need to sign this and this. They relate to the marriage. You haven't told anyone about it, correct?"

"I wouldn't want anyone to know."

"Keep it that way. I need it legal, but harder to discover. No one can know, or I will seek to end representation."

"Fine. Fine." I signed the papers. "Is this legal?"

She said nothing.

Maybe it was better if I didn't know. "So you can't help?"

She delicately slid the papers I'd signed into a drawer. "No. My help is what I told you. Nothing more. Nothing illegal. I bend. I do not break."

CHAPTER 23

"No. Absolutely not," Dana replied, once I got her to stop typing her latest corruption story. "Sire's not some teddy bear. You think you're having legal problems now?"

"Does he have access to a private plane?" I asked. Dana ignored me, her fingers once more blurring across the keyboard. "Dana."

"Boise, I have a deadline. Sire is off somewhere unknown, anyway."

"That's not true. He's not in the business of leaving you untethered." The assault of clicking continued, the press area a roomful of chattering plastic teeth. Walter Pickering's door hung open, his ergonomic office chair vacant. "Where's Walter? And why's his door open?"

"Hold on," she mumbled, moving her face closer to the screen, the glow catching her primal intensity. When she got like this, it was difficult to get through the reporter's onslaught. The slogan on the wall said it all: "The News Never Sleeps."

"What's going on with the *New York Times?*"

"Don't try that crap with me, Boise. I know your games." She kept typing.

To impress upon her the importance of her father's help, I leaned closer. "Dana, I don't have much time. This is about me staying out of prison, and maybe the noose. Remember?"

She paused her Liberace impersonation. "Sire's your white knight?"

"I need to get to L.A. before my trial. Even with Miguela's help, the evidence is …"

"Yeah, yeah. You can't leave the jurisdiction, though." I gave her a knowing look, and she gave me an are-you-fucking-kidding-me stare. "No, no, no. If you get caught off island, Annie loses the bail money."

"I'll pay her back if that happens. That's not going to happen, but if it does. Why? Will it wipe the Von Kurks out?"

"Not the point. She's trusting me and helping you, but that doesn't mean we should kick her in the groin. Her family is careful with money, they don't throw it around. Well, some of them, but not Annie. You may not realize this, but women in wealthy families have to earn trust with money a lot more than the men. Everyone assumes we go on shopping sprees constantly to deal with our unstable temperament."

"Isn't the whole point that I show up in court with a means of acquittal? If I show up, then she won't lose the bail. Leaving the jurisdiction is a slap on the wrist comparatively, right? Come on, Dana. L.A. is my only hope. If Sire can't help, I'll have to find someone else." I paused. "Someone even shadier."

"What about that investigator friend, what's-his-name?"

"He's not getting back to me." I looked down at my ratty tennis shoes. If I had the money, I'd scuttle them. "I gotta have my feet on the ground. You know that's how it works. It's the same with a story, right? Isn't that why weather reporters stand in the middle of a hurricane? I need to …"

Dana slapped her laptop closed, stood and stretched, letting out a massive yawn. She winced, removed her cap to adjust her hair before fitting it back in place. "I got the memo. Got it! I'll page him." Dana punched a number into her phone, set it back down, and dove back into her computer.

The other reporters were on their phones, talking and typing. Pure stress. I wanted to tell Dana about my nuptials, but didn't dare. That deal was too precious. I barely stood a chance with a great attorney. If Miguela withdrew, I might as well save the cost of going to L.A. and plead guilty.

"Well?" I said impatiently.

She opened the laptop again. "Shut up, Boise. Working. Jeez, man, go get some food. Come back in, like, an hour."

Out on the balcony, I gazed down at the cracked pavement, tiny weeds, clustered together, coupled, trapped between bits of concrete. Never-say-die. Relentless. Doing whatever it took to get sunlight.

Footsteps, rhythmic, regal. A tall, lanky man topped the stairs, his suit perfect, and other than a sheen of light sweat, which he constantly wiped from his bald scalp using a white handkerchief, he looked like he'd stepped out of the pages of *Gentleman's Quarterly.*

"Boise Montague. Heard you sprung from the big house. Looking to get back into your office?" Pickering's teeth gleamed. All that was missing was one of those photoshopped reflection effects glinting off his pearly whites.

"Hey, Walter. No. I'm waiting for Dana to finish something and help me out."

"The usual." Walter leaned on the metal railing next to me. "The landlord agreed to let you stay in your office. I kept a copy of the key in case there was any problem."

"Hang on to it. I don't have the heart to go in there yet."

Walter slapped my shoulder. "Back to the grindstone, my boy." He waltzed into the press room, a king entering his kingdom. I studied the parking lot some more, thinking that once I beat this thing, I'd hassle them to repave. It was unlikely. They wouldn't even give us decent doors.

"Boise. Boise!" Dana's shouted from the doorway. "He's in the area. He'll moor at this beach on the east end. Private dock. Be there within the hour. I don't recommend you make him wait."

"Thanks," I said. "Keys?"

She tossed her car keys over. "Leave it where you're meeting if you take off with him. Keys on the rear passenger-side tire. Don't make me regret this," she warned. "And send Annie a thank you note, for Christ's sake." Dana had printed Annie's address in her scrawling hand below the beach name and location where I was to meet Sire. When I looked up, she was gone.

CHAPTER 24

The deserted beach jutted inland, a finger of water, a fringe of sand, hoards of broken shells. A one-boat-per-side dock clung to some rocks at the eastern point where the beach ended and rose into rust-colored basalt formations. A cluster of clouds imprisoned the sun. My feet dangled over the calm water. An angel fish spiraled between the stanchions dotted with seaweed and barnacles. A slurping sound erupted from beneath the dock each time the water ebbed. The wind shifted and increased a few knots. Instinctively, I reached to catch my hat and grabbed a fistful of thick, oily hair. The sun peeked out then vanished once more.

I texted Dana, "Where is he?"

No response. She'd had enough of me for one afternoon. A hump of land jutted up from the horizon, hazy in the distance, but no boats. My insides grumbled. In my zeal to connect with Sire, I'd forgotten my second dose. I had pills, but nothing to take them with. I attempted to swallow it dry, and wound up heaving it back into my palm. A few yards off the beach, in the brush, I spied a stand of banana plants, their large palms swaying. A bunch of mildly yellowed bananas hung on the back side. Balancing on a rickety box, I managed to reach the fruit. I chewed the not-quite-ripe banana, then popped the pill as I was about to swallow.

From behind me, someone said, "Hey there, boy." I shifted and the box collapsed.

From my back, I grumbled, "You trying to kill me, Sire?"

"Had to make sure you were alone, lad. Never know what Dana's friends might be into. You look vaguely familiar."

I sat up and reminded him of when he'd helped Jimbo off-island. "Oh, yeah, you're that P.I." He said "P.I." like it was bad tasting medicine. "You wanted for murder, right?"

"You read the paper."

"What you want with me?"

"I need to get to L.A., asap," I said, standing and dusting my butt. "I have no money, but ..."

"Whoa, whoa, whoa, doggie. Did you just say you have no mullah?"

"Banana?" I said, offering him another that had fallen with me.

He snatched it. Despite his silver hair and messy facial growth, the man's eyes spoke of someone who missed little. Had he actually forgotten who I was, or was he playing at the confused old-man?

He munched the banana, watching me the way people watch an iguana climb a tree: all flailing tail and twisting gait.

"I'll make this easy. You know a decent to middling lawyer?"

"I have a lawyer for my case."

"I need legal advice. You figure out a way to pay for it."

I called Miguela and laid the guilt on thick. She asked to speak to Sire. I excused myself to take a piss.

When I returned, Sire handed back my phone. "So, how do we get to her office?" I glanced at his sailboat. "No, too long. She said she can see me, but we gotta get there by two."

I texted Dana that we'd be driving her car back to Miguela's office, then heading back to take off. I'd packed a light bag of toothpaste, floss, and other essentials, including one change of clothes that included a sweatshirt and jeans.

***

Sire disappeared into Miguela's office. I hoofed it up the hill to The Manner to grab some more pills in case I wound up being in L.A. longer than anticipated. I had to be back for my trial on March seventeenth, which was dangerously close to the anniversary of Evelyn's death. I wasn't sure what I'd do for money while in L.A.

When I returned, he was still inside. It had been over an hour-and-a-half. The porch outside served as Miguela's waiting area. No magazines, so I watched traffic and studied the government-grey industrial architecture of the courthouse.

Ten minutes later Sire exited. He looked less than thrilled. "Bad news?" I asked.

"Let's sail off this rock."

"Where we headed?" I asked.

"Best you don't know."

"I get that a lot."

***

I downed the Dramamine that he offered, then plunged into a deep slumber in the cramped cabin as the boat glided. The dream-horse kicked me in the face once again. I jerked awake. From the deck, the faint sounds of Beethoven. I flipped over and peered out the porthole. The air had cooled and the horizon had nearly melded with the sun. A small island loomed.

"There you be. You been out a bunch o' hours, lad. Those meds knock you, don't they?"

I yawned, reached into my pocket, pulled out floss and leaned over the water, aft. We motored at a good clip, the sail full, the winds strong. I spat some red saliva. The videos I watched on flossing recommended getting deep into the gums.

"Where we headed?"

"Huh? Speak up, the wind ain't kind to soft talking."

I repeated my question.

"That's Culebra. We'll anchor here for the night. I gotta get into town, get some supplies."

Sire returned in the morning grumbling about the testy nature of younger women.

We plowed on for two more days, anchoring in a harbor at night, going to shore, then leaving at the crack of dawn. On day three, we arrived at a smaller island with a rough landing strip on the southern tip. I saw no inhabitants. An hour after we arrived, a plane landed.

"Where are we?" I asked for the first time in two days.

"No where," he said as we watched a battered, military-green cargo plane jounce onto the weedy runway, halting in a cloud of dust and engine noise. "This is your flight. No boarding passes here. You only gotta know where it's going, not where it is. Don't ask why. Do you want to go to Los Angeles?" I nodded in agreement. "Then shut up and get on the plane. Stay in the front. Ignore everything in there. I'm stickin' my neck out to get you this lift."

Once inside, the smell of feces and damp straw bedding assaulted me. Scurrying sounds came from the rear. Out the filmy window I watched as Sire handed the pilot a brown package, who handed back a small military-style canvas duffle-bag. I moved to the back to inspect the noises. As I neared the compartment, a *squeal* erupted. I slid open a speak-easy slat in the door. Silence and opaque light. From the side, a monkey leapt into view, howling and slapping the opening, its finger nearly gouging my eyes. I stumbled backward, crashing into one of the seats.

"Hey, hey! Get away from there!" The pilot commanded. A nasty scar interrupted the stubble across his cheek. "I agreed to ride you on account of Sire, but I believe that man told you to stay at the front of this aircraft in your seat." He crossed his arms over his bulging chest. I returned to my seat. He looked at me like a Christian fundamentalist studying the face of Charles Darwin, trying to piece together the sinister intellect that had attempted to banish the foundations of truth.

I attempted to smooth the sheets. "Don't worry, sir. I'll stay in this seat."

"You gotta piss? Shit?" His scar twitched. He pointed outside at some brush, then tossed a box of tissue into my lap. "Make it snappy. We got a long haul. One more stop in the middle, during which you can take another shit. Otherwise, I don't wanna hear squat from you." He squinted at me. "Stay in the front of this plane. You understand what I'm sayin' to you? We're not friends and I don't care to share."

"Understood." The guy meant business and took pleasure in his frightening demeanor. Probably ex-military.

Once finished in the bushes, I popped another pill using a bottle of water I'd pilfered from the boat. I fell into a Dramamine sleep an hour into the flight, while studying the Virgin Islands' criminal code I'd downloaded to my phone. There wasn't anything that would get me off of a murder charge. The cops had done nothing wrong. Evidence implicating someone else, or exonerating me, was my only hope.

A bump, heralding our descent, jarred me out of my horse dream before the inevitable kick. Thousands of trees dotted the landscape. The jungle heat pummeled me as I disembarked and picked my way over to a shack selling soda, candy, jerky, and other backpacking necessities. On the airstrip, Mr. Personality filled up the plane and spoke Spanish with one of the workers. I guessed we were in Mexico, but it could have been any Spanish-speaking place in Central or South America. Mexico was the biggest in Central America, but others had even less law enforcement, more danger, and for a non-native like me, it was difficult to discern the differences in landscape or dialect. I attempted to ask the store owner where we were in the broken Spanish I'd learned during all those years in Los Angeles.

He responded in English. "I'm not to say. It's secret."

Gas pumps shimmered in the distance. Mr. Personality pointed his fingers at his eyes, then pointed his v-splayed fingers at me in a slow, deliberate manner. I'd always done that move as a joke. I smiled. He did not return the sentiment.

As we powered up, I considered the danger of having only one pilot. I hollered toward the cockpit, "So, you fly solo all the time?"

No response.

Several hours later, we touched down at a small airport in the high desert outside L.A. I would need to find my way into the city. Mr. Personality watched me disembark. I waved at him, trying to melt the ice, but nothing changed in his dissociated expression. Something occurred to me.

"Hey, uh, did Sire mention anything about a return flight possibility?"

The scar pulsated as his only means of expression, while his lips remained as straight-line as my bank account.

I had an Uber account with a credit card that still functioned, but that would cost a fortune. I had nothing of value, I was a man, and I was desperate. Hitch-hiking seemed the best value. After nearly an hour on Ranchero Road making sure no cops spotted me, I picked up a ride with a Mexican couple heading south on the I-5. They would get me within shouting distance of West L.A., namely Glendale. Getting to Marina del Rey shouldn't be too difficult from there.

The dilapidated truck crawled along the I-5, other drivers zipping around in their Mercedes and BMWs. The truck could manage sixty, but on a Los Angeles freeway, without traffic to slow down the lunatics, sixty was like a toddler running in the Olympics.

After thanking the couple for their generosity in more broken Spanish, I texted Henry. He picked me up outside a Starbucks where a cluster of Armenian men discussed basketball over espressos. The air was January-dry, and winter-in-So-Cal warm.

Henry pulled me into a man-hug before ushering me into his late-model Mustang.

"When did you get this?" I asked, impressed.

"Two weeks ago. My mid-life crisis is in full swing, no?"

"Aren't you a bit late for that?" I said.

He laughed. Henry liked joking about age, and didn't mind getting, while giving.

"At least I made it past thirty-five without a murder charge."

We both laughed, although mine was a bit forced. "Hey, if I play my cards right, I might have a conviction as well."

We pulled onto Los Feliz Boulevard and Henry gunned it through a yellow light, pinning me against my seat. Before long we hit the 10-West, zipping in and out of traffic, picking up a Dodge Charger along the way who followed our lead, like a remora, toward Santa Monica. As we passed La Brea, Henry squirmed in his seat, then said, "I know you've left me some messages."

"Yeah, a couple," I agreed.

"Been mighty busy. A lot of cases. Testifying."

I watched the red lights mount, afternoon traffic going west starting to crush. Scattered trees dotted the sides of the freeway, a vain attempt to keep nature involved. Los Angeles had more trees than most cities of ten million, but in some ways the little bit of green made it more obvious that nature had no place, an uncomfortable reminder of all that one had sacrificed to live here.

It flooded back: Evelyn, the law firm, my struggles to make it in the sprawling metropolis. My failure as inevitable as the horse's kick. I had to be careful. If the sheriff figured out my situation he'd either arrest me, or ship me back.

"It would have been better if I hadn't had to come here," I said, wiping a smudge off the inside of the passenger window. The sun boomed into the car from its low southwestern position, spraying my face. I refused to lower the visor.

"That's my fault?" he asked.

"Look, Henry, you've done a lot for me all these years," I started.

"But! But now I need to do more. Boise always needs more. I gave you wings and shoved you out. Now fly, kid. Fly."

Like a spirit floating in the smoggy air above the freeway, I looked down at the two of us in the sportscar. I wanted desperately to be that reasonable person who lived outside the emotion of the moment. "I have been flying. I've been an investigator for almost five years, thanks to you. It's fantastic. Tremendous. It makes me hard."

"Again. 'But …'"

"It's true. You put me on the path, and I'm on the path."

Henry shook his head, then laid on the horn as a car cut in front of him to go around a slower car without signaling. "You see this shit!" He leaned out the window and bellowed, "Learn how to drive!" The driver in front shot into the next lane, cutting off another car before continuing off the Venice exit. Henry leaned back inside and rolled up his window, still cursing. "I need a vacation from this crap."

I wanted to agree, but thought it best to keep quiet or he was going to dump me off on the freeway beside a discarded mattress. Inexplicably, the four-oh-five had little traffic and we zipped along into Marina del Rey.

I'd brought the key to my mother's place in the west tower of the Marina City Club. She owned a one-bedroom on the second floor facing north. White walls without a scratch on them. My mother kept a tidier house after my father passed. She liked order. He worshiped chaos. I opened the sliding door to the balcony. Traffic and helicopter rotor sounds filled the condo.

"How does she live with that?" Henry mused, studying photos of my parents' old life together. "Mind if I use the bathroom?"

The coolness of the couch felt good. I closed my eyes, waiting. After a while I opened them. "You okay in there?"

He came out. "Yeah, all good. Nice towels."

Mother had bottles of Stella Artois in her fridge. One bottle of beer couldn't hurt after the week I'd had. I grabbed two. He watched the helicopter while leaning over the chipped brown metal railing. I stood outside the sliding door watching the back of his head. Admiralty, a formerly sleepy lane, had become a cut-through to avoid the congestion on Lincoln. The police helicopter circled over an apartment building in the distance, perhaps helping ground units corner a perpetrator.

"So, you somehow left the jurisdiction, despite a court order. How'd you manage that?"

"This beer always tastes good, not too heavy, not too light," I said, handing him a bottle, clinking a toast, and taking a swallow. *Hello, old friend.* Henry's clink and subsequent swallow were less enthusiastic.

"So, I mentioned that I'm working on a trial. On a case," Henry said, returning his gaze to the hovering copter.

"Sure, sure," I said, leaning on the metal railing. "Keeping busy. You never struck me as being especially good at retirement."

Henry muttered something under his breath. I asked what he'd said.

"'Fuck it' was what I said." He took another swig and touched the bottle to the side of his neck. "Mighty hot for January, even in L.A. More hot days." He took another swig. "The case is Patrice."

The glassy air, the clarity of the brilliant light of Los Angeles, where desert and sea merged into some bastard child of illumination and human greed lay still, no trees moving, the angels in a holding pattern, except the blades of the helicopter and the fleeing criminal somewhere out there. It was one of those virtual-reality days. The beer bottle slipped from my fingers in a slow-motion tumble of glass and cascading amber toward the hedges bordering the sidewalk stories below.

"Patrice who?"

We occupied Patrice's balcony, drank Patrice's beer. Henry had, presumably, based on the length of his stay in Patrice's bathroom, just shit in Patrice's toilet. The bottle hit the hedge, weaved through the branches, and stuck, golden dribbles from the downturned mouth. The liquid caught some of the fading sunlight streaming from our left. No cars passed, stopped by traffic signals on either side of the tower. The helicopter hovered, the blades' noise becoming part of the landscape.

"You know what I'm saying," Henry muttered and took another sip. I snatched his beer and dropped it over the railing.

"You can't have any more of that beer!" The declaration came out hollow, like I was standing in the giant heart of a whale trying to find a lost child. "Why? Why? Why would you?"

"I did it for the job. I figured I was getting paid to solve the murder of a friend's wife. Your wife. You gotta understand, I'd already started asking around, figuring I could finish what you'd started."

"Who hired you?" Before he could answer, I continued. "Didn't you get a clue, mister detective man, when I didn't ask for your help? When I left?"

Traffic resumed, beer dripped into the hedges. A crow cawed from atop a street light.

"I thought the sheriff scared you off. I didn't know. Thought I was doing you a solid."

"Putting my mother in prison?"

He dropped his gaze to the sulfur pond across the street. "If she killed Evelyn."

"Everything's always so cut and dry for Henry Bateup. Someone does something, violates your code, they go to jail."

Henry planted his feet and crossed his arms. "Sometimes you need someone else to get justice for someone you love."

"She's my mother, not someone."

"I'll go. Nothing I can say is going to make this right."

"Now you're going to ignore this in person, like you ignored me the last few weeks when I needed your help."

"I'm not your keeper. I didn't get you drunk and into a murder charge. I did ignore you, only because I couldn't do it."

"What?"

"There's something else." Henry reached behind himself. I started to move away.

He pulled a manila envelope from the back of his pants and handed it to me. "You've been served."

The envelope felt like sandpaper.

"You asked why I had to ignore you. For what purpose. It was to keep after the mission for the murdered. I thought that was a might more important. If you didn't kill anyone, it'll work out down there. Evelyn needed me here."

"Evelyn is dead. Evelyn abandoned me. Whatever you can say about Patrice, she's still my mother." The helicopter banked away toward downtown. "Who hired you?"

"Someone else who cared and didn't mind where the truth led." Before I could respond, he opened the screen and marched through the condo. The bell attached to the front door *binged* as he shut it.

CHAPTER 25

Henry served me. They wanted me to testify on what I'd uncovered in my investigation of Evelyn's death that contributed to the case against my mother. They wanted my testimony to help put Patrice behind bars for killing Evelyn.

I was scheduled to testify on Friday, in six days. I'd need legal advice. My mother's murder charge threatened to derail my reason for being here. Sure, I loved my mother, but often, very often, I didn't like her. She had problems. Sure, we all had problems, but hers afflicted me. When I needed to accomplish things in life, her need for attention intervened.

I couldn't afford that this time. I called Miguela to report that I'd been served.

"That's convenient," she said.

"How's that?"

"You went to L.A., against advice of counsel. Hard to serve someone outside the county. You should have stayed focused on what should be your only task at this time. I could tell you were going to do it. I've spent enough time with criminals to read the signs."

"I'm not a criminal," I shot back. "I'm innocent."

"We already entered your plea," Miguela replied. "I'll seek to amend your release papers to permit you to appear in court for your mother's case. Send me a copy of the subpoena immediately. I told you not to go out there. If they find out …"

I urged her to finish the thought with a, "Yeah?"

"It won't be good. I'll work it out."

The morning was almost gone. I needed to go check out who worked with Felicia. It probably didn't matter, but I was here now. I'd banked everything on a feeling that someone in L.A. had something to do with their deaths, or that I could at least make the case to the jury that someone here had them killed. I had needed to make a move. This was the best move I could come up with.

Felicia lived in L.A. Evelyn lived in L.A. I'd lived in L.A. That seemed like something. Not many people from L.A. wind up in St. Thomas getting offed.

There had been an urban legend in my elementary school that, at Magen's Bay, a boy, who nobody personally knew, had had his legs bitten off while sitting on a rock in the shallow water. Every time I went to the beach after hearing that tale, I glanced around for kids with prosthetic limbs. Perhaps it had happened fifty years ago and the boy was middle-aged. As I got older and more cynical, I wondered if he, or the story were true. I reasonably doubted it.

The keys to my mother's SUV were in an old ashtray on an end table. Driving through the Ballona Wetlands, I planned to stop briefly at the spot on Culver Boulevard where Evelyn's body had been found. After the accident, people had taken to putting flowers there. No doubt everyone had moved on, as they do in major cities where people come and go, live and die, with fruit-fly frequency. As I approached, I spied a vibrant bouquet of cardinal roses in a glass vase, supported by a metal pole. Above the roses, affixed to the pole, a large card proclaimed: "We miss you, Evelyn!"

The violent whooshing of passing cars, buffeted the petals. A cyclist chugged by, heading toward the beach in full gear. The flowers were fresh. Not a grocery store arrangement. These came from a flower shop. A large yellow ribbon and bow encircled the clear crystal vase, likely to get stolen. Whoever bought it, had decided Evelyn's memory was worth it. The card was handwritten in flowing calligraphy.

I racked my brain trying to come up with someone we'd known who would go to this much trouble. Evelyn had friends in the area. She also had enemies. One of her enemies could have killed her after she left work at the non-profit for the day. Evelyn walked, or rather biked, the climate-change walk. She biked often, except when dressed for court. There were other people, besides Patrice, who could have committed the fatal hit and run.

Henry knew a lot about investigative techniques, but one thing you also learned as an investigator was that if you had a personal connection, that led to misses. Sometimes those misses were conscious. Other times, unconscious. I'd told Henry bad things about my mother's opinions on my marriage. About her stalwart jealousy. Perhaps those opinions, discussed over beer in wee hours, colored his conclusions. My mother made a good candidate. If viewed in a partial manner, the evidence would confirm her guilt.

I didn't believe it. Couldn't believe it. Henry was wrong. Dead wrong. The sheriff's department was wrong, too. Even if she did it, it had to be an accident. Reckless driving, or a huge coincidence. My mother lived in the area, and Evelyn stupidly rode her bike on these roads—at night.

Get back to your case. Secure your oxygen mask, then deal with your parent's.

BWPP was housed in a mini-mall next to a post office and a taco stand, where Culver Boulevard veered left to follow the coast. A nineteen or twenty-year-old woman manned the counter. Various displays of wildfowl and sea animals, as well as photos of the grassy ponds in the surrounding wetlands, dotted the walls, printed on poster board and blown up to increase detail, to make the victims more real. Birds were often only viewed in the distance, their wings spread, like the two lines in a painting. Evelyn contended that was why we failed to empathize with the destruction of their habitat.

"Hello," the woman said, a pleasant smile on her face.

"Hi. Do you know," I checked my notes to be sure I got her name right, and to seem less interested than I actually was, "Felicia Nichols?"

The girl pulled an inhaler out of a pocket on the side of her wheelchair and took a hit. "Yes," she said shakily. "I know Felicia." She grabbed a tissue from the box on the counter and blew her nose in a loud, long *honk*. "Excuse me. We've been wondering where she's been since her trip."

"Did you know my wife, Evelyn?"

She dropped the tissue in a waste-bin. "Evelyn? Sounds familiar. When did she work here? Hold on, I'm coming around."

I stepped back. She rolled around the counter. Her blue and white name tag said, "Grace."

"I'm sorry," I said automatically.

"For what?" she said.

"Uh, you didn't have to come out here."

"'It doesn't matter, if you don't mind.' That's my mantra. I like being on the floor. I was just watching a nature video on the computer back there, but you seem more interesting … for now." She laughed playfully at this last statement as if she knew I was more interesting than the big cats I'd heard growling. "Evelyn, Evelyn. Seems … wait a minute! You mean the lawyer? The one who died?"

She rolled over to a group photo on the far wall, in the middle of some notices of meetings. Evelyn had spent many a night at those meetings. She'd pedal home in the dark, insisting that her headlamp and the lights that illuminated the bike would keep her safe. Evelyn often did things that dared danger.

***

"What if they're drunk?" I asked.

"Drunk! It's nine o'clock on a Tuesday, not midnight on Saturday, Bo." Evelyn did not think there was any danger. Or, she enjoyed that there was danger. "Besides, there's a bike lane most of the way, and I ride on the sidewalk whenever convenient. Don't look at me like that. Is it because I'm a woman? If I were a guy, would you be worried? If I was your male roommate, would you be worried?"

"It's not because you're a woman," I'd say. "And yes, I'd be worried about anyone riding a bike in the dark on the streets of lunacy. Cars are in charge here. Pedestrians and cyclists beware the mean streets of L.A."

It was because she was a woman. She knew it. That made riding at night, in the dark, all the more enticing. She was an environmentalist, and a feminist. That made the meetings even more important. Sure, it was about saving the wetlands.

***

"Hello, sir? Is this her?" The wheelchair woman pointed a laser attached to her keyring at the photo, the red dot centered on Evelyn's forehead.

"Yes, that's her."

She looked horrified. "Do you know something about Felicia?" She wasn't calling the police or wheeling out the front door screaming in terror, so it was safe to assume she didn't know I was the prime suspect.

"I'm trying to figure out what happened to her. I'm investigating …"

"… her disappearance," she finished in a whisper of awe. "Did her family hire you?"

"Uh, no, not her family. Is there anything you can tell me that might shed some light on what happened?" I hesitated, then added in a conspiratorial tone, "Grace."

"How did you?" I pointed at the nametag. "Oh, right!" She laughed, patting the top of her head with both hands. "You investigate things. Notice things. That's good. Good." She looked confused, muttering something incoherent.

"Are you okay?" I asked.

"There's just a lot going on around here lately with the new grant approval and the latest change in the law that should give the wetlands added protection. The climate change thingy has everyone in a tizzy, which is great for us. Donations are coming faster and furious-er--but, Felicia disappearing? Not so good. Mark says they'll figure it out. Also, Felicia was impetuous."

"Pardon? Who's Mark?" I knew Mark.

She pointed the laser at the face of a well-muscled man standing next to my wife. "He's the head of our organization. Hires us."

"Are you a volunteer?"

She nodded proudly. "I've been here for almost a year. Not as long as Felicia, but pretty long. I love seeing the changes. Mark has such a big heart."

I had investigated Mark briefly, but stopped, despite my lingering interest in his extracurricular activities, once I'd eliminated him as a suspect in Evelyn's death. Although I discovered that Evelyn and Mark, a former mixed martial arts fighter, had sex together on many of those late nights when she was supposedly at a town hall meeting or fighting with land developers. At the time, I only cared about finding her killer.

It's extremely unsettling, feeling the expanding universe of grief, coupled with hatred and posthumous abandonment. After almost two years, my vitriol had subsided considerably. I could remain impassive, even objective about his presence in the photograph with the red dot sticking up his nose.

The dot disappeared and Grace turned toward me, her features a mask of confusion. I shuffled my feet, feeling the grit of sand on the floor. "Why are you here? Your wife died like a couple of years ago. And why are you asking about Felicia?"

"It's a coincidence that my wife and Felicia both worked here." *Which was exactly why I came*, I thought.

"Felicia's a volunteer, like me. She's not an employee."

I almost corrected Grace's use of the present tense. "Right. So, no one's heard from Felicia? Any theories or rumors?"

"She went to the Caribbean to visit family and get away for a few weeks. She should have been back like mid-December, but she hasn't returned."

I was playing this wrong. "Grace, I've got a confession. Felicia isn't missing anymore."

"What do you mean?"

I wanted to get more from her before others returned. I studied the photograph. Although Evelyn had worked here for years before her death, Mark was the only person I remembered. She kept this life separate. To be fair, I didn't do much to get involved. I was caught up in my own little world at the law firm, trying to make ends meet in a city that devoured money the way Payne and Wedgefield swallowed island real estate.

"Hey, what's happening today at my non-profit?" The question came from the doorway where the man Grace pointed the laser at in the photo now stood in the flesh, holding the door open to the beach air. A fog had moved in, and outside water ghosts floated around behind his silhouette.

"Oh, Mr. Green ..."

"Grace! Don't call me Mr. Green. You say that and I look for a famous R&B singer who deserves your respect much, much more than I." The executive director of BWPP examined me. Recognition, along with a flash of something my instincts read as fear.

"Boise? Is that you? My God, man! Where have you been all these months?" He tilted his head like a dog. "Or, maybe even years?"

"Hello, Mark," I said soberly.

Mark Green had a disarming manner that threatened me. He was hard not to like. You felt like the center of the universe when he spoke to you. Despite his cuckolding me, during my investigation he had been very cooperative and friendly to my inquiries. I, on the other hand, had trouble questioning him. It's easier to be magnanimous when you're the 'screwer'. He knocked me down like a bowling pin when I tried to punch him. He could have hurt me, but he didn't. Still, he'd screwed my wife, which was decidedly indecent.

"I've been living in the Virgin Islands," I blurted. So much for subtle tactics.

"The Virgin Islands. Interesting. Have you family there?"

"No, none."

"Forgive me, Boise, I'm here to get a document I need for court. Grace?" Grace reached behind the desk and produced a paper. "Thank you, dear." He examined it. "Perfect. Tell them this will work and I'll be in touch." He bent and put his arm around Grace's shoulders in an awkward sideways hug over the arm of the wheelchair, then turned back to me. "Grace here is one of our shining stars. A true believer. Right, Grace?"

Grace made a salute. "Oh, yes, Mr. Green, I believe in BWPP's cause very strongly and hope to stay for a long time to come. I'm so grateful you brought me into this amazing world."

Mark shook his head and gave Grace a second shoulder squeeze. "Thank God for the true believers, huh, Boise? So, tell me, what brings you back to L.A.?"

"One of your volunteers, actually. She was in St. Thomas about six weeks ago. I met her at a show."

"You're kidding." He looked genuinely confused. "Who?"

Grace burst out, "Felicia!" She looked at me. "Sorry, I took your line." She looked back at Mark. "Can you believe it?"

"Felicia. She hasn't turned up here for a while and we are concerned about her, but since she's only a volunteer ... well, they come and go ... We surmised she moved on to another cause. This happens so many times. Believers and their beliefs. Young people are finding themselves through good work, and we're thrilled to be a part of that for as long as they'll have us. Grace is another of these wonderful people who make this organization possible." He fingered his chin. "I'm still confused. Why would you be in Los Angeles about Felicia? Do you and she have some connection? You're not still upset about what happened? I'm sorry I did that. I mean the hitting. It wasn't right. You have no lingering physical effects, I hope."

If the authorities in St. Thomas called Mark as a witness, he'd tell them I'd been in L.A. I also had the excuse of my testimony, but how would I explain I got here the same day the summons arrived? Miguela said not to worry about it. Cops gave people bad news every day, but had some kind of training. No amount of empathy training fixed facts.

"I have bad news about Felicia."

Grace typed something into the computer below the counter. Her head darted up. "Oh, right, you were going to confess something earlier."

A tatted up dude in bicycle gear, binoculars slung across his torso, entered. He asked for a bird guide. Grace pointed to a stack of pamphlets. He took one, slapped it against his palm, left, and pedaled away.

I resumed my explanation, with nothing but to say it. "Felicia has passed away."

Grace's hand went to her mouth, her wheelchair sliding backward a couple inches. I watched Mark closely. He put his hand on Grace's shoulder. Her other hand gripped his wrist. He jerked his hand away as if he'd touched a hot stove.

"Oh, my God," Grace cried, grabbing tissue. "Was it some kind of accident?"

Mark turned to Grace as she gave him an evil stare. He whispered something to her. She said, "I know!" and wheeled off into a back room behind the counter.

"Everything okay?" I asked.

"Please, sit." He yanked two folding chairs from a pile leaning against the wall. The metal chilled the back of my legs. He rubbed his forehead, fighting tears.

Finally, he asked, "The police have any leads?"

I'd been careful not to suggest foul play. "Yes, but I don't think they're on the right track," I said. "Where did you get that idea?"

"What idea?" he asked, his eyes down on his fingers between his knees.

"That the police might be involved?"

"You're here, Boise. You're an investigator. Why else would you be here? Just to deliver the news of a volunteer's death in person from what, three thousand miles away?"

He had a point. Why else would I have come here. "Right. Right. It's a long way."

"Yes siree, you could have made a phone call. I'd hazard you would have made a phone call, unless you had some other reason for being in L.A., which I'm sure you don't. In person is another matter entirely." He repeated, "Entirely," under his breath as he dropped his eyes. He flexed his hands. He brought his head back up, his tanned face practically glowing, the spider webbing around his eyes blossomed when he smiled. "Boise, it's been great seeing you and catching up. I'm in a bit of a hurry. Leave your number with Grace and maybe we can talk again."

He left, at a trot. Grace rolled out from the back, holding a sheet of paper. "Where's Mark?"

"He left. He asked me to leave my number." I pointed to it written on a scrap of paper next to her computer. "I'd also like you to call if you think of anything else that might help me piece together what happened."

She pursed her lips, fighting the urge to break down. "Fine. But the file. This paper. He sometimes does that. He has a clean-up this afternoon on the beach. He gets concerned about events and spaces out. OMG. Would you mind chasing him down and giving him this?" She held out the paper.

"If you think of anything, please call or text."

My knee ached, but after a couple minutes of jogging it loosened up. I examined the paper jostling in my hands. A response to a motion to dismiss some environmental cease and desist action by BWPP. It was marked to be filed downtown in federal court.

I caught up to Mark in a sandy parking lot behind a red and white striped Italian restaurant. A worker set chairs on the sidewalk.

"Hey, Mark!"

He stopped his speed-walk. "Boise, I'm in a hurry. People are waiting to clean up trash that other people throw into our environment. If you want to re-hash history ..."

I panted, "No ... Grace ... asked me ..." I held out the paper with one hand and gripped my kneecap with the other.

He snatched it. "Did she make that phone call yet? I told her I did not ... oh, never mind. I'll call her later. Thank you for the kind effort, Boise. You really didn't have to do this for us." He started away, then turned back. "Hey, do you want to clean up the beach?"

Anything to delay my visit with Patrice. Besides, the fog made things temperate. He read my face. "Good! It'll be a blast. What else are you going to do on a Saturday?"

CHAPTER 26

I spent Sunday getting drunk and dozing. After the cleanup, I felt nauseous, like a large empty well had opened inside my gut. At first I couldn't sleep, then I finally drifted off, somewhere south of three am, only to start awake at six when the dream-horse kicked me in the chin. Pain shot through my cheekbone. It vanished when I opened my eyes.

Down at The Grog Shop, I managed to convince the counter guy, who didn't really give a damn, that I was Patrice Montague's son and she would be fine with me charging the items to her account.

"That's all you got?" I asked, pointing at the plastic liter bottle of Vodka of the Gods.

"Yeah, you lookin' for Grey Goose, Mr. Bond?" He sniggered at his bad British accent.

On my way back to the condo, Vodka and Sprite in tow, the phone rang. "Hi, Ms. Goode, what's the latest in St. T?"

"Spoke to Leber earlier. He's being very cloak and dagger. Must like you, 'cause he's acting like he's working for you, not the police."

"He wants justice."

Dana laughed her loud laugh where she threw back her head and you could see down her throat like a Peanuts character. "Cops want to clear cases. Justice comes a distant second."

"Not Leber," I said.

"Sure, sure, the cop with a heart of steel, pure and unoxidized."

"Not everyone's out to screw everyone else, Dana."

"Sure, Jabuti, you keep believing that, I'll keep writing stories that prove otherwise."

"Why are you calling?"

"Leber thinks that the doer is some guy from Jamaica who was involved with ..." I could hear Dana flipping pages in a notebook. "Ronica. He knew all of the victims and is a very jealous-type."

"From Jamaica, huh?"

"Boise, it fits. I mean, you see the L.A. connection, but that's tenuous. Who's coming to St. Thomas from L.A. to kill three women from Jamaica. Murders are usually local affairs and have more to do with significant others, not some grand plot to stick your head on pike."

"You don't think L.A.'s a factor?"

"I don't know. You have to have an open mind, so I'm keeping one, but you're less experienced about these things than Leber."

"True. But I'm also the one who's all in."

Dana sighed. "That's the problem."

I envisioned the painting outside my room at The Manner. Christina sprawled in the weeds, gazing at the ravaged house, the rusting gun. Her hopelessness. "Dana, it's for the best. Leber and I pursuing different leads. That's good. We're covering bases.

Besides, the more alternative theories Miguela Salas can present, the better, right?"

"You need to figure out a strong, plausible theory, or better yet, convince the prosecutor to drop charges by figuring out what really happened. Scatter-shot can backfire. Juries sometimes see it as desperation on the defendant's behalf."

"You sound like you have some experience."

"I've watched my share of criminal trials."

Henry always said, see where an investigation takes you. If you have a strong instinct, follow it. I had an instinct about BWPP and Felicia.

I drank vodka and Sprite as I considered these thoughts and watched a Padres game from 1991. The last batter I remembered that night was diminutive Bip Roberts, batting seventh. He'd swung, and I couldn't even remember if he fouled, hit, or struck out as the vodka took hold like a Russian wrestler bear-hugging a hapless opponent.

***

I kicked off the down comforter on my mother's bed, relieved at having neither been kidnapped nor accused of murder since arriving in L.A. If I hurried, I might get to the federal courthouse downtown in time to see what Mark Green was up to in the trial mentioned in that paper I'd given him on the beach. I scrambled down the stairs and figured out how to take the metro downtown to avoid spending money to fill up Patrice's gas-guzzler.

A text from Miguela Salas demanded I regularly check my email because things on my case might start happening any day. If I had to leave, my mother would have to figure out her own destiny.

There was a message from the prosecutor's office in California as well.

> Hello Mr. Montague,
> You need to come to Los Angeles to testify in the trial of Patrice Montague. This is in the best interest of your mother that you assist. It is also in the best interest of getting the truth of what's happened to your spouse.

Prosecutors often claimed that one of *their witnesses*, in this case yours truly, was being called to help the defendant. Ha! The email concluded by declaring I should call "immediately" to confirm my availability. Oh, the terrifying urgency.

Someone working over at the prosecutor's office didn't know that Henry had already served me papers and I would be going in for the summary judgment hearing. Apparently, the prosecutor thought I could strengthen their case and prevent the judge from dismissing. Why did they really need me? Had some evidence been tossed out? Henry Bateup generally buttoned things up tightly, but sometimes judges disagreed, despite good evidence, and dismissed cases.

I called to find out when I had to appear. "Anything sooner?" I asked, concerned that something might come up.

"This isn't open to discussion. You must alter your schedule to suit ours."

"And what if I just refuse?"

"You can do that, but it might not be in the defendant's best interest. Do you want the judge to think you have something to hide? Also, prosecutors tend to bring avoidance tactics up at trial. It never plays well. I recommend you cooperate now to save Mrs. Montague headaches later."

The clerk asked for my email to make sure I understood where to park and how to get to the courthouse. I was already in front of the civil courthouse, not far from where my mother's trial would be held. Like auto dealers, courthouses tended to congregate.

I hurried past a couple of men. One hollered at the other, apparently wanting the drugs he'd stolen from him the night before. The other guy saw things differently, alleging that he'd given the drugs over willingly.

"Now why the fart would I do that," the older one said.

"'Cause I'm your pal, pal," said the other, a too-new skateboard tucked into his armpit.

The bearded one doubled-over, guffawing like a donkey. Without missing a beat, the guffawing one asked me for a dollar or a smoke, whichever was close at hand.

"I don't smoke and I'm broke," I said. "I'm also wanted for murder."

"Yeah right," he said. "No one smokes anymore. What's the world on now? If we ain't smokin', there's gotta be something else. Everyone's got the death wish."

I struggled up the steep steps, melting like a witch from a Miyazaki cartoon. The guards directed me to the courthouse where BWPP's case was being heard. Few people occupied the gallery. Mark Green and another Caucasian man in a business suit whispered to each other over a long table at the front of the room, Mark gesticulating wildly, then saying, "No, that's not an option!"

Mark's companion raised his hands, then tapped his leather-bound briefcase lightly. Mark rose to his feet and almost shouted, "I don't care what the court wants. Justice demands …" he sat back down and finished his statement in a more controlled tone, punctuating his sentences with finger stabs. Even his jaw looked muscular. Where did he find the time to stay in shape *and* obsess about the environment?

A judge entered, everyone rose, then sat. The great seal of the state hovered above the scowling judge. The California flag on one shoulder and the star-spangled banner on the other. Lots of wood paneling. The hush of reverence.

Mark and his buddy, probably a lawyer, continued to have an animated conversation as the judge had asked for a brief time-out to discuss something with the court reporter and the bailiff.

"Okay, we are back on the record in the matter of Mark Green versus Alpha Land Management, Incorporated. Mr. Green, you are requesting documents from Alpha and they are claiming work product, is that correct?"

The attorney for Alpha stood and confirmed the judge's assessment. A brass plaque read, Judge Amy Couch. What was this case? Why was it under Mark Green's name? I'd assumed it was a BWPP case based on the interaction yesterday.

I opened the browser on my phone and pulled up the BWPP website. A search for Alpha Land Management, Inc. brought up several documents and articles revealing an on-going suit between Alpha and BWPP going back over five years. The original attorney of record for BWPP had been none other than Evelyn Montague. She had handled many cases for BWPP during her tenure at the non-profit, so seeing her name on the by-line of the case didn't surprise me, however, nothing in the articles revealed why the case had switched plaintiffs.

Evelyn had been replaced by new counsel shortly after her death. Scott Anders continued as the attorney of record from then on. Scott's photo appeared on the website for BWPP as a pro bono lawyer slumming from one of the big firms downtown. The do-gooder bug had bitten old Scott, because less than a year after taking over the case, he'd quit his high-flying legal job and high-tailed it over to BWPP, defending defenseless animals, protecting our watershed, and, in short, fighting the good fight. His smiling face on the website looked markedly different from the sneering countenance displayed in the pulpit after another heated exchange with Mark Green.

My phone buzzed. I ignored it. Then a text came in from the same number I didn't recognize. I scanned the text as I stepped into the alcove to return the call.

"Hello, Grace. To what do I owe the pleasure?"

"Mr. Montague. This is Grace from BWPP." I waited, then, "Oh! Right, you knew that, I just texted. I'm not an idiot, just a bit nervous."

"Don't be," I said, trying to ease her tension. "What is it, Grace?"

"You asked about whether someone here might want to hurt Felicia."

"Go on."

"There's a person here at BWPP who was none too fond of Felicia, and well, I just don't want any stones to go unburied, you know, for the sake of justice. Also, Felicia was nice."

"Who?"

"Scott Anders. He's our lawyer. Handles the biggest cases, I think. You know, I'm just a volunteer, but I don't know."

"It's okay to talk to me. You can tell me whatever your concerns are."

"Maybe I shouldn't. I like working here. Maybe I'll stay on. Mark was telling me there might be an actual position by the time my internship is complete."

"Internship, not a volunteer?"

"My dad thinks it's the same. I try to tell him it's not, but you know dads. It's about making money, or making sure he doesn't have to pay my car insurance at least. I've had a few too many moving violations. I don't want to lose my potential job."

"Grace, anyone would be lucky to have someone as conscientious as you working at their N.G.O. I get the feeling you're a very dedicated person."

"Yeah, that's nice of you to say, Mr. Montague, but really, I don't have any prospects and my dad, he's ready to cut me off if I don't start earning a living soon."

"What do you need help with?"

She paused, then said, "Can you get me another job?"

"I'll do whatever I can to help you, if you help me. This thing with Felicia is very, very important."

"Will you take me to dinner?" she asked.

It was my turn to be confused. "What kind of dinner?"

She spoke like an assault rifle. "Someplace nice. Someplace Mexican. I like Mexican. L.A. has good Mexican, you know."

"Okay," I said without thinking much about the consequences.

"I've always wanted to try La Serenata on Pico. You know it?"

I thought about my mother's cash stash. She could afford it. Besides, when I looked into Patrice's case, I could justify the charges based on my hourly. She owed me more than the price of dinner.

"I finish at five. Can you pick me up?"

Looked like I'd be driving the gas-guzzler after all.

CHAPTER 27

La Serenata occupied a nondescript building on Pico Boulevard sandwiched between a luggage store and another restaurant claiming to be authentic Cajun. We ordered a poblano quesadilla of corn masa. The steaming blob arrived drenched in green sauce--a chewy bit of heaven. It, and a margarita, on the rocks with salt, which Grace agreed was the only way to have a margarita, shot us out of the catapult into the starry night.

"I don't trust people who order frozen margaritas," she said with a giggle. She licked a grain of salt off her upper lip.

We made small talk about the state of the world, and she filled me in on the latest in environmental justice and waning enforcement at the federal level.

"Was that what Mark Green was so upset about this morning in court?" I ventured.

"That and other things. I think he's under a lot of pressure from our board. We haven't had a big win in some time."

"Huh. Couldn't tell that by the way he spoke to me the other morning when we were all together."

"Right. Grace!" She patted her head, then gripped the margarita in both hands, took a big swallow and licked salt off the rim. "Hmmm. Let's talk about something else. I have a big mouth. You're terribly thorough, what with going to watch Mark and Scott and the proceedings and all."

"Can I squeeze the lime into the drink for you? It makes more than a garnish."

"Oh, I never do that."

"Well, most don't know, but real margaritas are made with lime juice, not those crappy mixes." Of course people knew that, but clearly she did not. "This place makes 'em real, but you can't have too much lime juice, IMHO."

She giggled some more and downed the last of the drink. I followed suit. We ordered two more when they removed our empty plates.

"There's things I need to explain about Scott Anders." She paused and wiped her mouth, then looked around as if searching for an invisible fly. "Where's those margaritas? I need another drink." She belched, then giggled.

We waited. The drinks arrived. She gulped a mouthful, sloshed it around like mouthwash, then swallowed and licked. "Mmmm. Salt so good. Okay, okay, there's a swirly happening. With the swirly, comes the liquid courage. Scott." She wheeled from sitting across, to sitting next to me after I pulled a chair out of the way. Our backs against the wall provided an unobstructed view of the pastel room. Patrons occupied three other tables. One group appeared to be taking in some drinks and food after work. One whooped and whipped a jacket around his head, fluffing the hair of a co-worker. She took it in stride, laughing along. Apparently, they had either all been fired and didn't give a crap anymore, or they'd had a good day at the office, especially for a Monday.

"Now, we can see the competition and make sure no one is spying on us!" Grace announced conspiratorially.

"Are you in the agency?" I asked.

"Ha! I won't tell. But, I do need another job. Something that pays bigger money. You aren't sitting there feeling sorry for me, are you?"

"No," I said, a bit too forcefully. A beat, then I asked, "How'd it happen?"

"Nothing that interesting. Drunken father driving me and mom. He crashed. I woke up no longer being able to walk. Cool, huh?"

"Cool? Er, no doesn't sound cool."

"Thank you for not saying 'I'm sorry.' That gets trite after seven years. I'm better off. I was always a thinker anyway, so now I don't have these legs distracting me from my thinking." She nudged me and took another sip. "Come on, don't give me a long face. I'm fine. You put me into the car earlier to get over here. That made you feel chivalrous, right? See, taking care of me is good for you. I can tell you like it. I have a sixth sense about people who will show me kindness. But remember, I'm not helpless, and don't want pity." She pointed a salt-encrusted finger at me. "No pity!"

"Gotcha. No pity."

She licked her pointy fingertip. "Besides, there's this whole new way of looking at these former handicaps. I know blind people are into it. They don't view it as lacking anything. They embrace blindness or, in my case, immobility, as a strength. Something to be celebrated. The salt that makes us who we are. Can you help me get paying work in my field?"

"Rescuing wetlands?"

Her shoulder-length hair bounced and shook, even separating at the ends into a blur as she racked herself with laughter. I laughed along. Couldn't help it.

The stem of her margarita glass pointed straight up as she polished off her second. We ordered two more along with crispy chicken tacos. A hot, crispy shell with the perfect amount of fresh oil. My stomach groaned in anticipation.

Her laughter halted. "Someone wanted Felicia dead, right?"

The sudden change jarred me, like the police interrogation techniques designed to confuse suspects. "It certainly was no accident. Fully intentional," I said.

Her tears reflected the brightening lights, as winter darkness enveloped the building. She picked the napkin off her lap and dabbed at her face while mumbling something about emotions running amok.

The food arrived.

"It's okay. Your friend died. You can have feelings about it."

"Thanks," she snapped. "Your approval of my feelings is so warranted. Can we get back to why we're here?"

I wasn't sure if she meant her job or what she wanted to report on her co-worker at BWPP, so I picked at my beans and sipped the fresh margarita as the ice melted.

She revolved her food around the plate with a tortilla chip. Her fingers came to very pointed tips. "I think if anyone at BWPP could have done this, it was that lawyer, Scott Anders. He had a thing for Felicia. Aren't love-sick men often the guilty parties in these cases?"

"Why do you say that?" I asked.

"Well, books and movies about murder. Duh. And, and, newspaper articles about murders. Okay, okay, it's especially when it's a woman murdered. Guys like sticking things into women. Sometimes it's good and sometimes, like now, when the woman won't let the man stick, then they force the stick, sometimes. Lots of times, it's rape. Sometimes they stick with other things, like knives and bullets. Right?" She said 'right' as she raised the drink, her lip gripping the edge of the glass.

"I suppose all of that is true, but I need more."

"Hmmm. He was very mad at Felicia. Mad-dog mad. She wouldn't go out with him. I'm not sure why. He's handsome in that Scandinavian way, and he's got nice blond hair. Over the top in the gel department, makes his head look like a lawn. Oh! And he's really successful, but he still helps with the nature preserving and wetlands stuff. It's great. He's great. But she wasn't interested. One day outside by that Italian restaurant next to the BWPP, they were arguing. He was angry."

"That does sound like he could be a suspect."

"Sounds like? Could be? Uh-uh, Mr. Montague, he's a suspect for sure. Prime rib suspect. First, a woman couldn't have done this. She was strangled or hit by a rock. I hear conflicting things. Women kill with poison or maybe a gun." She had taken an ice cube out of the empty glass and was sucking on it.

"Can you get me some information on Anders? Like where he lives, if he's travelled recently, etcetera? Would you guys have that information?"

"Yes!" she said. The reduced ice cube flew out, plunked on her plate. She popped it back into her mouth. "Yessss, he guzz snot around por a pew days right when Pelicia left."

"Really? Where'd he go?"

She crunched the ice, sending a chill down my spine. I resisted the urge to tell her how bad that was for her teeth. "I bet he went to the Virgin Islands to follow her. Where else? He didn't come into BWPP for over a week."

"That unusual?"

She paused. We sat close enough that I smelled lime, salt, and makeup when she shifted in her wheelchair. "Not completely. Sometimes he's not around for a few days. But this was a whole week. It was the same time that Mark was gone."

"Wait. What?"

She put her hand on my shoulder as the waiter came by again. "Do you mind if I get another Margarita?"

"Well …"

"Oh come on, I'm fine. Don't worry, there's no chance of me falling down! And you're driving."

"Don't you have work tomorrow?"

"Maybe. I'm always such a good girl, meanwhile other people are killing. What should be so bad about me blowing off work for a day? I deserve it. I've come in every day for the last five months, like a good little girl. I deserve a break. Don't I?"

My margarita had become a watery mess. Her state somehow took the magic out of drinking. I thought about AA. I should get back to that, if I stayed out of prison. Yes, if I managed to beat this thing, I'd go back.

After the waiter dropped off the drink, I tried to move the conversation into deeper waters. "So, both the lawyer and Mark took off from BWPP the same week?"

She squinted at me. "They did? I mean, yeah, they did. But Mark Green? He could never. He's not that type. Besides, he went to some conference in Vegas."

I checked online. Sure enough, there had been an environmental conference entitled, "Two-Degrees Vegas," the week Felicia had been offed. "Do you know where Scott Anders might have been that week? Might he have gone to the conference, too?"

"No, Scott isn't that dedicated. He's in it for the glory. You know, prestige. To get more clients for his money-making lawyer gigs. Speaking of which, you haven't forgotten our agreement about you getting me work that pays, right?"

"No, I haven't forgotten. Is there a way you can see from the records at BWPP what those guys expensed that week?" I could contact my buddy who hacked things, however, I didn't have some hot-shot client with unlimited financial resources on this case. I'd have to get more imaginative.

"I'm not feeling so good," Grace said. "Can you take me home?"

Grace had a ground-floor apartment. As I eased her into bed, she mumbled something about playing a DVD. After switching on the television, I started the DVD player, assuming whatever was already inside would be suitable. Pam Grier shot a man in the face. A perfect bedtime story. It bothered me, putting her to bed without brushing her teeth, but that seemed a tad intimate. The volume low, I whispered goodnight, and slipped into the desert chill of the evening.

CHAPTER 28

The next morning, way before I was ready to get up, my phone buzzed. A text from Grace: "I need a ride to work. Please? Don't want to pay for Uber, and the bus is a pain."

I grabbed cups of coffee from the Grog Shop. She dumped cream and sugar into the cup while thanking me profusely.

"Jeez, Mr. Montague, you're a good guy. A really good guy." She sounded more and more like a cartoon from the 1930s.

The prime suspect in her friend's murder, and a good guy. Who said you couldn't have it all? "Thanks. How's your head today?"

"Groggy, but that was fun. Did we come to some agreement, like, on my job prospects?"

"Why do you think I can help you get a job?"

"You seem resourceful. Mom says to trust my hunches, like I have good natural radar about stuff. Did you know radar is a palindrome? I wanted to change my name to a palindrome, like

Hannah, but I'm attached to Grace. But, like, if I ever go into witness protection, watch out for that palindrome name."

"Good to know," I said. "I will help however I can, although I have a lot on my plate." She stared at me and then leaned forward into the line of my peripheral vision as we weaved through double-parked cars and Amazon vans.

"I'm going to help you nail that Scott Anders fella. Solving the case should get you more clientele, right?"

"True."

"Then, even though I don't work as a private eye person, I bet I'm helping you get jobs by helping with this case, right? So, you can do the same for me with the N.G.O. work, I'm sure. I don't need a huge salary, but I want to be paid. Surely you must know someone."

"What about working at a law firm?"

"I don't know. I hear they suck your soul. Besides, I'm not into practicing law."

"You could do research or admin."

"I want to work in non-profits. Something environmental."

"Okay, okay. I'll think about it and try to come up with a game plan."

"I trust you, Mr. Montague. Now, yes, I can check on that trip Scott Anders took. Like, where he went. I know someone he works with who knows his goings on."

"What about Mark Green?"

"I already told you where he was. Besides, Mark's too good a guy." She tapped her temple. "Radar."

I wanted to tell her about him punching me. "Please don't mention to Mark anything we've discussed. Or to anyone else who might speak to Mark. Okay?"

She slurped coffee, then asked, "What do you take me for?"

I helped her into her wheelchair, then into the office. It amazed me that she could manage this by herself all the other days of her life.

"I'm sorry to push, but how soon can you have the information?"

"Tonight. Let's go back to that Mexican place." The previous night had cost quite a bit. She read my hesitation wrong. "I promise to drink less. I get a little aggressive when I drink. I was a bit demanding."

"You were fine. Sure. Same time?" Off I went, wondering how else I could find out about Mark Green's whereabouts during that fateful week in November without alerting him.

I had an appointment to visit my mother at four in the afternoon. The jail was on Fiji Way, about ten minutes from BWPP. Considering how quickly things could escalate with mother, having an appointment would be wise. The scheduling program had offered no more than one hour per visit.

I ran a Google search on Mark Green, which brought up a host of Mark Greens who were not the Mark Green I wanted. Adding "BWPP", narrowed the search to several pages, mostly involving his antics in the world of environmental regulation and law-making strategy. Mark had even given a TED Talk in 2014 on the rising sea-levels and its effect on the Ballona Wetlands. The talk lasted ten minutes, and I learned zip about his personal life. Nothing online suggested any shady dealings, except for his involvement in mixed martial arts, a sport of violence, but he'd never so much as had a complaint from opponents, and now only trained to stay in shape. The man appeared perfect. A dedicated political activist, who favored bringing people together rather than tearing them apart. His public image held together so well, I had to wonder what else?

My phone rang.

"It is Miguela Salas, your attorney."

"Hello, dearest."

"You have a settlement hearing on Monday."

"About what? Can't you do it without me?"

Miguela did not find this amusing. "Judges get curious when defendants fail to appear in person. They are being generous giving you five days. They can, as a condition of bail, ask that you appear any time."

"Is that what this is really about? Making me appear. I told you California summoned me into court to give testimony in my mother's case."

"I took care of that. They are aware. The judge cares about her docket, not California. I'm not even one-hundred percent certain you won't lose the bail money. Annie Von Kurk and her family will not like that. Besides that, we have hearings you must attend. You are on trial for your life."

"What time exactly on Monday?"

"Nine a.m. I will not ask why you sound worried. We are not taking a deal short of dismissing charges, but we are required to at least discuss settlement. If you do not appear ..."

"Yeah, I got the picture. Shit."

"Be at my office on Monday at eight-thirty."

How am I supposed to get back there. Don't have identification for flying."

"How'd you get out there?"

"That's unlikely."

"I'll overnight your official driver's license. The court gave it to me when I told them you had to appear in California. Text me your mailing address. Anything else?" She waited. When I said nothing, she continued. "Do not be late."

I smashed the phone against the pavement before I could stop myself. "Great going," I grumbled. I had two appointments the same day over three-thousand four-hundred miles apart. The possibility of attending both seemed remote. Charlotte Amalie and Los Angeles had a four-hour time difference. I had to be in St. Thomas first at 8:30AM, then I somehow had to find my way back to L.A. in time for the trial at 11AM. Even a non-stop took over seven hours, but that point was moot, since no commercial flights had non-stops. The shortest trip took well over seven hours.

Asking the Von Kurks crossed my mind, but my self-respect, or was it pride, wouldn't allow. A private jet probably couldn't move me that fast either and would cost thousands, if not tens of thousands. No way. Forfeiting the one-hundred thousand in bail money was not an option. Mother's trial had to go to the back of the line. It had to. I called the prosecutor's office and left a voicemail. An hour later, someone called back.

"You can't just move a trial," an officious man pronounced. "This is not like asking to reschedule your tennis lesson, sir."

"I have no choice. I know you all want this done on your time schedule, but that's not happening. I have to be in the Virgin Islands that day for a hearing on my murder case."

"You have quite the family, don't you?"

"Do you want me to hang up this phone?" I inquired. "Do you?"

Silence. Then finally, "What about Friday? Maybe the prosecutor can call you earlier."

I agreed to be there on Friday. I had only enough money in my coffers to make a one-way trip back to St. Thomas. I bought a ticket to return on Sunday to give myself through Saturday to get all I could out here. The other option was to solve this case, figure out the doer, and make law enforcement shrivel into their shell like a scared turtle once Dana slammed them with the story of my mistreatment and innocence.

A boy could dream.

Grace texted. "Where are you? I'm waiting to go to dinner!" I tried to apologize, but she was angry. Grace did not like being "abandoned." Even sober, I acted like an addict. In truth, I could have met her if I tried, as the drive from South Central would take about thirty minutes, but I needed to get something on Mark Green. Jealousy had taken control. It had to be Mark, because I wanted him to be bad. This would make me better. Make Evelyn wrong. I needed Evelyn to be wrong.

Earlier in the day, I had followed Mark Green back to the courthouse where he and Anders met again presumably to discuss the case and attend another hearing. They ate a late lunch and when the judge adjourned early, Mark made his way to a park. He spread a towel on the grass beside a basketball court and laid on his back watching the blackening evening sky. A couple kids played basketball in the dark, the hollow sound of the bouncing ball echoing in my empty head.

CHAPTER 29

A couple hours after picking up the envelope from Miguela Salas containing my driver's license, a text from someone claiming to have information on my case chimed into my phone.

The biker bar only had a few Harleys outside on a Friday night because of low visibility. As sometimes occurs in L.A., a swirling fog overtook the western edges of the city, particularly thick right on the ocean.

I got a few stares. A woman in a corner booth waved me over. She looked like she could be Evelyn's sister: jet black straight hair, the skin-tone of a vampire, wide eyes. She had a no-nonsense attitude and a tight ponytail. She looked at home, slurping scotch.

"I took the liberty of ordering you a margarita," she said. "Rocks and salt."

"You got my number from Grace, I take it?"

She nodded, her eyes narrowing. "Very good, private."

Law enforcement people dropped the "detective" because they didn't take private detectives seriously, especially when we weren't former cops. It was also a play on the lowest rank in the army. This woman had checked me out.

"Are you a detective?" I asked. "Or a uniform?"

She showed me her LAPD detective badge. Allison Armitage.

"It appears you might be a fugitive, Boise Montague." I tensed. She let me squirm before saying, "Don't worry, that's not what we're here about. I don't do Marshal work. But, you should get back to your jurisdiction."

"I'm actually here to testify in a murder trial. Totally legit. Isn't St. Thomas outside your purview?"

"Enough," she said, glancing around, seemingly satisfied with the situation. "We need to talk about your case. I'm concerned you didn't do this."

"And you want to help me out of the goodness of your heart?"

Her eyes narrowed to slits. "You're suspicious. I like that. Could be you aren't totally out to lunch. I think my ex-husband might be involved. Very involved."

"Who's … Mark Green?"

Her eyes darted away to watch someone at the bar hoot. Threat dismissed, she shifted back to me. "I heard about Felicity, or is it Felicia?"

"Felicia. Felicia Nichols."

"My ex has a thing for the women he works with."

"No shit," I agreed. "Are you saying Mark killed my wife, too?"

"Evelyn Montague? I don't believe that. He was actually with me the night she died. In fact, I had just confronted him about his infidelity. You might say he was my first case as a detective. His meetings involved your wife opening her legs and him …"

"Whoa! Don't need it spelled out. I'm aware of what they did. What's this got to do with anything?"

"Your wife made me suspicious of my husband for other reasons. It turned out, he wasn't just into Mrs. Montague, he was obsessed with her. He called me when the private detective he hired figured out your mother killed your wife."

"Henry Bateup works for Mark Green?"

"The big brain." She continued. "I am helping you. You see that, right?"

I banged my fist on the table, making our drinks jump. "Your considered opinion won't keep me from going to prison. What actual evidence do you have that Mark Green had anything to do with Felicia's murder?"

"Two things. First, I realized three years into our marriage, six months before I discovered his relationship with Evelyn, that he had a sadistic side. Once I realized this, it became clear that it was probably only a matter of time before he either got help or did something drastic."

"Why didn't you do something to stop him?"

She took a swig of her scotch, set it down and doodled a peace-sign in the condensation on the outside of the tumbler. The bright red of her lips contrasted sharply with her pale skin, made paler by the foggy city night.

"What could I do? He never did anything I could arrest him for. He liked to hunt. That's not a crime. He even kept his hunting, as far as I knew, to the season. After a while, I just sensed I'd married someone who fit some of the patterns of a psychopath, although that's not what it's officially called. Mostly, there were hints of danger, but he kept the public persona strong, even in private."

"Two things?"

"I checked to make sure he was actually at that conference in Vegas. He went there, but according to his email inbox, he took a flight to St. Thomas and returned the day before the conference ended." She read my face. "Yes, Mark Green was in St. Thomas the day Nichols was murdered."

The last sentence was the only time she'd used the name, "Mark Green", in our discussion.

"Do you have proof of the flight? Did you print out the email?"

"I never got a chance to. I could view it, but not print."

"That's useless," I said. "Sorry. I didn't mean that. What you've just told me could save my life, but I'm not sure how to prove Mark's involvement without that flight information."

"What you can do is prove he was in St. Thomas during that time."

"You think a jury is going to make the leap that, because of a coincidence, they should acquit me? Two people from the same organization happened to visit the island the same week. So what? Your ex is a well-respected member of the community. He needed a vacation and didn't want anyone to know, so he said he was going to a conference. He played hooky, big deal."

"You follow the leads and go where they take you."

I rubbed my temples, trying to ease the pain. "Why did he kill the others? Maybe there's an angle there?"

"You were on the right track with Felicia. She's the key. Figure out what he was doing with Felicia and why she was his victim."

"But wait, maybe she was collateral damage, and so were the others."

"The frame on you was the objective?" She drew a ying-yang on her glass. Short fingernails, no nail polish. "Maybe, but why use someone like Felicia? He could have just used someone with no connection to you who already lived in St. Thomas. Why risk you coming out here and putting it all together?"

"Arrogance? The thrill? He's an MMA fighter. He's book smart, not emotion smart. I once had a cat who lost an eye because she wouldn't leave a crow alone."

She rubbed the glass clean. "He does believe that he has a legacy. He also held you responsible for Evelyn's death, even if your mother did it. He wanted it to be you. For a minute I thought it might have been Mark, until I heard when it happened. Besides, he got more upset about her than when I told him I was leaving. He loved her, as much as he can love." Her face looked like stone and night, worn by erosion.

"You didn't already know that?" I asked.

"My ex could be persuasive. He's an expert at acting like he's sorry for the things he's done, like he'll never do them again." She had a far-off look as she gazed over at the bar. "Making you believe they care. Making you believe they'll change. He made me believe that, despite his infidelity, we could work it out. What I failed to recognize was how obsessed he was, and that there was something wrong far more sinister than infidelity."

Obsessed. People tossed that word around like a beach ball, however, this woman didn't strike me as casual in her usage. "How do you mean obsessed?"

"Well, your wife was thinking of breaking things off with him. I spoke to her before I confronted him, tried to make her feel badly about ruining my marriage. I blamed her, like many stupid women do. I suppose she deserved some blame, but based on what I know now about Mark's need to be adored, particularly by younger, attractive women . . . According to her, and I believe her, he seduced her."

I scoffed. "No, not Evelyn. She's not weak-minded like that. If she did it, she wanted to do it."

"He makes you want to do what he wants." She excused herself to use the restroom and asked if I wanted another drink. I hadn't even noticed I'd finished.

She returned. I threw out another question. "Why Evelyn? If he likes adoration from multiple sources, like any young thing he thinks he can conquer, why would he obsess about Evelyn?"

"Weren't you obsessed with her?"

"Obsessed? Nah. She was my wife."

"Come on, be straight. I saw her. Spoke to her. If I were a man who liked women, Ms. Montague was a woman I'd be obsessed with. Maybe even if I wasn't straight. I hear a lot of gay guys still sleep with women. You ever hear that?"

She was right. We were definitely that couple whom people looked at and asked, "What's she doing with him?" I knew this because I said it to myself all the time.

"You hate your ex? He cheated. You got divorced. Why are you still following him around? That worries me. I don't want to get caught up in a squabble."

The bar darkened as if a shroud had been thrown over the already dim lighting. "You can trust me, Boise. I'm police. Everyone should trust the police. We're only interested in justice." She handed me a slip of paper with an address on it. "In case you feel like looking into things."

CHAPTER 30

Sirens screamed in the dimpled night. I hovered above and around sleep, then finally fell into the well. The spot on its leg, stubborn as a rusty screw. The horseshoe kick. A throbbing headache. So real.

A whir of helicopter blades followed closely on the heels of sirens. Reading *Crime and Punishment*, I found myself disgusted with Razumikhin's co-dependence, his sickening need to fix everything wrong with Raskolnikov's family, at the expense of his own sanity. I sat up in bed and re-read the part where he dropped to his knees in front of mother and sister, wondering if Dostoyevsky was serious with this guy. Loser. Maybe Raskolnikov would kill Razumikhin. He deserved it.

I put the book aside and ventured onto the frigid balcony, nude. After five minutes of shivering, I knew what I needed to do.

***

The drive to Mark Green's house in Baldwin Hills lasted twenty minutes in the dead still of morning. I made almost every stoplight.

Black, concrete lions perched on either side of the steep stairs. Below the lion on the left, a large garage. Green's black Mercedes blocked the driveway. Parking a block down, near the corner of Don Diablo, in view of the quiet blinking lights of L.A. Live in my rearview.

The streetlamps in this part of town were encased in concrete from the base up to a point just below the metal fixture at the top. The old-time lamps that buzzed when lit had been replaced by LEDs, so even at three in the morning, the silence resembled a taut rubber band. Somewhere in the hills, an owl hooted.

What was I doing here? The chances that Mark Green would be doing anything at this hour besides sleeping were slim. Even if awake, how would I see him?

"Only one way," I whispered.

A single car had motored by, plowing through the stop sign at twenty-five. The police weren't watching this corner for prowlers or moving violations.

I trudged up the incline as close to the curb as feasible, skirting around two parked cars, exposed in the glow of a streetlight. The area directly across from Mark's address did not have a light. I could see my breath and feel the dryness on my lips.

Besides a pair of security lights above the corner of the garage, the house lived in fairy-tale darkness. I huddled on the curb, near the corner of the front bumper of a Volkswagen, slightly downhill, in case a car came up. Cars on the other side, going down into the residential area known as "The Jungle", would be able to see the stranger sitting on the curb in the middle of the night, but I hoped wouldn't notice since I was on the opposite side and had dressed in black.

A light popped on inside the house on the second floor

through a pair of French doors. Eggshell curtains obstructed my view, but a human shadow floated in the opaque light. 3:20AM. Who wakes at that hour? Lots of people. Nothing suspicious about that. I rubbed my hands together and blew hot breath into my cupped palms. Another car's engine revved up the hill from my left, zipping through the stop sign at Don Diablo, in low gear.

The front door of the house creaked open. I bolted behind the rear tire, landing between the car and an agave plant, scraping my hand and cheek across the sharp tip of the leaf. I stifled a groan, my breath racing.

I inched toward the middle of the SUV, watching from underneath as the black Mercedes' door clicked open. The toes of the tennis shoes pointed toward Don Diablo, not moving for thirty seconds before levitating into the car. The V6 roared to life, idled, then the lights veered and illuminated the Volkswagen while executing a three-point turn and heading up the hill. I hobbled to my car and gave chase.

CHAPTER 31

We weaved through Baldwin Hills, ending up at a light in front of some ragged apartments on the corner of Don Lorenzo and La Brea. I hung back, acting like a Lyft, double-parked in front of the apartment building, close enough to the corner to watch the Mercedes signal a left turn.

The light changed green and a car appeared, blocking me from making the left in time. The stoplight turned red. I whipped around him, running the light.

The next intersection was one of those complicated L.A. spots where five streets converged. The light on La Brea was red, but the Mercedes had already vanished. Unless it had just changed, he'd taken the right.

I raced down another steep incline as the light at the bottom turned green. The Mercedes hung a left. I tailed. Despite the early hour, a crowd of cars made the following less conspicuous, allowing me to follow more aggressively.

Before long, we exited the ninety into Marina del Rey, moving through the quiet natural beauty of the Ballona Wetlands. Turning left onto Culver Boulevard, I spotted the Mercedes on the shoulder, the lights turned off. Mark stood in the darkness in front of Evelyn's roadside memorial. He waved me over as I tried to drive past.

"Was I that easy to spot?" I asked as I got out.

"Why are you following me?"

"You might be up to something."

"What's that?"

"Why are you here?"

"Is it not obvious?"

Hands in pockets, shoulders tight, I shivered in the cool air while Mark dropped his head like a weary traveler. "She was loyal. That's rare," he said. "Special." Illumination from the boutique hotel two-hundred yards away threw enough light to make out the wrinkles in our faces. "You know who I thought might be loyal?"

"No. Who?" I asked. Keep him talking.

"Grace. She fit the bill. She was a peach."

I fingered a length of floss inside my pocket, weaving it around, wanting to pull it out and thread, although I'd eaten nothing. "Where is Grace tonight?" I asked.

"Do you have any loyal people in your life, Boise?"

"Sure."

"Name one."

"I had thought Evelyn 'fit the bill.'" I released the floss and signaled air-quotes.

"I like that," he said, a smile creasing his face. "You went there, out here." He gestured at the deserted street, the reeds, the wetlands. "I remember talking in the dark in bunks at sleepaway camps to other young, impressionable campers after lights out. Kids I'd only just met. Strangers, really. But in the dark, we'd say things that couldn't, wouldn't be said in the light of day. You ever do that?"

"Why are you here at four in the morning?" I asked. A toad ripped a giant *croak*. Something white sailed overhead into the trees.

He nodded at nothing in particular. "Forgive me, but if we're going to have a candid discussion, I'll need to see your chest and, well, your junk. I mean, you don't expect me to toss away the game completely, do you? You're gonna have to make some layups. Put away some overheads. Land an uppercut." He studied my hesitation. "What's the hold up? I know you're not shy."

I lifted my shirt and dropped my pants. He seemed satisfied. "Phone."

"Excuse me?"

"Your phone. Take it out. Turn it off."

I shut down my phone.

He lifted one of the red roses out of the vase on the memorial and sniffed. "Still fresh. Like my love for Evelyn. Don't you want me to show you mine?"

"Got nothing to hide," I said. "Record away, asshole."

"Who's creeping around outside whose house in the middle of the night? Ever heard of stalking laws? Wondering how I spotted you? Easy. Cameras in front, plus I'm knowing the car you're driving very, very well. I've studied it. I tell you, Boise, you surprise me. You're either dumb as a grain of rice, or you're a goddamn genius. Which is it?"

"Don't know what you're talking about, asshole." My ears felt like they could liquify lead despite the chill in the air.

"No need to be rude. We're having a civilized conversation here, right?" He put the rose back and rearranged the flowers. "I bring flowers here once, sometimes twice a week. Still I do it. When was the last time you brought her flowers?"

"I'm not big on flowers. Neither was Evelyn."

"Ha! Women are all into flowers. All of them." He sniffed another rose. "She liked getting them from me."

"Look, I'm sorry, but can we talk about something else?"

"Hi-de-ho. Let's talk about you driving around in that." He stepped toward me. I involuntarily stepped away, nearly losing my balance on a clump of loose dirt. I winced from a twinge in my knee, but the joint held. "Don't drive that thing near my home. You understand? How could you think there was any way I wouldn't see it? A billboard of evil. Now you have it here. Have you no shame? No sense of decorum?"

"Whoa, whoa, whoa. You really don't like Range Rovers."

"Your mother fits the bill. She still fits the bill. She'll always fit the bill, because she killed Evelyn." His breathing had sped up, his teeth clenched in the faint light, then his phone chimed. He put it to his ear. "What?" Pause. Crickets and the smell of a skunk. "Yes, that's right. Well, find out! What am I paying you for? Oh, you did? And? No, I want proof that it was premeditated. What do you mean?" If Mark had had a knife in his fist, he would have plunged it into his thigh repeatedly with the motion he made. "This is bullshit!" He waited. I studied the memorial. He clicked off and leveled his gaze at me.

"Why are you here?"

"In L.A.? I'm testifying at my mother's trial."

"How did you get out of St. Thomas? I thought you got remanded. It's triple homicides. Triple homicides don't get bail."

"I guess whoever told you that was wrong. I'm out and they granted me ..."

"No! Somebody's fucking with me. This can't be right. This is not how it was supposed to go." He dialed a number and spoke rapidly, disjointedly. "What's he doing here? And you, you brought him. This wasn't supposed to go. This doesn't fit the bill." He stopped prattling and listened. "Don't come. Stay there. It's fine. We're fine." He paused again. "I said we're fine. We don't want that." He clicked off.

"What's happening? Who are you talking to?"

"Nothing, nothing." His eyes bugged. He swatted at something. "He insists it's nothing. Go home, Boise. Better yet, go back to defend yourself, if you can. The others, they're sorry." He tugged a petal out of a rose and rubbed it against his cheek.

"I'm not going anywhere till after I testify. Do you understand that my mother is on trial for murder?"

"It runs in your family, it would seem. You. Your mother. I heard dad wasn't such a stand-up man himself."

The crazed look in his eyes finally forced me to step back. His lips continued to move after he stopped speaking, as if someone had muted him. Suddenly his face neutralized, like base to acid. He picked my phone off the rock next to the flowers and handed it back.

"Turn your phone on, Boise. It's all good in the hood. We're good. You can do what you like, it won't make a hair of difference." He nodded for a while as if answering an unheard question. "I wish you nothing but happiness and good tidings. Did you have a Merry Christmas? A Happy New Year? I hope you defeat those who would … be harmful to those you care about. I value your values, why you're here. More than you know. Let me ask you one thing: would you be here if those women … if you weren't accused?"

"I don't quite follow."

"Felicia and the others. Are you loyal to them?"

"I get paid to solve crimes. I can't afford to go off solving every murder I hear about involving people I don't know. So no, I'm not loyal to Felicia and the other victims. I don't know them. Their families didn't ask me to solve their murders. They believe they have the killer already. Why would anyone ask the accused to solve the murder of their children?"

"Yes, yes, how completely silly of me. That doesn't fit the bill of what people would do when hiring a private detective. You would know. Forgive me for my ignorance." He leaned over and sniffed the roses one last time, then turned toward the offices of BWPP. He turned back. "Boise, don't let this dissuade you from stopping by tomorrow if you please. Really. Stop by anytime.

Grace likes you. You keep things interesting."

CHAPTER 32

I wanted, very badly, to call my mentor and ask his advice. Henry and I now existed in limbo. He helped put my mother in jail, and I didn't think that I could abide that, no matter his good intentions.

"It's not going to bring her back," I muttered. Same lame argument, always used by the guilty. It wasn't about "bringing them back." It was about the living. Everyone, myself included, acted like what they did was for the dead. Justice was for the living. Entirely selfish. It was wrong to let the guilty wander free among us once we knew the truth.

But, my mother wasn't guilty. I wasn't guilty. We weren't guilty. Now, I had to solve two murders to protect two innocents. Very much about the living. I didn't really care about Felicia. I didn't know her beyond a couple hours of dancing and sharing a joint. The others, I could barely retain their names, yet their deaths now consumed my life.

I'd always thought Mark Green strange, a bit unhinged, a bit too … perfect. People like that rarely lived up to their billing upon closer inspection. He needed to be the killer.

Grace's thought was ludicrous. What did she know, a twenty-something intern? I was the investigator. These thoughts rattled around my head as I lay in bed, trying to make up for not sleeping the night before. Finally, I flicked the comforter onto the floor. There would be no midday napping today.

***

There was no one at the BWPP counter. I called out. A boy of eighteen sauntered out, shoulders hunched. He mashed his fingers on a phone screen urgently. "Damn!" he said in a British accent. He looked up, pushing his glasses back into place. "Help you?"

"Yes, I'm here looking for Grace."

"You see her, tell her I'm not too keen on having to cover her two days now. She's not answering or nothin'. You some bloke interested?"

"Excuse me? I'm just coming by …"

"Look, fella, if it's Grace Walker you want, you'll have to go find her another place. Suppose she's moved on. No loyalty, I suppose."

I tried calling and texting as I struggled through the insistent Friday afternoon traffic jam that, during my years of living here, had progressed from afterschool, to anytime after noon, as the cars and people crammed into a city built for nineteen-fifties traffic tried to function in the twenty-first century. Grace's car was parked in front of her small apartment building, a ticket plastered on the windshield. Friday street sweeping. No parking 10am – 2pm.

Odd, she didn't seem the type to leave her car to be ticketed. I replaced the ticket so she wouldn't get another. Up the block, a tank-shaped street sweeper moved glacially, the whirling bristles edging the curb with an incessant hum. I stepped to the sidewalk as it circled around Grace's car and continued down the road, the driver a picture of indifference to trash, pedestrians, and cars violating the rules.

I knocked. No answer. I peeked through the crack in her blinds, but only saw a vacant living room. A reflection of the kitchen in the television appeared clean and unoccupied. I called. I texted. I pounded on the door. A neighbor came out after a while.

"Do you know Grace?" she asked.

"I'm a friend. Have you seen her?"

"I saw her leave for work yesterday, but not since. She's a nice sort. Too bad about her walking. Still, a nice sort. I think she moved in because we have an elevator."

I handed the woman my card. "If you see her, would you give a call?"

"Sure thing, Boss-y?"

"Boise. Like the town in Idaho. The university has a good football team."

"Don't watch football. Is Grace okay?"

"I hope so."

I had to testify at mother's trial. Grace had disappeared. Mark Green had spoken to me in the middle of the night like a man experiencing dementia. The hourglass was getting low on sand.

My phone rang as I stood next to the Range Rover, still in front of Grace's place, trying to wipe some dried bird crap off the door handle.

"It's Boise."

"Will you accept a collect call from Marina del Rey Jail? Press one for yes." I punched one.

"Boise. I hear you're in town. Why?"

"Hi, Mom."

"You haven't come to see me. Don't I rate a visit? You are staying in my home and you don't come to visit?"

"Well, Mom, I've been called by the prosecution to testify in your case."

"The prosecution! Why would the prosecution call my son. What did you tell them?"

"Mom, calm down."

"I won't calm down. My son is testifying for the enemy. I protected you from a collapsed lung all those years. Kept you safe. Fed you. Clothed you. Birthed you ..."

I mouthed along with her diatribe, the same laundry list of parental duties she guilted me with every time I did or said something she didn't like.

"... Bathed you. Gave you a roof, hot water. Hell, I even made sure you got a good education."

"The education wasn't that good, Mom."

"Compared to the African kids, like your grandmother, any education in an American school is like attending Stanford. You got math, science, English, even some physical education. Don't be ungrateful, Boise. Your lungs are strong. You are healthy. No HIV, right? Am I right?"

"Yes, Mom, you're right."

"Come visit. I want to see you before you testify against me."

"I'm not there to testify against you. I hope that I'll help keep you out of prison."

"Why would the prosecutor call you if it's going to help me?"

"Mom, it may be bad for us to speak, that's why I haven't visited. Maybe that's what they want, for us to say something that they record or use against you when I'm up there. You know I have to tell the truth under penalty of perjury." Although I'd come up with this bullshit on the spot, it wasn't true. The truth was much farther down in the bottom of the cave where the bats lived.

"You've always been overly cautious about rules. Why stop now?"

"If you say something to me or I say something to you, they could impeach. Better that we don't speak. There's no privilege."

"What could we say? I'm innocent. That's it. What is there to say?"

"Mom, you know I've been through some trials? You recall I worked for a law firm? These things are dicey. You never know what they could use against you. I've wanted to visit. It's not that I don't want to, but you see, even this conversation, I promise they are listening and maybe recording it."

That silenced my mother.

"Are you driving the Rover?"

"Yes."

"It's paid off."

There was more I wanted to know about the car, about that night. I kept it innocuous. "Mom, how are they treating you?"

"This place smells like fungus and Pine-Sol. What do you expect? It's a jail. My lungs don't like the air here. You got in some trouble too, right? How are you here?"

"They subpoenaed me to testify, so they let me come up for that. My trial isn't for a little while."

The phone clicked, indicating that her fifteen minutes of time had come to an end. A woman in the background complained that Patrice was taking too long, in far more colorful language.

"I'm almost done," she proclaimed. "I gotta go. Fine, don't come see your mother. That's fine. You already abandoned me here, went to that god-forsaken rock, just to spite me. Why should I expect anything else?"

I wasn't going to see her. It was a bad idea. That conversation we'd just had was a bad idea, but I guess it had to happen.

The neighbor I'd spoken to exited Grace's building and hurried north on Centinela toting a small black and white flowered bag and a purse slung over her shoulder. A single-engine plane swooped overhead. The Santa Monica Airport was right up the street, in the direction she'd headed. She wasn't headed to the airport, however. At the corner of Palms and Centinela, a black Mercedes picked her up.

CHAPTER 33

Mark Green's Mercedes motored to a café on Venice that had a French name and served breakfast and lunch only. They took a table on the street, a couple yards from the entrance. The morning pallor had burned off, transforming into another virtual reality day: a brilliant blue sky dotted with green explosions. I belonged on the small rock, slinging my services to drunks and tourists. It felt wrong here now, the Von Dutch hats and expensive cars scattered amongst immigrants and desperados looking for their next fix. The island had the vacant-eyed men, but lacked the overwhelming numbers.

The unmatched pair ordered from a thick waitress and moments later a food runner brought over two waters and two mugs. The neighbor placed her hand in the center of the table, inviting Mark's touch. Mark picked up his coffee and leaned away.

After they finished, he dropped her back at her apartment building. She sat in the car longer than necessary and appeared to get upset before exiting and hurrying into the building. I followed her inside and knocked on Grace's door again, waiting and knocking repeatedly. When she didn't answer, I knocked on the neighbor's door.

"Who is it?" she said from the other side of the peep-hole. Her tone betrayed upset.

"Hello, ma'am. It's Boise, the man who stopped by an hour ago to see Grace. Can we talk?"

"About what? I told you, if Grace came home I'd give her your message. I have your card."

"I want to ask about you meeting with Mark Green just now."

Silence. It was a gamble. This might scare her off. She might call Mark, but I didn't think so. If she called, he might be angry at her, as well. I wanted to warn her off of him, that he might be using her, but that could cause her to clam up completely.

"He's a friend of mine, I know him from BWPP. My wife worked with him for many years."

Again, silence, but I could hear her like a mouse in a hole. "If he's a friend, why not talk to him?"

"I'm concerned for Grace. She hasn't been home. Do you know where she is?" I looked around at the other three closed doors lining the hallway. "I'm really not comfortable talking about this in the hallway for your neighbors to hear. I promise, I'm harmless as a mouse."

I waited, silently negotiating my entry. As I was about to suggest we meet outside and take a walk, the lock clicked. She belonged in the nineteen-fifties, but had some slightly modern angles added, like highlighted hair.

She gripped a tennis racquet in a batter's stance. "First, let me tell you, I will use this ..." She looked down at my business card held in her non-racquet hand. "Boss-y. I'm sure Grace Walker is just fine. She's a capable woman who keeps her own counsel."

"How do you know Grace?"

"Duh. We're neighbors."

"So you lived here and happened to meet Grace and her boss somehow."

"Is that a question?"

"Sorry, I'm not being clear. You met Grace as a neighbor. How did you meet Mark Green?"

"I knew Mark Green first. I introduced them. I suggested Grace take the internship with Mark's outfit to get her started on the road to being a do-gooder. Mark likes to mentor young women."

"I'm sure he does."

"Pardon?"

"Nothing. That's nice of him."

"Mark values loyalty, and Grace Walker always struck me as loyal. She's been a good friend to me."

"Do you have a key to Grace's apartment?"

"Why are you asking me that?"

"Well, neighbors often exchange keys so that they can take care of a problem, feed the cat, etcetera." I was being bold, perhaps because of the time constraints. I kept asking myself, "What would Dana do?" every time I thought of breaking off and putting my tail between my legs. So far I'd managed to keep after ... shoot, I didn't know this woman's name. "I just realized, I don't know your name."

"Dedra Detrick."

"Is that your real name?" I asked, knowing many in this town changed their names after moving here.

"How rude! Who says that?"

"That'd be someone named Dana."

"Thought your name was Boss-y?"

"Never mind. So, Dedra, please, I'm a private dick and I need to get into Grace's apartment. Any ideas?"

She stopped looking at me like I was a baseball and lowered the racquet slightly. "You really think something happened to her?"

"Does she often stay away this long without telling you?"

"I'm not her mother. Anyways, maybe she finally got a man. It's tough for a person, well you know, like her, to meet a partner. She's pretty, but I don't know, maybe men don't think it works."

That was not a fifties statement. "I think I recognize you!" I said, snapping my fingers.

"Really?" She definitely was an actress and Dedra Detrick was not her name.

I took a stab. "Yes, I went to a film festival last year. You were in a short. What was it called?"

Her face blossomed. "*Five Strangers*. That was me. I had three lines! You saw that?"

I sat down and rubbed the arm of the flowery upholstered chair Dedra probably inherited from her grandmother. "You really did a good job."

If possible, Dedra's face grew brighter, now resembling a California forest fire. She lowered the tennis racquet to her shoulder, considered the situation, then dropped it on the round dining table that occupied half the living room. A book of Lanford Wilson plays lay open on one of the dining chairs.

"Are you in anything right now? A play or another film I should see? Or better yet, I'd love to watch that short again."

A black and white cat sauntered out from the hallway to my right and curled itself around Dedra's muscular legs. She had the build of a gymnast. Opening the entertainment cabinet that housed her television and stereo, she pulled out a DVD jewel case and held it between her fingers like a game show hostess, dancing the case around in front of her slender chest.

"This is it!" she cooed. "You really, really liked it?"

"Yes, I really, really liked it."

"You really liked me in it? What did you like best about my

performance?”

"Oh gee, umm, well, it's been a little while. I say we watch it again, you know, to refresh my memory.”

She grinned. "Oh, fun!”

When she turned to put the DVD into the player, I checked the time. I'd been here too long.

"Hey, uh, Dedra …”

"Oh, this stupid thing. It doesn't always read the DVDs. Hold on.”

The television blinked on and a title card illuminated the screen with options to play, watch special features, and other menu items.

"There we are! Now, my mother calls me Dedra. Call me De-De, like the ice cream place.”

"Okay, De-De.”

"See, cause my name has the same letters beginning both first and last. I thought it was clever. I thought of adding a middle name or at least initial, but de-de-de sounds like I'm singing a show tune. Too much, right? I like musicals, but I don't want to be named after one or sound like one, you know, the casting agents might not take me too serious if I went that far. What do you think?”

I resisted the urge to look at the cat clock on her wall again. Her bulging eyes seemed to take in my every move. "I … I think I really want to see …” I read the title off the screen, "… *Five Strangers* again. I loved all five of you, but you were the best.”

Her face grew uncertain. I could be such an idiot. "I'm not one of the strangers, silly. You really must have forgotten some of this. Wait a minute, when did you say you saw this?”

"Last year,” I said hesitantly.

She scratched at her dimple. She tugged the blinds over all the windows and turned out the light she had on over the dining table.

We watched the film. She was very arguably the worst actor in that, or any film I'd seen in years. Everything was too big, her face too animated. She might have had a career if audiences once more craved silent films. After a torturous fourteen minutes, the last credit rolled.

"Well, was it as good as you remembered?"

I grinned as big and false as her acting. "Oh wow, it really was. You really stand out. What a performance!"

She scratched her dimple again. "Awww, that's nice of you to say. You know, I just like to bring emotion into people's dreary lives. All those people …" she made a sweeping hand gesture one-hundred-eighty degrees as if waving to an adoring public from atop the Eiffel Tower, "… working in offices." She shook her head as if she understood the plight of the masses. "It seems so empty."

The screen had returned to the menu. "Do you want to see the special features? There's an interview with me that the guy doing the behind-the-scenes did next to the craft services table on the second night of the shoot. I told some things about my background as an actor and my childhood. I come from the Lee Strasberg School, you know."

"Gee, De-De, I don't know, do you mind if I check on Grace? I'm a bit worried."

Her demeanor shifted to a darker shade of pale. "Grace Walker. Funny name for a cripple. I'm so sick of everyone asking me about Grace all the time."

"Who's asking you about Grace?"

She put her hand over her mouth. "Ooooops! I'm not supposed to talk about her with anyone. Shoot!"

"De-De, you can tell me." I held my hands up. "Harmless as a mouse."

She drummed her fingers on her knee. "You do have a trustworthy face. I guess that's why you're suited to your profession. People have to trust a private eye, right?" She looked down at her penny-loafers for a while. "You know, I have a scene for my acting class tomorrow morning, and I still don't have the lines memorized because I'm always talking to Mr. Green about Grace. I need you to run lines with me, then I'll let you into Grace's place."

"What if we went into her place, then ran the lines?" I suggested.

"What if I killed myself?"

"What?" I exclaimed. "Why, why, why would you talk about that? Are you suicidal?"

"When I don't know my lines, it's a viable option."

After another ten minutes, I convinced her that Lanford Wilson would have preferred Grace's living room as a setting. I based my argument on the idea that Wilson preferred the furniture in his productions to match the current time period and I took the risk that Grace had more modern furniture than De-De. I had no idea how Wilson felt about furniture.

I pushed through the door to Grace's apartment before De-De could remove her key from the lock and yelled, "Grace! Grace!" as I stormed from room to room, the urgency growing as rapidly as my impatience with De-De's narcissism.

Grace wasn't much of a homemaker. Dishes from at least three meals filled the kitchen sink. On the wall of her bedroom, hung a home-made sign in black sharpie on white paper: "Don't Feel Sorry For Yourself." Below that on a smaller sheet of paper it said: "Help others."

De-De came into the bedroom a minute later holding a glass of water. "I got my prop. Don't think Grace will mind me drinking from one of her glasses, do you? I mean, my teacher says to get comfortable in the space, especially if it's the character's. I gotta make myself at home."

I sat on the edge of the unmade bed and considered Grace's wall of declarations. Mark Green picked the women in his life who would be loyal. Women who felt the need to help others in need and would be loyal to him because he made them feel that being loyal to Mark Green was the same as helping those in need. Grace wanted to be someplace where the people needed her help more than they focused on her tragedy, giving her the illusion of being whole. I also considered that Mark Green favored loyalty above all else and had somehow found out that Grace wanted to leave BWPP.

As I re-read the admonition to "Help Others," my eyes descended to the waist-high chest of drawers. Grace Walker's inhaler rested atop the dresser. De-De yelled from the living room. "I'm done with my water, I'm in the zone; this space is mine! Time to act!"

I picked up the inhaler, depressed it. A puff of air splashed the palm of my hand. Shoving it into my pocket, I headed out the front door to protestations from De-De that sounded like a bad Susan Sarandon imitation. After getting to my car, I doubled back to the apartment for one last request. De-De hadn't moved and was now smoking, her eyes half-closed in a dreamy "come hither" state.

"I knew you'd return ..." she looked down at her script, then held a second copy out to me, "... Larry."

"De-De ..."

"It's Anna! My name's Anna. See, it's right there." She tapped the script. "We're in character now." Then she whispered, "Great idea to make me think you were walking out. Heightened stakes. I thought I was losing you. You ever thought of doing some acting?"

"I didn't ... listen, uh, Anna, I need to know if you know where Grace is. I think she's in trouble, and I can't waste time running around from place to place guessing where she might be. What did Mark Green say to you?"

"You said we were going into Grace's place to get into the spirit of the play. Now you want me to help you leave and go look for her? Mark said she's fine, that she's crashing at his place for a few days. I was upset and asked if they were sleeping together, but he insists it's strictly platonic, that he just feels sorry for her, the pitiful thing."

"His place. In Baldwin Hills?"

"How do you know that?"

"Is it his place in Baldwin Hills?" I repeated impatiently.

She shrunk away. "You are not loyal. You are not nice. Leave me alone." She stormed into her apartment and slammed the door. I heard the lock click.

I shut Grace's door. As I made my way down the hall, a muffled voice called, "Boss-y? Are you out there still?"

"I'm here. I need to go, but if you can confirm that it's his house is in Baldwin Hills, I'd appreciate it. Does he have any others?"

"I deserved that. Your anger, I mean. I get wrapped up. You seem like a good guy. Promise you won't hurt Mark?"

"I have no intention of hurting Mark unless he's hurting Grace. I just want to protect Grace."

"You men and your protecting of Grace. Poor little thing. She is pretty and helpless. Well, not really helpless, but she'd like you to believe that."

"De-De, I really have to go."

"He keeps a place near LMU. Here's the address." She slipped a sheet of paper under the door. "Please don't mention I helped you. He doesn't like it when people aren't loyal."

***

A few blocks from Loyola Marymount University, I parked in front of a small apartment building and walked up the quiet residential street. A woman in high heels walking a Pomeranian, sauntered by. The dog had little pink booties on his tiny feet.

"Excuse me?" The woman shoved her graded sunglasses to the tip of her nose and looked up from her Apple Watch, her expression one of polite disinterest. "Do you know who lives in that house?"

"If I did, I wouldn't tell you."

"I'm a private investigator. I'm worried the man who lives there took a woman and is holding her inside. Does that seem ..."

"In there?" The woman chuckled. The little dog yelped once, sniffed my shoe. "No, the people who live there have children. The father works at the university and the mother plays a lot of bridge." The dog strained at the leash and squeaked at a cat that scurried across the street. "Mitzy! No! Ugh."

"Do they have a daughter named Dedra?"

"Dedra? No, but, oh wait, yes, that's Samantha's stage name. Dedra and something with a 'd'."

"Detrick," I said. It wasn't a question. "Son of a ..."

I raced back to my car and beelined it to Baldwin Hills. On the way, a call came in. Henry.

"What are you doing?"

"What do you want? You planning to put me in jail, too?"

"No, I just want to explain. My intention was not to put your mother in jail."

"Great, you've explained. Feel better?"

He sighed. "Olive branch, Boise."

I screeched to a halt behind some idiot trying to turn left below a no left turn sign. I blared the horn, waited for a small break and ripped into the right lane as another driver honked at me.

"Boise? Boise? You there?"

"Yeah, I'm here. You want to justify putting my mother away?"

Henry guffawed. "Wow, man. Don't have anything to justify. I followed the trail. It led to Patrice. I'm mighty certain I didn't make her do whatever she did."

"Tell yourself that. You know what I would take? You tell me who you work for. Who thought so much of this that they spent money to put you on the case?”

“Not gonna happen.”

“'Bye.”

Through Baldwin Hills I drove as fast as I could, jouncing over the numerous speed bumps. I climbed the steps, past the black lions and the Mercedes, and pounded on the door. “Come on. Come on.”

Mark Green leaned into the door frame, his bulbous head like a pit bull. “Hey, there …”

I shoved past him. “Hey! What the …”

“Grace! Grace!” I careened about the cavernous house.

“What the heck are you doing?” Mark said, his face calm.

“Where is she?”

“Who?”

“Grace Walker!”

“Oh, golly, Boise, haven’t seen her. She doesn’t come over here much. I don’t have an elevator and all those hillside steps coming up here are tough.”

“Look, fuckface, tell me where she is. I know about De-De, and I …”

He chuckled, his eyes alight with mischief. A piece of lettuce or spinach stuck in the gap between his front teeth. “Do you know much about life, Boise? De-De does help me out. She watches out for my interests. We’re friends. She gets compensated. People don’t much look at a young woman except to ‘check her out.’ They can move around, watch, etcetera. Unlike men, who are the stereotypical ‘watchers.’” He kept making obnoxious air quotes and smiling his lettuce-smile.

“Just tell me where she is.”

“De-De slips around like an eel.” He turned away from me, fingering the back of a gaudy Victorian-era chair with lots of buttons. “If I could facilitate an older woman, that’d be even better, but for now, she’ll do. She’s very determined to, you know, make it as an actress. The work she does for me is very flexible. Pays better than waiting tables."

"You pay for her apartment?"

"She is roundly compensated for her work in a manner agreeable to all parties. Barter is a nice medium of exchange, don't you agree?"

"Avoids the IRS."

"Very good, Boise." He spoke like he was praising a puppy for using the training pad.

"Enough." I tried to sound tough. He could probably crush my skull between the pecs beneath his Tommy Bahama shirt. "Where is she?"

"Why don't we call her? I'll call BWPP and check if she's there."

"I tried that. They said she hadn't been in."

"Well, I had her doing something outside the office today, but certainly …" He glanced at his watch. "Certainly she's back by now."

He dialed on speaker phone. Grace answered. "Ballona Wetlands Protection Project, how may I be of service?"

"Grace." The relief on his face was notable. "Hello, it's Mark. How did that errand go today?"

"Fine, fine, I filed the papers. You were right, they respond to me."

"Well, you're much better as the face of BWPP than I ever was. I have Boise Montague here with me. You remember him, right?"

"Yes," she said, her tone like granite.

"Hi, Grace. How are you?" I asked in a cheery tone.

"Fine."

I thought about asking about her inhaler, but decided that admitting I'd tricked her neighbor into letting me into her apartment wasn't the best idea.

A tense silence held the room. Mark broke it. "Well, day's

almost over. Enjoy your evening, Grace."

"You, too, Mark."

"There, you see, she's working away, nothing to be concerned about. Grace covets her work with BWPP and I wouldn't let anything happen to her. She's a valuable asset."

"She's a person," I muttered.

"The most valuable assets always are."

"I'm still curious. Why is her car at her place? What's she driving?"

"Oh, I let her borrow one of my cars. She likes driving a Mercedes instead of her boring car. I had my car outfitted for wheelchair drivers. I have family with difficulties, too, so I understand her predicament. She was so excited, she asked to use it for a few days. I couldn't say no."

He'd done this just to screw with me, but what was the point of going on, he'd out-played me. "Does she use an inhaler?"

"Ah, the inhaler. De-De called and mentioned that. Why don't we make that our little secret, huh? If you give it to me, I'll make sure it gets back into Grace's apartment and she needn't be the wiser."

I handed it over. As I stalked out, I shouted over my shoulder, "Maybe you have my phone."

Mark had the home field advantage. He knew the players. Hell, he'd drafted them. Here I was trying to recruit with nothing except my charm to convince these people that someone as charismatic, generous, and confident as Mark Green, was also responsible for the deaths of three women.

"Stupid," I mumbled, my forehead resting on my steering wheel. I leaned back and stared at downtown L.A. A small cluster of skyscrapers, smaller than most cities of ten million, I'd always assumed because of earthquakes. An image of my mother and I buried beneath rubble flashed in my mind. On the rubble, chiseled like hieroglyphs in an Egyptian tomb, criminal statutes, complete with numbers and italics, recounted our sins. "The killing of a human being with malice aforethought." The rocks weighed tons. My arms were trapped like snakes locked inside a safe deposit box.

All of this would be over before long. I'd sleep on a crippled cot inside a urine-soaked institution and perform unskilled manual labor, or I'd sleep on mustard-colored sheets at the West Indian Manner, comforted by Christina and crickets.

My phone buzzed. A text from Dana. "Call me." I dialed.

"Hello, mon ami."

"You know those guys who helped you arrive in L.A.?"

"You mean the super-friendly dude who flew the plane and the primates?"

"Sire says there's some payment due. Report to Topanga Canyon."

"Whoa, whoa, whoa, I got stuff to do. I don't have time to go gallivanting around in hippie-ville."

"Oh shut up, Boise. You already live in St. Thomas. I'm texting the address. Don't get on Sire's bad side, or he won't help you out next time and that pilot … I told you to steer clear."

"What did you get me into?"

I explained that I'd be returning soon and Dana grunted her approval. "Just do what you're told, and keep your clothes on."

CHAPTER 34

"Can I help you?" A woman in denim overalls, set down a pail full of something, then placed her hands on full hips, a cowboy hat riding sidesaddle. Her smooth, tanned obliques peeked between her shirt and the loose folds of her overalls. A mud stripe ran across the bridge of her nose.

An old-fashioned farmhouse staked the center of the land, rolling hills of grass and shrubs, along with Eucalyptus trees from which birds squawked in various tones and volumes. Horses, cows, llamas, a few alpacas, and a large tortoise milled about. Piles of freshly cut branches littered the ground around one of the Eucalyptuses.

"Sorry to bother." I bowed slightly. "Yes, I'm looking for a cranky guy by the name of … well, I don't recall his name. I met him on a flight out here. He was transporting some monkeys."

"Uh-huh. From where again? And what's your name?"

I explained it all to her, leaving out my semi-fugitive status, making sure to drop Sire Goode's name. Her distrustful eyes scanned me. "And you want to know where this monkey-smuggler might have gotten off to? What for?"

"I'm supposed to come here today … didn't he ask Sire for me to come do some work? Is this the right place? Cranky, doesn't talk much?" I drew my fingernail across my face. "Got a nasty scar down his right cheek."

"And you know Sire Goode?"

A man wandered out of the barn. I yelped, "Hey, that's him! You're you! See." I pointed. "Scar."

"You! What's he doin' here?" He directed the question at the woman.

"Xavvy, I don't have time for this shit. You always got someone snooping around looking for you. Take it somewhere else. Too many folks knowing our business, you ask me." She hoisted the pail and headed over to a slop area where a couple pigs caked in mud snoozed. "Sire sent him out here to pay for his ride."

"Oh, crap." Xavvy slapped his forehead. "I plum forgot I told that fool to send this fool. Shoot, I never thought you'd show up on account of me telling you our business was concluded."

"Yes, you did tell me that." I took a big sniff as the fresh-cut eucalyptus cleared my sinuses.

Xavvy hooked my arm in his vine-like fingers and dragged me over to my car, his tone hushed. "What I need is for you to help me get these monkeys out to a refuge about one-hundred miles north. It takes two and my guy bailed last night. We load and unload, but it's the drive that really matters. Sharon there ain't to be the wiser."

Sharon had turned away, but backed toward us in a blatant attempt to eavesdrop.

"Shhh. I don't …" He pulled me farther away. "… I ain't keen on her knowin' about my brother bailin'? You say that it was a mistake and drive on down to where the dirt and asphalt meet. Park your car there. I'll pick you up."

Subterfuge between Sharon and Xavvy. Fun. "So, I help you with the monkeys you didn't even want me to know about, and what, then you call Sire again and I have to keep doing crap for you whenever you want?"

"Naw, man, it's not like that. This one solid, that's all it is. One solid, then we solid." How much nicer they got when they needed something.

"All right," I murmured. "Is this legal? I've already got enough trouble ..."

"We're legal. We're going to a refuge to keep these animals out the black market. It's the black market fellas I need you to watch for."

***

At the edge of the asphalt, I crouched in some California dry grass and dust, swatting gnats. The truck was large, like one of those U-Haul moving trucks. Stenciled across the back was the logo for an organic farm in Ojai.

"Where'd you get the truck?" I asked.

He pointed a finger at me, his dusty goatee bobbing up and down. If he didn't always have a scowl on his mug, he might have been a decent looking guy. "Just 'cause you helpin' out, don't mean I've become Eleanor Chatty. I drive. You focus." He reached behind the seat and pulled out a shotgun. "Know how to use it?"

I raised my hands and backed away. "Not much a fan of firearms."

"You don't need to be a fan. Just need you to load ..." He put two red shells into the back of the barrel. "Cock." He shut the barrel. "Pump." He pumped the action. "And dump."

He pointed it at a defenseless bush to my left and fired. The leaves of the tree shuddered like it was in a momentary rainstorm. I dropped to the ground and covered my nappy head. "Jesus!"

"I got your attention?" he asked. A malevolent smile dawned on his sour-puss. "This ain't no game, boy. We playin' for keeps. You know Sire's daughter, so you know Sire ain't no pussycat. He's a goddamn coyote, and I'm a fucking puma. Drink this." He handed me a 5-Hour energy drink. I downed it. "You alert?"

He reloaded the shotgun and handed it to me. "Pump and dump." He pointed at the bush.

I pumped and dumped. The bush shuddered again. I dumped the shells and reloaded. "Yup, I'm alert, but I'm not your boy. Can we stop for some food?" Xavvy had already circled around the truck and started the engine. I muttered to myself, "Guess that's a no."

CHAPTER 35

We drove through the canyon toward Ojai on some odd route that weaved through Moorpark and continued onto Route 23. Although I'd lived in L.A. for quite a while, I mostly knew the west side, downtown, and some of the San Fernando Valley through serving papers and tracking cheating spouses.

We swung through, Santa Paula, a small town of tract housing. The shotgun bounced like a newborn on my lap as the truck navigated smoothly, never too fast or too slow. Xavvy had found his calling: navigating and operating vehicles. His flying, his driving, were easy and unencumbered by his nasty personality.

"Hey! Hey!" Xavvy yelled in sharp, clipped tones.

"Wha?"

"I see ya dozing. No dozing. We got a job. You need to keep checking that side mirror. These guys …"

"It would help me to know what I'm looking for."

"Danger, man. Danger. You don't need no fancy degree to spot danger. Good ol' fashioned common sense. How'd you stay alive this long?"

"Why would we be in danger? We're rescuing some monkeys, right? Who cares?"

Xavvy slapped the steering wheel and the truck swerved before returning to a steady gait in the middle of the lane. "We going into the mountains now. One lane each side. This here used to be a stagecoach route back in the day. I take it because it's easy to spot folks following. There's no where to hide, but it's also dangerous. These here ol' monkeys, let's just say there's a market for 'em. They're more valuable than all that Bitcoin everyone goes on about, and they's real. You can touch 'em. People like owning animals no one else has, but these here beasts, they weren't meant for that."

"Xavvy, you almost sounded like you cared for a minute."

"Shut up and pay your attention to that mirror. We get ambushed, I'm gonna shoot you after we shoot them."

We ascended into acres of rolling greenery. Hawks or falcons, I wasn't sure which, circled in the uninterrupted morning sun. As I studied a single hawk off to our right, Xavvy let out a hissed curse.

"Gun!"

I whirled my attention first to the sideview mirror. Nothing behind. Then, he hollered, "Front, left!" as we rounded a corner bearing left, a parked muscle car surrounded by three meatheads sporting beards and blade sunglasses. They all held weapons casually pointed at the ground.

"Use the gun!" Xavvy shouted.

I leaned across as Xavvy leaned forward to give me room out his window and fired. The casualness of the men vanished as they dropped to the ground and scrambled behind their car. They didn't fire.

"Why aren't they shooting?" I asked.

"Precious cargo," Xavvy growled. "We crash, could hurt the primates. There'll be more. Be ready."

Sure enough, as we came onto a straightaway, a car blocked our lane. Xavvy pulled the truck hard left, clipping the corner of the vehicle and nudging it into the side of the hill.

I yelled, "Car!"

In front of us, a minivan approached, a middle-aged man's mouth open, his horn screeching. The van braked as we veered back into the correct lane. Behind us, the muscle car gained, the headlights like eyes, the grill a hungry mouth. The car trapped against the side of the hill spun its wheels to no avail.

"What do we do?" I asked.

"I'm figurin'. Gimme a minute. You a detective, come on then, detect us a solution."

I leaned out my window and aimed for the hood of the black Nova, which swerved to the driver's side, out of my line of sight.

"You gotta go out," Xavvy yelled.

"Out?"

"Yeah, see the ladder on the side, grip that and move to the back."

I looked out the window and noticed the ladder going up the side of the truck.

"How am I gonna hold the gun?" I asked.

"Here," Xavvy pulled a revolver out of the glove box. "Waistband, pal."

Pistol in the small of my back, I opened the door. Wind howled, billowing my shirt, my nipples hardened and goosebumps prickled my chest in the chilled air. A shot fired and the truck groaned before listing toward the hillside. Branches slapped me before I could fully exit. I yanked the door shut before it got ripped off. We halted in a turnout.

Xavvy squinted out his window at the ground. "Shit! Forget it. Flat tire. Too dangerous to keep driving." Xavvy banged the wheel, then checked the time on the digital dashboard clock. He mouthed something, then asked, "How long we been on the road?"

I chose this moment to notice that the truck had a cassette deck. "Long enough that I wish we'd brought some music. We left a little over an hour ago."

"That oughta do." He stroked his goatee, then repeated, "That oughta do." He shot off a text, then said, "Wipe down your side." I wanted to know why. "Shut the fuck up and wipe."

He pulled rags from behind the seat, dumped some water from a bottle on them and handed me one. I wiped every spot I could think of, then leaned out and wiped off the door handle.

"You sure we don't want cops?"

He slid so close, I smelled chewing tobacco. "Use the rag over a hand and don't touch anything on this truck from here on out." I wrapped the rag around my right hand.

The Nova pulled behind us. One of the guys had a bullhorn: "Open up, pretty little bitches. Throw out the weapon."

Xavvy snagged the shotgun off the floor, wiped it off, and tossed it out the driver's side window.

"Now, exit real slow. Everybody out the driver's side."

Xavvy climbed down. I stuffed the rag into the back of my pants with the gun after wiping it off, then slid across the seat on my hip to keep from discharging the weapon before pulling my baggy flannel over my pants and joining him. Xavvy pulled a set of keys from his front pocket, dropped them next to his foot, and kicked them behind the front tire.

"Hands," bullhorn said forcefully. We raised our hands. Three guys sauntered up to us.

"Keys," said a biker-looking fat man, clad in an "I hate everyone" t-shirt under an open denim vest.

"Lost 'em," Xavvy said.

"You're funny. You just pulled over. Where's the keys?"

"Ignition."

During this intellectual exchange, the other car pulled up,

smoke billowing out of the hood. A man climbed out the window, race-car-driver style. His cowboy boots and a Sacramento Kings basketball jersey confused me; maybe confused him, too. Thick wads of armpit hair stuck out around thin biceps.

"So, boys, where my 'keys," he drawled to his crew.

"I'm trying to get the keys from this here pendejo," said Bulky Biker. "I'm gonna ask one more time …"

"Hey man, I'm just interested in the live 'keys. No need for the hostility, although, I gotta admit you did ding my car, which I don't much care for. If I get the 'keys smooth-like, then we can all separate. How's about I just take the whole truck?"

Xavvy spit a brown stream of chaw on the ground next to Bulky Biker's work boots. Bulky stepped to Xavvy, who leaned in, nostrils flaring.

"I'll sting you so fast, fat man, you wonder where the swelling came from."

Bulky punched his right fist into the open palm of his left. "I'm gonna …"

"Billy! Billy! You ain't doin' nothin'. Step back! Let a grown-up talk to the children. Who's this one?"

Billy turned to Sacramento Kings and said, "Man, why you gotta always be a peacemaker? I never get to hit anyone. I miss …"

"Hey, hey, hey! Don't you say his name." Sacramento Kings wagged his finger. "Ah-ah-ah! Don't say it. You remember what happens if you mention him again." He waited, then said. "Who's the king?"

The men behind him said in a monotone, like kids reciting the national anthem before they'd fully woken up. "Loren is the king."

Loren "The King" turned to the men behind him and raised his arms wide and splayed his fingers to the sky. His Sacramento Kings jersey lifted, exposing his pierced navel. "That's right boys." He turned back to Billy. "You see what they said, Billy. Only one problem, the teacher couldn't hear those students way in the back of the classroom, so you're gonna have to speak up. Oh, what the hell, you better yell it. I'll get out my decibel meter."

Loren clicked an app on his phone and held up a green screen. "When it turns red, then I'm satisfied you were loud enough." He leaned into one hip like a cheerleading coach awaiting the squad's exceptional cheer.

More pissing matches between superiors and drones. "Hey?" I said loud enough so the decibel meter moved nearly to the red.

"You see, that's how it's done." The King faced me. "Mr. Sidekick, what is it you wish to address to The King?"

I sighed. Time to play the game with this loon. "So, Mr. King."

"Just King."

"So, King, can you and your … Billy, air your grievances in another time and place? Do my colleague and I really have to be a party to this workplace scuffle?"

The King held my eyes for a long time. "I see that for a small man, you have spunkiness. Very cute. But we are not here to serve your purposes or get you on your way in a convenient time frame. That said, we might want to move things to a quieter location." He watched a car drive by, a dog hanging out the window, its tongue lolling in the wind. "Yes, this is true. Okay. Let's get this opened up. Keys?"

One of the henchmen checked the ignition and shook his head at Loren.

"I lost 'em," said Xavvy.

"That's funny. Maybe we just shoot your friend here." Billy moved closer and put the barrel of his gun against my forehead. I flinched slightly. "Whoa, this boy don't like guns. That's wise. See, he's the smart one." He gazed at me, a twinkle in his eyes. "But don't ya move too fast, could cause accidental discharge."

Xavvy sneered. "Whatever man, if you want go shootin' folks over whatever you think is in that truck. We're moving farm goods."

King leaned his head against the side of the truck. Some kind of scurrying sound and an occasional monkey noise faintly vibrated inside the metal casing. I'd heard it throughout our drive.

"Yeah, no. I know 'keys when'n I hear 'keys. You don't want to open up for the 'keys? What do the itty-bitty primates matter to you?"

We both stood there, me with the warm barrel of the gun on my forehead starting to itch, my crotch schvitzing, while Xavvy played roulette with my life. I wanted to tell them the keys were behind the tire. I'd repaid my debt. He'd treated me like a third-class citizen. Some displaced devotion, maybe to Sire and Dana, paused me. If Xavvy really saved 'keys from being owned and abused by men who wanted them as a conversation piece, maybe that was as good as anything to die for.

"Billy, bring the gun over here. Don't you go wastin' a bullet on that Samoan boy." I could always tell the dumbest one at the party was whoever made the first Samoan comment.

"I'm not Samoan," I said. "Just 'cause a man tends to gain weight in the middle ..."

They headed to the rear of the truck. "You just shoot the lock off like the good little soldier you is."

"See, why'd you have to go and say something like that?" Billy asked, removing the barrel from my forehead.

"Just point and shoot, like I'm gonna make you do with the phone later when I fuck your girl in the ass again." The King laughed, turning to his other henchmen for support. They gave it, guffawing along like a pack of dogs. "You know, Billy, if your brother wasn't my brother from another mother, then ..." The King never finished his last thought, instead a bullet entered the base of his skull and exited between his eyes. His sunglasses split at the bridge, exposing jaundiced eyes faded to black. King crumpled like a liquid mannequin.

Billy cocked his revolver and pointed it at each of the others in the gang. "Any you bitches got a problem with a change in leadership?"

In unison all the men said, "NO!" Their hands by their ears. A stain spread in the crotch of the middle man. His knees buckled.

"Man, get up," Billy commanded. He turned to Xavvy. "Now, I need those keys to the back of this truck, or has your usefulness run out, too?"

Xavvy reached behind the tire and threw the keys to Billy, who unlocked the trunk, the muzzle of his gun *clinking* against the truck as he removed the lock. On Billy's instruction, the others loaded the body into the back of the truck.

Billy climbed up on the rear bumper, trying to see over the boxes. "What's all this?"

"I told you, we're transporting farm produce," Xavvy said, his natural impatience continuing to cause me consternation. Billy stared at him with a don't-make-me-pop-a-cap-in-your-knee gaze. "The monkeys behind; in the rear, man. What do you think, I'm not gonna hide them?"

The King lay beside a pile of boxes filled with oranges and lemons. Blood pooled on the gouged floor of the truck, along with some meaty tissue and bone fragments. The two halves of the sunglasses glinted in the late-morning light. I thought about how men failed to seek out the right people. How I had trusted Henry and he had betrayed me. The men moved boxes. Billy yelled at the shorter one to move faster, stacking the boxes out of the way so they could see the inventory. The shorter guy tried, but lacked determination.

Xavvy smacked me in the arm and mouthed, "Run."

My knee felt good, but I hadn't really tested it in a full sprint. I mouthed, "Why?"

He mouthed back, "No monkeys."

The bottom fell out of my gut. Billy held his gun at his side. I still had a gun in my back, but didn't want to fire a shot.

Billy half-watched his crew and half-watched Xavvy and me. Xavvy inched closer to the back of the truck on one side while I inched closer on the other. We were both only steps away from either door. I counted one, two, three with my fingers, and we both lurched forward and threw the doors inward simultaneously as Billy turned and raised his gun. Shots fired into the door, but we were already running around the front and down the road.

The doors banged open and Billy screamed, "Get 'em," in a tone that said he'd discovered there was nothing in the back of the truck except a tape player.

As we ran, I panted, "This was a decoy? When the hell were you going to tell me?"

"I don't trust you," he said, his breath coming in quick gasps. He looked at his phone. "The monkeys already made it. We clear, just run."

"Oh yeah, we can outrun a Nova? Do you have a big-block in your ass?"

Up ahead at another turnout waited an inconspicuous Nissan Sentra, Sire Goode at the wheel. We dove in and sunk into the floor as Sire pulled out and drove toward our pursuers. He reported that the Nova was gone and the truck abandoned.

"Can they trace that back to us?" I asked. Xavvy ignored me as he texted.

"Did she get 'em delivered?" Xavvy asked Sire.

"Smooth as Lake Placid, baby," Sire purred. "That was one of my better plans, no?"

Sire Goode slipped his fist between the front seats and Xavvy bumped. I put my fist up for a bump. Sire obliged, but Xavvy went back to his phone.

"What? I don't deserve a bump? I helped," I grumbled at Xavvy.

"Xavvy, give the guy a bump. He played the role perfectly."

"This fool almost get me killed," Xavvy said. "If I hadn't left him ignorant, who knows what else he'd have fucked. I treat him like nube and that's how he acts. Like type-casting. No acting required. He just be himself."

We drove in silence for a while, then I asked Sire, "There were no monkeys in our truck?"

"Not a one."

"The woman."

"Is she safely away?" Sire asked Xavvy.

"She safe. And you." Now he was finally addressing me directly. "You need to stall more next time. That extra time with the keys? We needed that."

"Next time? Why would I do this again?" I countered.

"Never know when we'll need a patsy," Sire said, breaking into laughter. Even Xavvy cracked a small grimace.

CHAPTER 36

The next day, I ruminated about the possibility of a call from the sheriff that I was wanted for questioning in the disappearance of some monkeys or a dead King. My phone remained silent, and I passed Thursday in attempted decompression, fingering the tender spot on my forehead, while baseball reruns from the 2015 postseason played in a loop. In the early evening, my phone dinged.

"Yes, I'll accept the charges."

"Where are you?" she asked.

"Nice to speak to you too, Patrice."

"Don't give me that bullshit. You are testifying tomorrow for the prosecution. What are you going to say?"

"Mother, what are you worried about? I'm going to try to help you as much as I can."

"You could say I was with you."

"When the police interviewed me at the time I told them I was home alone waiting for Evelyn after work, like I did every night. Evelyn worked all hours. Did you tell them you were with me?"

Patrice didn't like the Virgin Islands at all, but she'd picked up habits there, like sucking her teeth when she didn't get her way. "It might be better if you shoot yourself in the foot as far as credibility goes. You know take one for Team Montague? We're not looking too good right now. Dominic ..."

"You heard that I'm also on trial for my life, didn't you?"

"Don't be so melodramatic." Long, painful pause in which I almost hung up. I bit into the corner of my bedsheet and sucked, stifling a scream. "I'm sure you had nothing to do with a triple homicide. The good people of St. Thomas will see right through that error."

"You think perjuring myself in a California court is going to help my case if I decide to testify in my own defense?"

"How should I know?"

"My testimony will be easy tomorrow. I've done this a few times. I'll do exactly what they ask you to do: tell the truth, the whole truth, and nothing else."

CHAPTER 37

The jurors, a mix of races and ages for another case in the courtroom, milled about the hallway, whispering amongst themselves, like a church on Sunday morning before the pastor makes his way into the pulpit.

A deputy ushered me through two sets of heavy wooden doors that opened into the gallery. All eyes turned. I wore slacks, a collared shirt, and a mismatched windbreaker that made my neck itch. The vibe coming off the defense table was almost as gray and chilly as the air outside.

The jurors looked so innocent, stowed like luggage behind the wooden enclosure as if to protect them from the effect of the decisions they would make. Laminated black and white numbers identified each juror.

Was there something in my teeth? That was generally my first anxious thought in front of ogling strangers. Today, the day my remaining parent might go to jail, my thoughts went to: If she's guilty, how will that play at my trial? Could the prosecutor somehow use this against me?

Mostly, I considered how much I owed my mother today, versus how much I owed my cheating, dead spouse two years after the fact. Mother was still alive. Patrice Montague in prison wouldn't bring Evelyn back. Patrice was not a killer by nature, so throwing her in the clink wouldn't insulate society from an ongoing threat. This was a one-off; either an accident or because she hated this one person, who happened to be the love of my life.

Did I owe Evelyn? She slept with Mark Green, a man who often seemed to have things caught in his teeth. She probably didn't love me and was planning to leave. Or, she was confused. Trying to figure it out. Enamored with a colleague fighting the good fight. Other women seemed enamored with Mark Green. The guy had something. Women had daddy issues. The guy liked to play the hero. He looked the part.

I raised my right hand, everyone somber as cats. "Good morning," the prosecutor said as I dropped my hand and settled into the wooden pew. We had spoken on the phone. He had a competitive smugness, that only those working for the government possess. You had to get something when they paid so little. He knew about my impending trial and consequently, the defense attorney also knew. We argued about it, but in the end, he decided that my testimony was important and he'd leave it to the jury to decide whether the murder charge made me unreliable.

Patrice's prosecutor, known only as Lohman, had said, "Murder's not a crime that inherently suggests you're a disingenuous person. But you should have told me about it. How are you ... never mind, I don't want to know. We won't mention it, after all, you were arrested, not convicted. If they use it to attack your credibility, we'll deal."

Through the hazy window of my surreal calm, I noticed people in the gallery. Some of Evelyn's family, who had failed to stay in touch, studied me, judging what they expected me to say about her life and death. Henry cross-legged in the back. Mark Green entered and settled next to him.

"Mr. Montague? Could you answer, Mr. Montague?"

My eyes stung, like someone had spent an hour blowing cigarette smoke in them. I blinked rapidly. "Repeat the question, please."

The prosecutor reached for his notes. He had already asked the prologue questions: name, age, astrological sign, relationship to the victim and suspect, etc. We had also reviewed questions which mostly related to my notes from my investigation back when Evelyn died and all these law enforcement assholes had insisted it was an accident. Thanks to Henry, they'd been proven wrong. It occurred to me that the last sexual encounter of Evelyn's life had been with Mark Green. They'd pinned her death on Patrice. Every member of my family could wind up doing time, simultaneously, in some way related to my having been involved with Evelyn.

"Yes, I believed at that point in time, Evelyn had been killed purposefully, based on my findings."

"Why did you cease?"

"That man," I pointed my chin at the sheriff, a bald man with a hawkish demeanor and a stare that natural-born law enforcement types must learn before the age of ten. The leaves on houseplants shriveled when Sheriff Jones put his attention on them. "He told me to cease interfering. He wanted the case closed, wanted the noise to stop." My head bobbed subtly. "Sheriffs like to brag about their closure rates come election time. I suspect that was his motive."

"Mr. Montague, we don't need the editorializing," the judge said before an objection arose.

"He asked, I answered. His question …"

"Let's move on," the judge said as he glanced up at the clock above the jurors' heads.

In my divorce investigator days, I'd learned to keep my hands in my lap when being questioned. Hands distracted. Henry had worked on this with me. My hands attempted to float from beneath the confines of the witness box. Once they escaped, I would get irate or nervous. If I could keep them in check, I could keep my emotions in check. Henry being here was hard. Helping convict my mother was hard.

"Do you believe your wife was murdered?"

"I don't know." My little finger twitched. "The Sheriff and his posse thought it was an accident. Hit and run. They thought a drunk driver or some stupid teenager. Now, because some other guy looked into it, they reopened and dropped on Patrice."

The prosecutor eyed me, trying to look like Sheriff Jones, but his background of Ivy League schools and pool parties, prevented his stare from even making house plants shiver. "So, you don't think Patrice Montague, your mother, committed second-degree murder?"

The defense attorney shot to her feet. "Objection. Asks for a legal conclusion. Is this witness a lawyer?"

"I'll rephrase," the Prosecutor said without waiting for the judge. "Do you think your mother killed your wife?"

"No," I said, trying my damnedest to sound convincing.

Lohman pursed his lips and threw me an incredulous look. "Even though Evelyn was having an affair and by your own admission they never liked each other very much."

I waited. Saying nothing often unnerved attorneys. Their outsized egos wanted validation. They wanted to brawl verbally. Funny thing was, they often didn't ask a question, and in court, if they didn't ask a question, best to remain silent.

"Mr. Montague?"

"Yes?"

"Answer the question," the judge intoned.

"What question, Your Honor?" I asked.

The court reporter read back the last statement made by the

Prosecutor. The judge spread his hands and shrugged. "Yup, that's not a question, Mr. Lohman."

The prosecutor watched me a while, then waved his hand as if warding off a pesky fly. "No more questions for this witness."

My mother's defense attorney started speaking before she'd risen out of her seat. "Mr. Montague, you say in your notes that Evelyn had been struck on the right side of her body from an SUV. How did you come to that conclusion?"

"Coroner's report and the insurance company both concluded that. I also looked at the bike myself. The impact point was high and indicated a rounded object moving very fast, probably the bumper of a car."

"But what was unusual about this situation that made you think it was more than an accident?"

"At that point on the road you'd really have to go out of your way to cut across the lane and hit someone in the designated bike lane. Anyone that out of control would have crashed into the building behind Evelyn's ..." I swallowed, my throat constricting as I pictured my dead wife's corpse. The Defense Attorney waited. Everyone waited. I looked at Henry who nodded at me. In that moment, I knew we'd be friends again, even with Green seated next to him, Henry was on my side. "Uh, Evelyn's body."

"So, that's why you believed it was purposeful. Still, strange accidents happen. And Evelyn was on the wrong side of the road, correct?"

"Yes, but in my experience it's a percentage game, and the percentages here said someone saw her and took the opportunity. She was probably trying to ride up, then cross over to the right side and begin her trip home in earnest. The spot was close to her place of business."

"Do you believe it was your mother?"

"No."

"Why not?"

"I know her. She came to my house that night. She seemed normal."

Denial. As powerful as love, and much more common.

I authenticated some more documents that showed it was certainly possible, although not certain, that my mother committed the crime. She was on trial for murder-two because no one thought she "laid in wait". The prosecution's theory was that Patrice saw an opportunity and took it. I said as little as I could about why I'd ceased the investigation.

I no longer wanted to drive Patrice's stinking SUV.

The defense attorney ended her questioning. The prosecutor and his assistant debated after the judge asked if they wanted any redirect. The judge pressed him. Lohman finally rose.

"What time did your mother come to your home on the night in question?"

I stared at Patrice. She stared back. I couldn't do it. For many reasons, but mostly, I just couldn't do it. I swatted a fly that landed on the wood near my hand. I missed.

"Do you need me to refresh your recollection as to the answer you gave the police?" asked Lohman.

"No," I said with more venom than intended. I held up both hands, one splayed and the other with four fingers. "Twenty-one hundred hours."

"Nine o'clock. Was this typical for your mother to come by unannounced at that hour?"

"No."

"Why was she there?"

My hands tapped the edge of the witness box, making a soft wooden sound. "She said she'd found out that Evelyn was sleeping with a co-worker."

Murmurs. Evelyn's family did not look pleased. The prosecutor waited for the noise to die, looking pleased with himself. Lohman then asked, "How did she seem about this?"

"Self-righteous," I answered, drumming on the wood.

"No further questions."

As I hustled toward the exit, Henry caught my arm, looked me in the eye, the way close focus can alight on one eye at a time, my eyes both on his left, the brown color speckled and bright with a mixture of disgust and respect.

"The whole truth," he muttered.

"Shut up, Henry." He released me, the tense firmness of his grip dropping away and leaving me nowhere to go, floating in space, heavy with pollution.

***

I called Sire Goode from inside Patrice's SUV. "You know a junk yard? I need a place, with no asking, no paperwork."

"I'll call a guy. He'll expect you. High desert. Address coming. Ask for Dewey. One more thing."

"What?"

"Dana sent me a message. She said not to tell you. She's coming out here. She's worried about you."

"You sure it's not the bail money?"

"Just don't tell her I told you. I got a reputation to uphold."

***

Dust swirled, my curls bounding in the brown sleet. Patrice's SUV had been crushed into a compact square of metal, piled amongst other metal that might become a weapon. I hoped that I couldn't be recalled to testify further in my mother's case. I had to leave for St. Thomas; get back to the wreckage of my life.

Mark Green fit the profile. I had one more day to get anything I could. Even if I got something, there were rules, chain of custody. I wasn't a police officer or a detective. I had no authority, especially here in Los Angeles. A tumbleweed rolled by outside the diner. I'd convinced a tow driver to drop me at for some breakfast and coffee.

The cold, relentlessness of the valley left my hands chapped, a crack in the fold of my index finger bled. I leaned my elbow on the top of the booth table, gazed at Ventura Boulevard through the painted letters and numbers on the large glass frontage. My hand pressed against the roof of my mouth--the small, familiar taste of my own blood, long and salty. Cars careened by. My half-eaten plate of eggs lost steam while I continued to declare, silently, that my mother hadn't killed my cheating wife--that she hadn't done it as some kind of chivalrous gesture to defend her son's honor. Mark Green wasn't the only one who demanded loyalty.

Patrice's visit on March twenty-second of 2014 served two purposes: to make Evelyn's death less devastating, and to give my mother some pretense of an alibi. The more I reviewed it, the more I believed she had had the time to do what she did before arriving at my house. And though it would take a trial, and Henry, to force the issue, I had to admit it to myself: I hadn't stopped investigating because of the sheriff's threats. I'd stopped because I didn't want the truth.

Maybe mothers hate wives no matter what. Patrice certainly never trusted or liked Evelyn. My blinders kept me from seeing the obvious at the beginning and when it got closer to being inevitable, I fled the scene. I didn't kill those girls, but maybe I deserved whatever that brought. Henry and Mark were on the side of right by any means necessary. I could have refused. I could have stayed in St. Thomas.

No amount of solutions could rinse the lingering aftertaste. That jury of her peers should come back right. I needed them to come back right. Majorities were often wrong, but unanimous verdicts . . .

CHAPTER 38

I popped a six-dollar pill and checked my watch again. Where was my ride-share? A Mustang sans the big "U" pulled over.

"What the fuck are you doing here?" I asked. A clean, black Lexus, pulled up behind him.

"Thought I'd give you a ride to the airport. Bury the hatchet?"

"I like my hatchet," I said, fighting every instinct I had to forgive him. "Besides, I already paid for the driver. Once they arrive, you can't cancel. I'll see you around," I slapped the edge of the open window, and strolled toward the Lexus.

Behind me I heard Henry open the driver's door. "Come on, don't be like that. It's only a ride to the airport. You may never see me again. Out of sight, out of mind. You know I don't …"

I whirled on him. "Save it, man. I gotta focus now. L.A. belongs to you and my derelict mother." I turned away and opened the Lexus' door. Tones of soft saxophone music drifted out.

The driver said in a syrupy tone, "Boise?"

Henry leaned inside the Uber with his I'm-gonna-slam-you-to-the-ground-and-slice-off-your-lips face. "He doesn't need a ride." He yanked the door out of my hand and slammed it. The Lexus bolted away. Henry yanked the handle of my bag away and hefted it into his trunk.

"I've got something to tell you and it's an in-person kind of discussion. Since you're leaving, it has to be now."

Once we were zipping along Admiralty, he tried to lighten the mood. "Nice message."

"Don't gloat, it's unbecoming a man of your intellect," I shot back.

"Being right isn't always satisfying." Out of the corner of my eye I could see the sunlight from the southern sky painting Henry's ear in a desert light. A different light from that of the Caribbean. An unblemished brilliance. Perhaps it was the light, hitting his ear through his spotless windshield that made me want to come clean.

"This car, it suits you," I said.

"You mean sexy and red?"

"A gas-guzzling loud-mouth who doesn't understand the meaning of friendship."

"Yup. Wash it twice a week in my yard. Got a drought warning once."

Right then, a seagull grazed the windshield, careening into the wetlands like a flung snowball, wing over wing. A small droplet of blood spread, opaque on the tempered glass. Below the blood, a white feather buffeted before lifting off.

"Damn it," Henry growled. "Birds. That's the second one since I bought this car. Never happened before."

"Maybe it's the color. You gonna tell me about you and Green?"

"Not much to tell. He called and hired me to find Evelyn's killer. He's pays mighty well."

I twisted the pocket floss around my fingers, before pulling it out and threading my teeth. I flicked some food particles onto the immaculate dashboard where they stuck like tiny darts. A woman at the light next to us squinted at me and I pointedly threaded the floss between my front teeth while glaring at her.

"So, what then? You knew Green and I had history."

"Yeah, I knew. I knew, but again, I thought it was for the best all around. You left off and he was willing. What harm? I couldn't figure why you didn't want to finish it. Something was off, but …"

I let go of the floss and slapped the dashboard. The floss hung from between two of my teeth, a pair of white strings making my words slur. "But you knew! You knew I wouldn't like it, or you would have told me."

"No, that's not it. I thought it might upset you, that's all."

"Bullshit!"

"It's buggin' me." He pulled to the shoulder where the freeway widened, waited for a car to pass, then got out, pulled a rag out of his trunk, and leaned over, blocking the sunlight. He spit on the windshield and scrubbed the blood, which had dried. First the middle of the stain came out, then the red ring. After more spit and shine, all traces vanished. He glanced at me, questioningly and I flashed the "okay" sign.

My phone vibrated. "Hey, Leber, what's …"

"Are you alone?" Leber asked, his voice like a bass drum.

Henry slid back into the driver's seat and I got out, shutting the door. The noise from passing cars made it challenging to hear.

"Yeah, I'm alone."

"What're you standing in traffic?"

"I'm on my way to the airport. I pulled over and got out of the car."

Henry scrutinized me through the passenger glass. I held up a finger. I turned away, facing the wooded edge of the roadway.

"Don't get on the plane," Leber said soberly.

"What? Why not? You want me to have a warrant out for my arrest?"

"The answer is in L.A. Stay there and stay on Mark Green. He's involved."

"Where are you getting this? Wait, what happened with Ronica Mathews' boyfriend?"

"I spoke to him. Simon Gaines claims that he followed you and the girls after the concert. He watched from the bushes, fully intent on killing you, if you made a move on Ronica."

"What makes him trustworthy?"

"I believe him."

"You thought I was crazy to come here looking at Green."

Leber sighed. "That's a misstatement of my evaluation. I said that you should consider other avenues."

"Yeah, well, I didn't have time for a protracted investigation."

"I get that. I'm telling you to stay on it out there. One thing though, he says he saw two white guys. One looked like he could handle himself and another was more of a pretty boy, the type that worked his whole life in an office, like an accountant."

From behind me, Henry said, "Boise, we gotta go. You're gonna miss your flight."

I told Leber to hold on, then said to Henry, "I'm not going to the airport anymore. Give me a minute."

Leber chimed in, "Who was that?"

"A detective I know. He lives here. He was driving me."

"Can you trust him?"

I hesitated, then said, "I don't know. Let's get back to this. Did you guys do a sketch with this wit?"

"No. Jamaica didn't have a sketch artist available. White, five-eleven, slicked back brown hair, beady eyes, high cheekbones. Gaines said the guy worked out, but wasn't 'real'. Like his skinny self knows anything about 'real'."

In front of me, a eucalyptus tree's slender leaves flipped, like streamers at a festival. The breeze sent a winter chill through me. There was someone who fit that description.

Once Henry pulled out again I waited, promising myself that if he didn't answer my earlier question, I'd read about it in the papers.

"Where do you want to go?" Henry asked. "Back to your mom's?"

"How about Mark Green's house?" I replied. So much for waiting on his answer.

Henry's lip twitched. "I'm getting on. You know I'm now a member of AARP? They asked me to join five years ago. Every year I get an invitation." He nodded, his eyes flicking to the side view mirror before changing lanes, continuing east. "I turn fifty-five in eight days. Fifty-five. You know what I do every year on my birthday since I was fifteen?"

"No," I replied as we headed east to Baldwin Hills.

"It's weird. Very weird. Only my mother knows I do this. You remember Kennedy's inauguration speech? The one that made us all believe?"

"I've never heard that speech. Before my time."

"Listen to it some time." He nodded again, like he was answering some unheard question. "Good things. It's a speech of cooperation. It makes me want to be better."

"Hmmm," I muttered. "That may be what Kennedy wanted or wished for, but I'm not sure that's what human beings are capable of."

"Oh, yeah?" Henry made a hard right on Slauson.

"I think it's more accurate, what Dostoevsky says in *Crime and Punishment*."

"Big book," Henry said.

"I took the time to memorize a line that I thought summed up what he had to say about the human condition. Wanna hear it?"

Henry watched the road.

"Sorry if I butcher it, but it goes something like, 'Everyone's'… no … 'Everyone must look out for himself and the best time is had by those who're best able to deceive themselves.'"

"Mighty cynical, Boise. Mighty."

"The copy from jail was falling apart. The last four pages were missing, so I don't know how it ends. Imagine trudging through all that story and coming out with no ending?"

"I helped Green despite your shared history. What do you want me to say?"

"You didn't tell me," I said sulkily.

Henry said something under his breath. I asked him to repeat. "Easier to ask for forgiveness."

"Ha!" I threw my head back. We'd arrived on Mark Green's street.

"I did the right thing. Patrice did it, you just refused to see it. I'm not blaming you for that, but you were wrong. Mighty wrong."

"Is that what you wanted to tell me? I needed to cancel my Uber for that? By the way, you're paying for that ride."

I showed him the amount. He handed me cash. I got out and headed up the brick steps, past the black lions and young palms in large planter boxes.

"Boise! Boise! Stop." He caught my arm half-way up the steps. "I just heard on the radio. Patrice got convicted of manslaughter and sentenced to twelve years."

He glanced up at the door at the top of the stairs, then whispered, "It should have been life without parole."

I firmed my lower lip. "Let's move on. Fuck her."

He played a video for me on his cell phone, a video that caused me to grab the railing. It felt like someone had taken a chainsaw to my knee. "Where'd you get that?"

"Traffic camera. Every night that car was there. It was useless as evidence since you can't read the license plate or tell who's inside."

"What about the night of Evelyn's … you know," I choked.

"It happened out of frame, but the SUV pulls away from the curb less than a minute before it happened."

After an eternity, my head cleared and I continued up the steps. "That car's gone. I junked it."

"I hope you know what the hell you're doing." The buttons of his white shirt struggled against his gut. Along with his convictions, his cheeks were sagging more than I remembered.

"You working out at all?" I asked while waiting at the door. He had trotted back down to his car and leaned against the bumper, arms crossed.

"Nope," he yelled up, watching me with more than a little distaste. "Too busy putting bad guys …" He paused for emphasis. "… and gals, behind bars."

A female voice behind me said, "Mr. Montague? What are you doing here?"

Grace Walker sat in the doorway wearing a red satin robe over a white nightgown.

"I might ask you the same thing. I came here to see Mark."

"Oh. Uh, he stepped out to get some bagels and coffee." She giggled. "Breakfast in bed. I like Starbucks better than his crappy Folgers crystals."

A silence descended like something between former lovers who see each other after years and know that things never fully resolved.

Finally, she said, "I'd invite you in, but it's not my place …"

"You know, I was worried about you? When I didn't see or hear from you, I thought …"

"You thought what? That poor little Grace needed big Boise to take care of her? To protect her from the big bad head of a non-profit that saves wildlife and land? Yeah, I'm in a very dangerous profession." She grinned a nasty grin. "On second thought, I've got no interest in letting you in. You sit in the waiting room if you like. I don't need you judging me."

"Tell that to Felicia Nichols," I said.

She rolled back and slammed the door. Down at street level once more, I leaned on the Mustang next to Henry.

"You still haven't learned much about getting to a witness."

"Stop trying to teach me for a change, okay. If I have a question, I'll ask." So far this wasn't going like I planned. "I goin' teach you somet'ing for a change," I said in my island accent.

Henry wasn't part of my life in an everyday way. He existed mostly in my thoughts, and my emotions, borne of his training. Some part of me had thought I might return to L.A. someday when my heart mended, but two things were obvious now: I wasn't ever going to call L.A. home again, and my heart would never mend. Despite all the evidence that Evelyn was done with me, I'd never be done with her.

"I am certain Mark Green killed those women and framed me."

Henry heard me clearly, but said that stupid, overused word anyway. "What?"

"How nice. You know it's true."

Miguela's name popped up on my phone. I had avoided her calls all week, figuring I had nothing to tell her, and knowing that ignorance would be her best defense come judgment day.

"Gonna answer it?"

I clicked the green button. "Hi, Miguela."

"It's your wife and your attorney who you've ignored all week. I do not appreciate that. I just spoke to Detective Leber. He says you missed your flight."

"That's true."

"You will be held in contempt of court. A warrant will be issued for your arrest. Someone will come for you and extradite you to St. Thomas to stand trial. You will be fined and perhaps charged with further crimes. You will lose the bond. Do you understand these consequences—what they are, what they entail?"

"Miguela ..."

"The answer does not involve my name." She didn't sound angry.

"Uh, yeah, I understand," I said. "But, can I explain?"

"No need. I'm sure you believe you have some good reason, or you are incompetent. Either way, the court won't care, thus I don't care." This woman was blunter than a baseball bat. "I'm telling you, as a member of the bar and a servant of the court, you need to be here tomorrow for your trial at ten a.m. If you are not, I will inform the court that I informed you of your duty and the consequences. I dislike losing. Do not make me lose."

"That's what I'm working on," I replied.

"Do it faster." Dead air.

Mark Green's black Mercedes appeared at the four-way stop a block north of the house, right beneath the murky view of L.A.'s ever-expanding skyline. The light from a single giant, electronic billboard on the convention center flashed reds and oranges above the tops of trees.

"For the record, I have no evidence, nor did I suspect that Mark Green was involved in anything down in St. Thomas. I still don't believe you. You sure you're not clouded ..."

"Look," I said in a harsh whisper. "I just got confirmation from Detective Leber that a witness saw Green and another white guy at the scene of the murders."

"What?"

"Keep it down," I whispered.

"You sure? Green was at a conference in Las Vegas that weekend. Anders confirmed it."

Scott Anders. He fit the description given by Simon Gaines. "Anders lied," I said.

Green was out of his car holding a white paper bag that said, "Coffee MV" and a cardboard cup holder with three coffees. His face resembled an old leather shoe. He glanced from Henry to me and back to Henry. He needed to shave.

"Henry. Boise. What's this about? Why are you in front of my house? Don't you have to get back to St. Thomas? And you, don't you ever go to the police station? Aren't you a volunteer? Don't they need you over there?"

Henry's face darkened. He rested his hand lightly on the roof of his red Mustang, running a finger over the bright paint job, then inspecting his fingertip for dirt. "My Mustang looks shiny and new, doesn't it?"

I wasn't sure who the question was directed at, but the silence intimidated me, so I answered. "Car looks like a million bucks."

"Not talking to you, Boise," Henry said, his eyes still fixed on his fingertip. "Look, Mark, there's this thin layer of dirt that builds up mighty quick. I've had the car only a few weeks, yet there it is. Air pollution. No garage. Don't have that luxury." He casually indicated the three-car garage at the base of Mark Green's impressive Mediterranean home. "Hell, I suspect your shingles cost more than my whole condo's worth."

"I can explain," Green said. "You guys want to come inside?"

"Why do you have three cups of coffee?" I asked. "From Coffee MV. Isn't that where Felicia worked? Did they get a new assistant manager yet?"

Green had trouble masking his dislike. "Your mother got convicted today. I got the text I've been waiting two years for."

This man had taken Evelyn from me and now he'd taken my mother. He'd already beaten the crap out of me once when I'd originally confronted him about Evelyn. I couldn't do much about him physically.

"It wasn't enough to get my mother. You had to get greedy. You had to put me away, too."

"You did that to yourself, Montague."

"Don't you feel anything for Felicia? For those other girls? All that to get to me?"

Again, he looked at Henry, then back at me. "I like two cups. It gets me revved. Now, if you'll excuse me, Grace and I are going to eat some bagels and stare into each other's eyes." He started up the stairs.

"Did you love my wife?"

"You have a mistaken assumption about my relationship with Evelyn. I valued her as an attorney. I valued what she could do for BWPP--for the cause. I valued her loyalty. If that's love, then yes, I loved her. If it's about romance and flowers, then no. Evelyn was a realist. We respected each other and from that, other things blossomed."

At the top of the stairs, Green set the coffee container and bag on the railing and turned toward the street where Henry and I remained. "You know, it doesn't matter much anymore. All of it happened mostly the way I wanted. I just didn't count on that. You know how you waited so long for something, but never ultimately considered what it would be like if you got it because you never ultimately thought you'd get it? That's the predicament I find myself in at present. I got everything I wanted for this thing, whatever it's called, this life, this existence. It goes and goes, swelling and fleeing. Now I find myself fleeing and swelling. Take this coffee."

Green delidded a cup and poured scalding coffee over his left hand. "Ahhhhhhh!!!"

I remained frozen to the spot, not sure if I should feel sorry for the son of a bitch. Henry darted past me, bounding the stairs two at a time. He unlocked the door with the keys that Green had left in the lock. From my rooted position on the street I heard voices behind the labored breathing of Mark Green's pain.

Henry yelled down to me. "Get your ass up here. Now!"

The "now" broke my trance. Inside the threshold of the doorway, Scott Anders had a gun pointed at the back of Grace Walker's head.

Chapter 39

My flight from LAX would be boarding right about now. It appeared that I'd be facing numerous additional charges for failing to appear at trial in less than twenty-four hours. Even if I showed up, I'd done little to prepare.

"Hi there, Henry Bateup. Please, take all weapons off your body. Better yet, strip to your skivvies."

"Skivvies?" Henry asked.

Grace keened, like a child on a swing, as Anders pressed the gun hard into her skull. He hissed at Henry, "I'm not in the mood for clever banter."

"All right." Henry disrobed to his tighty-whities. Henry, like me, appeared not to care much about being naked. He kicked his pants away, his belt clattering into the corner.

"Remove them too, but slowly." Again Grace made a sound as Anders squeezed her throat with his free hand and pushed the gun into the base of her skull. Henry reached down to unclip the ankle holster on his right leg, then the knife on his left.

"Take it easy, take it easy," I said. "He's doing what you asked."

Henry wanted to make a move. It was too risky for Grace. He tossed the gun and knife on top of his crumpled pants. Anders eyed me like I'd molested a child. "All you had to do was accept your fate. It's what you deserved. Look at him. I said look at him!" Grace flinched again. I looked at Mark Green, slumped on one of his bar stools nursing his burned hand.

"I deserve to go to jail for killing three women?" I asked.

"You deserve the death-penalty for aiding and abetting the murderer of your wife. Look at him! You did that. He used to be a man of strength, of pride. You left a shell."

Green laughed like a manic clown, then squeezed his injured hand into a fist and pounded it on the kitchen counter, letting out little yelps, his red eyes fixated on the wall as if watching a film projection of something only he could see. Red droplets burst from his pink, calloused knuckles.

Anders was right about me. I'd shunned L.A. and Evelyn's case for one reason: to avoid the truth that a jury would arrive at without any investigative assistance from me. Patrice Montague ran over Evelyn Montague because, in Patrice's twisted mind, Evelyn deserved it for cheating on her son, or something more sinister.

Grace let out an agonizing, "Whyyyyyyyyy?"

Her head shook and Anders smacked the back of her head. "Shut up, bitch! Mark, pull yourself together! We don't have time for this."

Green did not appear to understand. He continued to stare wide-eyed at the blank wall. The shininess of the white plaster reflected in his eyes. Mark Green keeled over, like a wind-up doll running down.

Breath pelted from my nostrils in quick bursts. I jammed my

hand into my pocket, twisting at the ever-present length of floss buried in the bottom, beneath my keychain pepper spray. Anders' eyes alighted on my pocketed hand. "What've you got in there, Boise? I know you can't have a gun. Too cowardly. Weak. What was it Mark said you carried? Pepper spray? Out with it, matey."

"In the corner," Anders commanded. It landed with a soft *thump* on top of Henry's pile. "You got anything else?"

"No."

"Good," Anders nodded. "I don't want to make a mess all over this nice hardwood. Blood can be a bear to get out of wood. What I don't understand about all this is you, Bateup. You've got a life. Mark here paid you well to check into his dead girlfriend, and you guys came up aces. Justice. Everything a lawman wants from a case. Extra cash. Caught the bad-girl. What's your angle? Why are you listening to someone like this loser?" He nodded in my direction, a devious twinkle in his eyes. "What's he to you?"

Henry's hands were planted on his hips. A little bit of a belly, but mostly muscle taking on the middle-age sag. The hair on his chest had turned white, but somehow, his tanned skin made it look good. Henry's lip curled into a sarcastic grimace that said: *You are out of your league. You better kill me now, otherwise, one way or another, I'm going to plant your head on a spike.*

Anders brandished the gun, holding it too high. "Don't look at me like that. You think you know something. You think you have this figured out?"

Grace let out a soft whimper, then said, "I really need to pee."

"Sorry, hon, you're not going anywhere. Pee in your chair. I don't mind the smell. What about you guys?"

"Hey, genius," Henry said. "What's your plan?"

"Plan?" Anders repeated.

"Yeah. Exit strategy. We're in a residential neighborhood with limited egress. There are three exits I noticed. Straight down the hill. Straight up the hill. Down a block and turn right."

"I need to talk to someone." The voice coming from Mark Green sounded like he'd turned into another person.

"Hey! Mark! Hold it together. I'm taking care of it," Anders replied. "Keep your lid on."

Henry snickered, moving his right arm across his chest and pulling the elbow with the crook of his other arm. After a few seconds he switched the arms and stretched in the other direction, as if preparing to play a tennis match with a buddy on Saturday morning.

"You got a big problem, Anders. I've seen this before. Guy starts talking in a different voice. Like he's been possessed. What is that, a Latino accent? How does Mark Green, a full-blooded American boy suddenly start talking like he's from Mexico City? You know how? He needs to be someone else, just for a little while. Something isn't right with the man. I'd chalked it up to his concern about the trial. He blurts out odd shit before we go into court. He stares at the statute of justice and mouths things at her. Mighty strange.

Then, Boise comes here insisting that something's happening, that Mark has something to do with those girls being murdered. I dismissed it because Mark had been in Vegas, except that other than you, I couldn't find anyone who'd seen Mark that weekend. Yes, he'd been at the conference earlier in the week, but none of his colleagues could confirm seeing him on the day before, the day of, or the day after the murders, except you. You confirmed it." He grimaced as he stuck his hand out in front and pulled back on his palm, now stretching his forearm. "This wrist always feels tight since I got that pin. I believed you because you had no skin in the game. Why would you care about Felicia? Why would you care about Boise? Those people had no direct impact on your life. You came onto the BWPP crew after Evelyn died. No benefit. Mighty strange. Why are you doing this?"

Mark Green snapped out of his reverie, his voice returning to the normal California-dude inflections. "What's eating you,

Henry? You're just a beat policeman in plain clothes. Right? You've always been just that." Then Green twittered, "Tee-hee-hee."

Anders removed the muzzle of the gun from the back of Grace Walker's head and leveled it at Mark Green. "You keep your trap buttoned-up or I'll close it for you. You understand? Shut up! That's all you had to do this whole time, muscle-brain."

Green had crawled up onto the kitchen bar and laid down with his legs bent and his torso threatening to curl into the fetal position. He resumed staring at the wall. His Adam's apple bobbed.

"That's better," Anders said. "Now, where were we? Ah yes, you were saying that Mark's alibi didn't hold up so well under your brilliant scrutiny?"

"Why are you involved?" I asked. "Green here put you up to it? Did he suck you in the way he sucked Felicia in? He's exceptional at that."

The smell of urine filled the room. Drops dribbled from the bottom of Grace's wheelchair. "Sorry," she whined. The brave, fun-loving girl I'd had dinner with had become the pathetic one who had no love and no real life. She looked like she wished Anders would end her misery.

Anders scoffed. "I said to do it, but I didn't think you would. What's wrong with your bladder?"

Grace cried harder. "Please, please, I have nothing …"

"You see the mess you've made? I had this all worked out, but you jerk-offs had to interfere." Anders leaned into one hip, shifting his aim from Green to Henry. His hand remained firmly planted on Grace's right shoulder, as if he believed she could push her way up and attack him. "Again, I understand why you want answers." He swung the gun to me. "She's your wife and your mother and it's your life that we fucked with. I get that. You on the other hand …" he pointed the weapon at Henry. "What the hell are you doing? You guys fucking each other?"

Henry's look of sarcasm and skepticism became more pronounced. "I could ask you the same thing. What's Mark Green to you?"

"Porfiry would have seen it sooner," Mark Green said without pulling his eyes away from the fascinating blank wall. I stared at him, wondering why he mentioned the storied inspector from *Crime & Punishment*. "That's what's bothering you, isn't it? That you worked for me, watched Scott and I argue countless times, and you assumed it was about the case, but it was about confessions. About me not getting what I wanted. You are no Porfiry. He figured it out." He'd been speaking to Henry, whose face turned red, fists clenched at his sides like a fighter waiting for the bell.

"What did you want?" I asked.

"Liberty. You and your filthy mother stole that. You didn't even have the decency to hold her to account. You never loved Evelyn. Not like I did."

"Not like you did. We agree on that," I replied. "I think you loved her because she was a good lawyer. You care about your non-profit. That's how you seduce girls." I motioned at Grace. "That's why she's here, right?"

Green's eyes flashed before returning to their blankness and the white wall. "Loyalty deserves reward."

Grace whined. Anders open-palmed her upside the back of the head. "Shut up!"

Leber had mentioned the victims, Ronica and Jill, being "arranged", when he'd come to see me a few days before Christmas. That word stuck like a dart. The more I thought about it, the more it seemed that the murders were separate events happening on the same night on the same beach.

As if reading my thoughts, Mark Green piped up. "Scott, why'd they have to die? Those other Jamaicans? Why? I didn't want 'em dead."

Anders spun like a rabid dog. "Shut up! What's the matter

with you? Jesus, man, you have one job, keep your ass shut! I'm losing my patience, you hear? If you don't shut up, there's going to be another dead chick on your conscience. How many can you handle? Just give me a reason."

Grace's terrified eyes locked with Green's vacant stare and somehow she brought him back. "Help me," she mouthed. Meanwhile, Henry's eyes darted back and forth from Anders' face to the pile of weapons and clothing.

"Can I sit down?" I asked.

"You two are making me nervous. Don't make me do something stupid." Anders' hand tightened on the trigger and his lips drew into a tightrope. "Stop eyeing your weapons, lawman. Move that way." He motioned Henry to move closer to me, away from the pile. "That's a fine idea. The both of you sit down over there next to Mr. Green. Sit on the stools."

We moved over to the kitchen area and sat in front of Green, who remained prone across the kitchen bar, gazing at the wall. Green whispered something to me that I couldn't make out. He repeated it, like a chant. The second time, I caught his meaning. "I killed Felicia. She betrayed me. She betrayed BWPP. She was not a believer."

I tried to hide my shock at the whispered admission, but Anders' nervous eyes read something in my countenance. His eyes swung upwards to Green whose mouth continued to repeat, "She was not a believer. She was not a believer. She was not a believer."

Anders trained his gun on Green. "That's it, Mark. That's it! You breathe funny, and I'm gonna put a bullet in you. You understand? Shut up!" He fired a shot that plunked into the wall above the dishwasher, spraying drywall across the counter.

Out of the corner of my eye, movement from the balcony. It caught Anders' attention, too.

A woman in a red cap had climbed onto the balcony.

"What the fuck?" Anders screamed, swinging his shooting arm toward the intruder and firing a shot into the sliding glass door.

I yelled, "Dana, get down!" and dove out of my seat, tackling Anders mid-shot. The glass door shattered with a crash as I landed on Anders' feet, feeling his ankle crumple. My shoulder thudded to the floor, a shooting pain rocketing through the tender nerve where I'd been shot. I bit my lip and tasted blood.

Anders howled and Henry said, calm as a rock, "I got him, Boise."

I rolled off my shoulder with a groan. Henry had the gun on Anders, who writhed on the ground moaning.

"You okay?" Henry asked.

"Is Dana all right?" I answered between swears.

"I don't know, go check on her. She's not moving. I got these assholes."

I stepped through the broken door and shook Dana's shoulder. She turned her head toward me and whispered, "Can I move?"

I chuckled, letting myself fall against the wall. "Watch the broken glass."

Without moving she reached a hand up. "Well, then, don't just stand there giving me advice, lend a hand."

Henry hollered, his voice tight. "What are you two doing out there? I need one of you to cuff these guys."

"Oh yeah, sorry about that." I got zip-ties from Henry's stuff and rolled Anders over with Dana's help.

"I need medical attention," Anders whined. "I'm gonna sue you for trespassing and breaking my ankle. Thing's swollen like a baseball. I was ultimately defending Mark's house from invaders. You guys have no P.C. Fourth Amendment. A policeman can't just barge into a private residence."

Henry shook his head. "No wonder you guys kept losing those cases. You're a growing breed--attorneys who don't know the law. Boise, share with him why we could enter, even if we were police."

As he spoke, I slipped zip-ties over Mark Green's hands and feet. The man could've fought back, could have used his martial arts skills. He didn't.

Once finished with Green, I leaned over, my face in Anders' grill. He smelled of some expensive cologne. "Extenuating circumstances, little man." I touched my finger to my lip. "Also, I seem to recall we were invited by the owner."

"Snap!" Dana said, as she picked a shard of glass out of her hair and dropped it on the ground. "What's his deal?" she asked.

"What's your deal, Mark? You gonna stare at the wall all day?" I asked. "I don't think he can live with what he did."

Henry pulled on his pants and relieved Dana of the pistol. He disappeared into the back hallway, then tiptoed downstairs, sweeping the house.

Green's eyes came to life. "I can live with it, but I can't live with him. Another disloyal dirt-bag horning in on my plans. They're everywhere. No one gets it. No one understands the struggle. No one since Evelyn."

That's when I remembered Grace. I spun around and found her slumped over, her pulse erratic.

"We need ..."

"I already called it in. Ambulance coming," Dana said.

Grace's skin appeared almost translucent as I transferred her from the wheelchair to the couch, covering her with a blanket. Reassuring words had no effect. She lay, motionless except for a dismal light in her eyes.

I turned to Henry and Dana. "How do we get them out of here?" Dana was busy dictating notes into her phone. I interrupted her flow. "Let me get this straight, you're here because Henry called you?"

"Kind of. I called him and he got me worried that you wouldn't come back for your trial date. He said you were caught up obsessing about this guy." She indicated Green. "Annie also got concerned. Despite her nonchalant demeanor, she is a Von Kurk. They're not fond of parting with money, especially six-figures. Well, not unless she gets a handbag and a nice pair of loafers out of it. To appease my partner, I jetted to L.A. Secret motive: when Boise Montague's involved, I know there'll be some fucked-up story that'll make the front page and get picked up by the Associated Press, which means more exposure and a bigger payday. It drove Walter crazy to pay for my trip, but he knew that you'd create a fucked up situation that bleeds. You're three for three, Jabuti."

Henry watched Green, who continued to stare wide-eyed at the wall and chatter to himself about loyalty and loss. Henry shook his head, then addressed Dana and me. "The place is clear. Dana, mighty impeccable timing. Like truly second to none. I see why Boise-Boy keeps you around."

"Hey, Henry, are you gonna put on your shirt anytime soon? It's starting to get weird." Dana turned to me. "Did you learn the naked thing from him?"

I indicated Green and Anders. "This is great. You can contact your dad again and convince him that we need to get what's-his-name to transport these two yahoos back to St. Thomas."

Henry stopped dressing to watch me with a look of stupefaction. Dana knitted her forehead, the still-recording phone held at her side. Simultaneously, they said, "What?"

"We need these guys in St. Thomas for my trial. I'm missing the first day."

"It's delayed," Dana said. "They can't have a trial without the defendant. That pesky Constitution even applies to the U.S. Virgin Islands, although most of the time it doesn't seem that way. The judge is very, very angry with you. She chewed out Miguela, but your lawyer's a pro. She sidestepped the land mine, although we are going to have to be very convincing to keep from losing bail. You could be working on cases for Little Switzerland for the next ten years."

I laughed, but Dana only stared at me. I stopped laughing. "You're not kidding."

"I'm not," Dana said. "You gotta repay. How else?"

"Maybe I start smuggling with Sire."

"Not funny, Jabuti. Besides, you move too slow."

Henry piped up. "We cannot just kidnap these men and ship 'em to St. Thomas. You'll--we'll--be arrested for kidnapping and transport across state lines. Shit, into international waters. Let me handle this."

I threw up my hands. Mark Green grunted.

Henry spun on him. "What, Mark? What is it now?"

"I think I can help." His eyes shifted off the blank wall. "The life I've led. I still think I did the right thing, but Ronica and Jill. Those other girls. The ones Scott ..." he seemed to search for the right word, "... executed. They weren't supposed to be there. I had no idea they would be involved. I wanted to back out, but he said he'd take care of them and make sure the whole thing got pinned on Boise. He promised."

"You'll tell this to the police," I said.

"Yeah, I'll tell 'em."

"One more thing. Where the hell is my cell phone?"

Green dropped his head and pointed to a drawer in the kitchen. Sure enough, my phone was in there along with a bunch of batteries. The wailing ambulance arrived, punching a hole in the quiet morning.

CHAPTER 40

After the questioning by the police and the revelation that I was wanted at a trial in St. Thomas, the LAPD were inclined to arrest and prepare me for extradition. Henry went for his own debriefing. The arresting officer Mirandized everyone, and that's when I realized our mistake. The defense attorneys for both Anders and Green would have a field day with Green's statements made to us in the house, mainly because Henry was a volunteer cop and no warnings were given after the two killers were immobilized.

Henry convinced them to let me go, provided Dana made sure I was on the flight to St. Thomas at nine the following morning.

The overcast sky huddled over us as we drank beer and ate burgers. Dana had nothing to say about my alcoholic tendencies, and I did nothing to reassure her that I'd return to AA.

"Can you get me in to see my mother before I leave?" I asked

Henry as he dipped a fry into his ramekin of ketchup.

"What? Tonight? Where's she being held?"

"I'm not even sure at this point. It was in Marina del Rey."

"Hold on." Henry made a phone call, then sent a couple texts. "All right, all right. She's still in the same holding pen. You can see her for twenty minutes if you get there before six." I checked my watch. Enough time to finish my food and have one more beer to deaden my emotions.

Dana watched a screen above the bar where a college basketball game had just entered overtime. "You sure you want to do that? She's your mother, I know, but I don't think I could forgive anyone if they ran over Annie. Just sayin'."

"You see what I mean," I said.

Henry agreed. "Mighty direct, Ms. Goode."

"Why thank you, Henry. I'm glad some people appreciate those who don't inveigle. Jabuti takes it for granted."

"I don't … look, Dana, there's a time and a place. You just don't know when to stop. When talking to man about his dead wife and killer mother, that's the time to stop asking 'reporter questions' and be a supportive … whatever you are."

"No questions. I told you what I'd do."

Wasting my breath. "Henry, drive me over there?"

"Oh, no. The po-po said I gotta watch you. I'm coming."

A grin spread on Henry's face. "This chick gets better every time she puts you in your place."

"Watch it, Henry. You're still on thin ice."

The smile evaporated from Henry's face. "I'll pay for the beers."

***

We arrived at the jail and were ushered into a room with a low glass partition and little privacy. Everything felt like crappy Disney World: fake, overly planned, too much disinfectant. My mother looked like she'd missed the last train out of France before the Germans arrived.

"I didn't want to see you, but I want to know what happened to my car," she stammered.

Patrice Montague did not often sound unsure of herself, but this trial, these tribulations, this jail that would soon see her off to prison for twelve years, a kindness extended only because she appeared so fragile, dressed in weight-loss and gloomy hair.

"Are you eating?" I asked.

"The shit they serve in here? It goes through me like a goddamn box-car on Laurel Canyon. What happened to my car? Lizzie told me it's not in my parking space."

"You don't need it."

"Boise!" Her voice deepened and rose all at once.

"I disposed of it." I didn't bother trying to keep the disgust out of my voice. "You could show a wee-bit of contrition. At least you should have sold the murder weapon."

"It was an accident."

"It's gone to that big junkyard in the sky. Maybe it's been recycled into one of those new-fangled air fryers I'm thinking of getting for my room."

"You got-damn bitch! That's my car. I wanted that car. I had some good times in that car."

"You mean like running over my wife? Are those the good fucking times you're referring to, mother?"

She pounded the heel of her fist against the pressboard counter, which brought the shadowy guard off the wall. He pointed a finger. "You two can't visit like civilized folks, I'll cut this short." Mother cocked her head at the guard and wordlessly mouthed his warning and imitated his finger-pointing. He scowled, then leaned back again. Her hair resembled a sea anemone. We'd already packed ten-years' worth of pain into the first five minutes of this visit. I wasn't sure I could survive the remainder.

"I don't want to fight. I came to say goodbye. Gotta hurry back for my own murder trial."

She scoffed. "Good luck with that, son. If I knew anything I'd come testify and help put you in the goddamn slammer, too. That's what family's for, right?"

"Mom. Patrice. I told the truth."

"You know I don't like it when you call me that. It's 'Mother.' You know, I was stuck here after you abandoned me, and you made sure you went to the one shit place I'd never follow. Now, I'm supposed to believe that you had only good intentions in testifying here? You never wanted me around. I sure as shit know Evelyn hated me."

I scowled back at her and leaned forward till my breath fogged the glass. "I abandoned you? I abandoned Evelyn to keep you from going to jail. I didn't make you kill anyone. I stopped before I was certain, and convinced myself that it wouldn't bring her back if you went to prison. I let it lie. And here I am, torn to pieces and miserable. Unable to have a decent relationship because I can't let go of her."

"That gives you permission to destroy my personal property?" Her voice rose, her nostrils flared. "I loved that car! Loved it. A lot more than you love me."

I broke eye contact, gazing down at the pock-marked counter, soaked by the tears of wives, mothers, fathers, who had to speak through glass to a child, a spouse, someone they thought would be part of their lives until one or both of their lives ended. I wouldn't add to that trail. Patrice Montague showed no remorse. Somewhere, behind the closed doors of the jail, a woman's wail pierced our emotional bubble.

"Are you even sorry for what you did?" I asked quietly. I knew it was drowned by the wail, but I said it for myself as much as her.

"What? You gotta speak up in here. Lot of ambient noise. There's no goddamn peace."

"Never mind." I pulled in a ragged breath. "I had this nasty dream about a horse. It's stopped."

"A horse. Who cares? I'm in prison for twelve, and you're talking about horses. Boo-hoo."

I nodded, my head, still looking at the flat wooden surface below the phone. I imagined lawyers taking notes as their clients asserted innocence. I imagined my mother laying in wait, committing first-degree murder and getting away with a lesser charge, yet still being ungrateful about a lousy car. "You're right. You're right. Dreams are boring and God knows you've got places to be and days to count."

A drop of water plunked and split into a thousand drops next to my elbow. On the way out, I told the guard, "You've got a leak above window number seven."

CHAPTER 41

Outside, the sky wanted to weep, but this being L.A., no rain would fall. Henry had waited, which was more than I hoped for. He ran me back to my mother's place. They wouldn't let me through the gate.

"Received a notice today that you are not a welcome guest of Patrice Montague any longer," the guard read off her computer screen. Henry busted a u-turn. I shot the bird out my window as he jammed right on red where it said we shouldn't.

Henry let me crash at his place. Alone in the guest room, I charged my phone and checked it against my better judgment. I hadn't checked it in quite some time. A dozen texts from a Caribbean country code appeared on my screen. I couldn't believe it. I texted her back. One minute later she called.

"Hello, Celia. My God, how are you?"

It had been nearly a year since her kidnapping, but Celia Jarl sounded like a different person--breathy and mature. "Hello, Boise. My hero."

"Stop that, Celia. I've tried calling ..."

"Daddy keeps changing my numbers, and I just stay on the island now. He's very strict." I waited for more. "It's pretty boring here, but I have my spies to give me information."

"Spies?"

"A girl's gotta know what's happening in her home town. Especially, what's happening with private eyes who save lives."

"You're keeping ..." Then it hit me. "You? The doctor? From Miami. It was you."

"Is the knee healing well? I asked Daddy to send him. He's the best. He has a technique, like only he can perform."

"Jesus. Celia. Am I ... Your father asked his friend to fly down and operate on me?"

She giggled. "What's the big?"

We talked about pop singers and her hopes to go study at the Sorbonne in Paris. After a while, I said, "Celia, I have a long flight in the morning. Will I hear from you again?"

Another giggle. "I'd like to come visit, actually, but for now, yeah, I'll call when I can. Peace." She hung up.

CHAPTER 42

The next morning, before my flight, bright and early, Dana and Henry showed up. "Is traffic always so awful, even at six in the morning?" She scowled as she handed me a coffee from MV.

Henry and I exchanged good-byes, as he claimed to have early morning business. He seemed distant, like he'd made a decision during the night as he lay awake staring at his popcorn ceiling, about what I'd done. Maybe my guilt imbued him. Either way, we said few words and shared a fist-bump in parting.

"Mind if we make one stop?"

Dana replied from the back of the Uber, "We've got time," as she frantically typed something into her phone.

"Do you ever stop typing on gadgets?"

***

I texted and called Grace. No response. I knocked on Grace's door. No answer. De-De edged out of her apartment, tennis racquet in tow.

"Hello, Mr. Montague. Why don't you leave poor Grace alone?" The Susan Sarandon accent. She motioned over her shoulder. "And who's the trashy redhead in the Uber?"

"Have you seen Grace? I just want to make sure she's all right."

De-De crossed her arms. "Are we still in character? I don't like your choice. He sounds too wimpy."

I groaned. "No! No, we are not in character. This is not a play. This is life."

"Life is ..."

"De-De, just tell me where Grace is and if she's all right."

"Oh, my God! You haven't even asked how my scene went."

"I have a plane to catch."

"Scene went great! This teacher, Ivanka Coco, she has connections with all the big wigs. She started Brad Pitt and Parker Posey. She says I have star power. You believe it? I mean, I don't know. What do you ..."

"De-De! Grace."

De-De dropped her eyes, her long eyelashes almost drooping over her cheeks. I wondered if her eyelids ever got tired of lifting all the mascara. "Grace split. She said she was going home. Wherever that is. Midwest somewhere, I think. She said she'd send for her things. Said she's had it with L.A. Too many crazy men."

I nodded and wished her luck.

"Sure you don't want to come in and watch *Five Strangers* again?"

"I have a plane to catch."

That's when Grace's door creaked open. De-De's hands shot downward to her hips and she pushed to her tippy-toes. She pointed the tip of the racquet at Grace. "Graaaaaaaace! You said to get rid of him. Ugh!" De-De stormed back into her apartment and slammed the door.

We stood there … well, I stood there. She sat there. She looked haggard. Her eyebrows knitted and her mouth puckered. She struggled for composure. A scarf covered the bruises on her neck.

"I'm a bad judge of character," she mumbled. "I wanted to run back home."

"Nothing wrong …"

"You have a plane to catch, remember? Is that redhead your girlfriend? Never mind, don't answer that. I wanted to flee. I'm a fool, a wannabe. I wanna save the universe, but I can't even get my life started. I'm like a Post-It that won't stick. I started packing my stuff, to run back to the Midwest. To live in an Edward Scissorhands neighborhood and be wheeled around by people who'd pretend to feel sorry for me, but really just like feeling superior. You know the type. Somehow, I heard that stupid, overplayed Frank Sinatra song about New York. I heard it in the drug store last night as I waited for my anti-anxiety prescription. He talked about making it there and making it anywhere. You know the one?"

My cheeks sagged like small sacks of flour. She kept furling and unfurling her brow, the battle with unseen things.

"Anyways, I want to make it here, so De-De wasn't really lying, but I came back." She rolled backwards to reveal suitcases in the entryway. "Do you think it's the right thing?"

I thought of Junior Bacon disappearing off St. Thomas. Running. There was nothing wrong with it, but there was nothing wrong with staying and fixing the broken glass of your life either.

"If you really mean it. Places are all the same. Trees, buildings, flowers, concrete. The people make the place. You could be one of the people who makes L.A."

Her mouth relaxed and her brow parted. A single watery prisoner escaped and dribbled down her cheek.

"Boise!" It was Dana at the end of the hallway. She tapped her wrist.

CHAPTER 43

Miguela arranged an emergency hearing with the judge in chambers. The prosecutor remained standing by her chair.

"I said, have a seat, Attorney Cleveland," the judge demanded.

Eleanor Cleveland had been insisting that this was not over. She wanted to interview the other suspects more extensively before releasing me. The judge told her to sit and shut it as her continuing defiance bordered on contempt.

"Eleanor, I have read the documents, all the evidence, and all that The People here and in California have provided." Prosecutor Cleveland looked taken aback by the informal address. "You may not be satisfied, but I am. This man, Boise, has been through enough. Additionally, I am dropping the assault charge against his fellow inmate. The inmate insists that Mr. Montague had nothing to do with it, although he's not saying who the perpetrator was."

This all sounded good to me, but Miguela's face remained impassive. My optimism was short-lived. "You've been a busy body, Mr. Montague," Judge Bugleson said with a stern glare. "Seeing as you've already wasted this court's time considerably, what with jumping bail and causing all sorts of delays to many people's lives, including my own."

"Excuse me, Your Honor, if I may."

If possible, the chamber got colder. Law books lined the shelves and a diploma from Columbia Law School adorned the wall above the judge's head.

After a cavernous pause, Bugleson declared, "Counselor Salas, I would recommend you put a leash on your client. Miscarriage of justice or not, I do not like being interrupted."

My mind drifted into a fantasy of laying around in my room watching Andre Dawson. If I got out of this, I'd find some way to watch a mid-season '89 Dawson at bat for the Chicago Cubs showcasing his broad shoulders and rapid through-the-zone bat speed.

"Mr. Montague!" Judge Bugleson jerked me out of my man-crush-reverie. "I would appreciate your attention. Now, despite your flagrant disregard, and I do mean flagrant, for the laws of this great territory, I'm only going to take ten-thousand of your bail money, although the territory would be well within its rights, and needs, to take the entire hundred."

I started to protest, but the judge's face made it clear, as did Miguela, who crossed her arms, that if I pushed, she would double the penalty, or indeed, tag me with the whole amount, effectively shoving my financial well-being off a cliff.

"You can rest assured, the ten thousand will go to a good cause, namely repairing the water damage on the east wall of the records office." She smiled at me. "We appreciate your contribution to the cause of freedom of information in the Virgin Islands. Otherwise, since these other fellows are being brought in from California to face trial, you are free to go as even our ..."

She cleared her throat. "… unorthodox legal system does not allow for two separate trials simultaneously for the same crime, despite the ambitions of the learned prosecutor."

I hugged Miguela, who stiffened.

"Mr. Montague! No inappropriate touching of your attorney in my chambers. Jesus, man, have you no etiquette? Were you raised in a warehouse?"

"No, ma'am, but I live in a guesthouse, Your Honor." I wanted to tell her smug face that we were married, but I didn't want Miguela to slit my throat. Nonetheless, nothing this judge said or did could dissuade my joy. I'd soon be laying in bed, watching the Cubs win one off the Giants.

"Mr. Montague, you will show respect and pay attention. Now, it has been a flagrant miscarriage of justice you suffered, however," she held up a finger to stop my blossoming grin, "you will not be getting any kind of settlement out of this territory."

"Ma'am?"

"There's more to this. These men. These killers." She said the last word like Katherine Hepburn, with a mild Caribbean accent. "They framed you. Why? Did you do something?"

I looked at Miguela. Still nothing. "What is this? Can she do this?"

Miguela's eyes rolled to me, then back to the judge. "She's the judge. She has wide discretion to question and debate."

The judge nodded. "Listen to your attorney, Mr. Montague. It took me twenty years of blood, sweat, and misogyny to get here." Miguela tolerated judges the way chefs tolerated heat. "Why did these men do this? Merely to be mean to you?"

What the hell, she'd eventually find out. "Judge, they came after me because I failed to bring a killer to justice, and they wanted to punish me for that."

"And the victims? What was their involvement?"

"This seems irregular for a judge …"

"Don't worry about it, young man, I won't be trying their case."

"The victims were convenient. I think the one guy is a sadist and this was an opportunity to kill two women and put it on someone else. He just wanted to kill. The other woman—Felicia Nichols—was killed because of perceived disloyalty to her boss, Mark Green. He's the second killer, but really, he was used."

"How noble of you to make excuses for your framer. Now, was that so hard? As I always say, only those with something to hide refuse to cooperate."

I said nothing. After she signed the order for my release and handed a copy to Miguela, she rose and we rose, since for some god-forsaken reason everyone had to stand when judges stand as if they're fucking royalty.

"I have to get working on these others," Prosecutor Cleveland said, not bothering to hide her annoyance at not getting to put her own questions to me.

After Cleveland left, the door slipped shut, and Miguela gave me a nod. We headed for the exit. As I stepped through the door, Judge Bugleson said, "One more thing, Mr. Montague, call my cousin." We waited for her to finish reviewing something on her desk. She removed her horn-rimmed glasses and pointed them at me. "Do it today. Once you tell me that you and Elias have spoken and that you and he will meet regularly, then I will release your funds, or rather Annie Von Kurks'. Mr. Montague, treat him better. You're the only man he trusts and his father was your closest friend."

St. Thomas was a small place.

CHAPTER 44

Before heading home, I stopped by Bob's Store. Old Wendel must have given up on me coming back, as he had an ad for part-time work in the paper that I spotted after reading the teaser story Dana had written about my fiasco. I wanted to make a living solely as a private detective, but I suspected that was going to be harder than ever.

Wendel paid in cash at the end of each day, and I needed cash, desperately. He agreed to rehire me, saying that innocent men were welcome. The simplicity of the store appealed after the complexity of the last three months.

"Glad you made it. Got superstitions 'bout jails. Hospitals, too. Hold on," Wendel hollered at a guy examining the liquor shelves. "I once gave this bastard a bottle because the label had a misprint. Now, he comes in searching for them every time I get a new shipment. Cheapskate! Pay for your rum like everyone else. I sell it cheaper'n anyone else 'round here. I already told you, no more freebies, even if the label's wrong."

The man kept checking one after the other. The cheapskate had a superpower that I didn't possess: the ability to ignore people, even when they were hollering at you. Miguela possessed it, too.

Wendell ushered the vagrant out, then motioned to the back of the store. "Something just came in. Thought it might look good in your private eye office."

We slipped into a cluttered area in the back. On a table sat a contraption with a marble and dominos set up.

He dropped the marble into a shoot. It filtered through the device, causing pulleys to move and things to roll. At the end, a set of ten dominos tumbled over. The last one fell into a slot that lowered, causing a small Virgin Islands flag to unfurl while the Virgin Islands March, plucked inside a music box. It reminded me of a tune from a Disney movie, but I couldn't recall which one.

The tune concluded. From behind us, a man said, "What's that thing run?"

"It's not for sale," I said. "Thank you, Wendel."

"Yeah, yeah, whatever," Wendel said, his salty beard spread to reveal crooked teeth. "I'll see you tomorrow for real this time, right?"

***

Back at *The Manner* I found Lucy and Marge in the bar, throwing darts as one ratty customer, who made a living ferrying people to snorkeling spots once a week, nursed a drink. Lucy leveled her gaze and crossed her arms. Marge wrinkled her nose, then headed behind the bar. "What you want?"

I couldn't look at Lucy, so I smiled and looked over at Silent Marge busying herself with dirty glasses. "I suppose I'm lucky she doesn't speak."

"What you want?" Lucy repeated.

I pulled a set of sheets out of a bag slung over my forearm. "I'm sorry for vomiting on your sheets."

Lucy's scowl faltered as she opened the package and fingered the satin sheets. "Deez ain't da right sheets for our guests. We ain't da Waldorf."

"They're for you and Marge. I already replaced my own. Those are two-thousand thread count babies," I muttered like I was sharing a dirty secret.

"Fine. You could stay." Lucy punched me in the arm.

CHAPTER 45

Dana slapped her knee, threw her head back, and howled with laughter. "Shit, Boise, you know how to pick 'em. Bugleson is Roger Black's aunt? And, you are indebted to Cecil Jarl?" I got up and closed the cantaloupe-colored door to my dusty office. The Rube Goldberg device dominated my desk. I'd just run it for Dana and the music box was still playing the tail end of the anthem.

"Yeah. It's Celia's fault."

"That's what you get for saving a young woman's life: her arranging for you to owe the shadiest character south of Cuba a debt. Don't you also owe that witch something for fixin' your knee and the flower thing?"

I'd forgotten about my debt to U. That would also have to wait until another day. "Please, I'm trying not to think about it. I'm focusing on the less scary prospect of Elias' great-aunt. Apparently, her nephew complained a lot about me. What happened to manly discretion?"

"I think that died in the mid-nineties." The march ended with a flourish. "Anyway, you better meet up with Elias asap, because Annie expects her money back soon."

"Relax. I already arranged to take him out to a ballgame at Lionel Stadium next week."

Dana snatched another slice of the banana bread that my favorite nurse had left in front of my cantaloupe office door. She'd already eaten half the tin. I'd only managed one slice. I hoped to save some to enjoy later a la mode. "Hey, I thought you said you didn't like bananas!"

Dana picked up the marble. "Fun contraption, but you really ought to decorate this place a little. A movie poster of something filmed here." She snapped her fingers. *"Weekend at Bernie's Two."* When I said nothing, because I was busy thinking about how I was going to pay off the ten-grand I owed Annie, she said, "You know, if you'd just have had lunch with the kid once in a while, he would probably be fine. He doesn't seem that needy. You have time."

"Not anymore," I said, sulking.

She slapped the desk. "There it is, glass-is-half-full Boise. So you owe ten-grand, and you're married to a lawyer. Annie'll let you work it off. If you recover this stolen Rolex and do a couple more jobs, you should be back in the black. The main thing is, you didn't get executed, or even significant jail time. The governor has decided to go after Green and Anders with the death penalty, but the attorney general's fighting him."

I began resetting the dominos in their slots to run the machine again. "What about Miguela? I don't even like her. She's awkward."

"That's why I've never been married. Everyone's awkward."

"You despise convention."

"I do, but that's besides the point. Come on, finish telling me about California so I can turn in this final article."

I wasn't supposed to tell anyone about the marriage, but if you couldn't trust a reporter to keep "off the record" comments secret, what could you trust? I still had no idea what purpose our marriage served, but Miguela had held up her end of the bargain, so I'd hold up mine. She now owned my name and address. I would never get married again, so what did it matter? Didn't even have much interest in dating.

"After that, I'm going after the prison system," Dana said.

"Please don't. I just want to leave it alone."

Dana scoffed. "Not doing it for you. Oh, almost forgot." She pulled a bulky, lightweight box out of her hobo-bag and handed it to me. I opened it.

"You shouldn't have." I stuffed my blossoming head of black curls into the hat. "Is it going to solve anything? Some decent people might get hurt."

"Someone from that prison is going down. This is bigger than you, Boise, although I'm not sure it's bigger than your hair. I couldn't look at the frizz anymore, so really that hat was for me."

***

I arrived at Julian's house on the third Friday night in late January, 2016. My ordeal had begun in November 2015, merely three months ago, but it felt like I'd been dealing with this murder rap for a lifetime. Julian had been kind to me in prison.

When I arrived at Julian's ramshackle house for dinner, Kenny and his daughter, the devil child I'd danced for while incarcerated, were in the kitchen. I pulled Julian aside. "What the hell is this?"

"They like to cook, and it's good." The food did smell enticing. It had been a long time since someone had cooked a meal for me in a house that wasn't a guesthouse.

"Hey, Boise! Told you we'd hook it up, mi son. Dis here me daughter. Say hello to your dancin' friend." She turned her little

294

face away. "Come on, come on, Tamara. Say hello. Dis man ain't goin' harm you."

"Dad-ee, you said he was a multiplex killer. I'm scared!" She moved behind her father. When she said, 'dad-ee', my knee throbbed.

Kenny smiled big. Awkward wrinkles spread from his eyes like fingers. I guessed he was around thirty and the girl looked twelve, but acted like six. "Sorry about dis. Her mother tell her not to come. She puttin' bad ideas in she head. Tamara, dis man ain't kill no one. He find da killers. It was two odda men."

Tamara's eyes widened. "So, he ain't kill no one?"

I jumped in. "Well, Tamara, I've kinda killed people, but in self-defense."

Kenny and Julian glared at me like I'd lost my mind. I winced, realizing I was trying to justify killing someone to a twelve-year-old.

Julian squeezed my shoulder amiably, but firmly, so I followed. "Boise, why don't I get you somet'ing to drink?"

Spending the evening with a man who had framed me for assault and beaten me, was not my idea of a good time. I let Julian know this.

"I understand," Julian said, his soft, clear eyes sitting on me with their knowingness that reminded me of a former client who'd vanished. Julian's lower lip drooped like it weighed more than the rest of his face. Perhaps people's inability to look past his hangdog manner had kept Julian confined to the recesses of the penal system when, in fact, he should have been a teacher or a counselor. He wanted to help people. "You need to hear me out on this."

"Julian, you ambush me with this bullshit. I'm exhausted. I've done nothing except worry about my freedom for months. I came here to spend the evening with you, maybe watch some sports, drink a soda. How is it we're here with a demon and his demon spawn? You're friends with this psycho?"

"He's not a psycho. Under a lot of stress. Tamara," he casually indicated the girl standing at the stove with her father, stirring a pot. "She got a rare form of M.S. that affects kids. She has a hard life. He is very angry. Been drinking a lot, but he's in a program."

I scowled at Kenny and his stupid helpless daughter. "Yippie-doo. Dude ratted me out."

"No. No. He's a lot of things. He's not a rat. You talking about the judge knowing you left the island? That was Jenkins, not Kenny."

Jenkins, that prick. Holding a grudge for his old man.

Kenny propped Tamara on his knee, letting her stir the pot. He seemed pretty sweet with his daughter, but then again many killers were sweet to their own children, it didn't make them good people. I had fantasized for months about putting him in prison. I hadn't felt much better about his rabid daughter, who'd egged on her father to make me dance for her pleasure.

"Just for tonight, can you just do it for tonight. He won't apologize with words, but he's a hell of a cook. It's his way." Julian shrugged an oversized shoulder. "You just gotta eat the food. Oh, and we got you something, but not till after dessert."

I clenched my teeth, licked my lips and fingered my pocket floss. "Fine," I muttered.

We ate. The food was scrumptious and spicy. The dessert was some kind of mango-guava sorbet that defied gravity. They gave me a brand-new hardcover version of *Crime and Punishment*.

Later that night, in bed at The Manner, I read the last four pages, which made me feel slightly less cynical about humanity and my marriage. Slightly.

Meet a new character from the pen of Gene Desrochers.

Rajiv Nap is a tennis professional struggling to figure out what to do after leaving the tour. He lands a job at a residential club in West Los Angeles shortly after the end of the Covid epidemic. Little does he know that the crazy characters who live and play at The Oceanfront Club will test his ability to make it in the real world like nothing he's ever encountered.

Keep reading to enjoy an excerpt now.

CHAPTER ONE

It's much easier to stay friends with people if you don't know them too well. Rajiv Nap was no exception to this rule. Waiting to turn left into the gated entrance, he kneaded a mushy red ball in his left hand. He did this in an effort to balance out the inequities between the right and left sides of his body. In this respect, as in so many others, he'd failed miserably.

#

Rajiv didn't much like his penis. It functioned. He had sex in the usual ways and with the usual people, women mostly.

At twelve years old, a kid on his soccer team pointed at his bare midriff in the locker room and declared that Rajiv had a small penis. Raj tried his best not to let the other kids see it, but sometimes people saw you naked. One of the meanest kids in the school, a kid they called "Freddie-Forearms", on account of his bulbous forearms, pantsed him while Coach Head squeezed one of his eternal dumps in the corner stall out of earshot.

Raj didn't remember the name of the kid who pointed out his short-comings, but he remembered his face. That face haunted him, like the chiding of a disappointed father. Long chin, spiky hair, an allergic complexion. Raj possessed the clairvoyance to recognize that the kid would rush and become the president of a frat, then proceed to drink beer at parties and date-rape sorority girls. He would swell on the power he garnered from demeaning every freshman who rushed for years to come. That would be the highlight of the young buck's life.

Getting back to Raj's penis. Regardless of size, it functioned in the usual ways. The tip of the penis causes lots of problems. Sometimes life altering problems that cannot be remedied. Possessors of a penis hoped that they matured or got lucky in their youth, when the penis' power was at its height, and didn't suffer those consequences for the rest of their lives. But sometimes the choices led you down a path, caused you to converge in a wood where there was no going back.

Rajiv Nap arrived at the gate of the Oceanfront Club, penis pointed straight ahead, the tip as sharp as the arrow on a compass. Seagulls hooted. A dollop of guano plopped on his windshield. He cursed, pulled the lever next to the steering wheel. The white dung smeared in a parabola. He cursed again.

The stench of Sulphur wafted through his window. A slimy body of water surrounded by recent landscaped succulents and eucalyptus trees, burbled behind him across the street. In front of him, a black Tesla crouched, waiting for the guard to let him through. The Tesla's license plate proclaimed "TOPBUNS" on one of the popular retro California yellow-on-black plates. Raj had recently registered his clunker and knew anyone sporting those vanity plates needed people to notice them or had money to burn. Probably both. They cost more than twice as much as regular plates and for the life of him, Raj couldn't see the value of yellow and black over blue and white.

A pair of tentacle arms waved from the driver's side window and an unnaturally long finger extended off one of the arms toward the building behind the guard shack. The guard's sleepy expression remained intact, a corded phone held to her ear as if waiting for the go-ahead to execute the Tesla driver. A black face mask covered her nose and mouth. Spittle ejected from inside the car as the finger pointed more pointedly.

Lots of people still wore the masks. Raj had his on, even while driving alone. It made no sense, but he felt relief of a sort from its now comforting presence in his life. The pandemic had worn on so long it really had become normal. The authorities sent mixed messages about whether people should still wear a mask. Vaccinations had reached the seventy-six percent mark and many had defected to the dark side, choosing the small rebellion as their only means of protest against the microscopic invaders.

Mr. Tesla screeched, causing a woman wearing an elaborately sequined face-mask and walking a chihuahua to stare. Raj pondered why anyone would wear a fur in Southern California during summer. Cold shoulders, he thought, chuckling. His amusement died as he contemplated meeting his new boss and starting his first real job.

Raj rolled down his window. He checked the console clock. The guard didn't seem predisposed to letting Mr. Tesla through the gate.

"What the fuck, lady. I have an appointment I'm late for!" Hollered Mr. Tesla. "Open this gate. He knows I'm coming. We have a meeting. Michael Carmichael. He's in the penthouse right there. I'm his goddamn agent. How many times do I have to tell you people?" A brief pause, presumably to catch his breath, then bull-horn loud, his hands cupped around his mouth, "Let's gooooooo!" The tentacles extended again and the single gangly finger pointed up at the top of the split round building.

Despite his displeasure, Mr. Tesla took the time to check his look in the sideview mirror. As he did so, the man stared at

Raj's face. He swiveled his owl-head and yelled, "What are you lookin' at?"

Raj raised his hands off the steering wheel, his face a mask of innocence, even as the pace of his breathing increased.

Mr. Tesla shot Raj the bird. "Yeah, what I thought. We're all in this together!"

If you enjoyed this excerpt, please go to your favorite retailer to pre-order *Oceanfront* today.

THANK YOU READER

Thank you for reading *Crime Paradise*. Your support of my book by spending the time to read means a lot considering all the other options you have. I love reading and enjoy hearing what other readers have to say about my books or any books. If you feel the impulse, please email or drop a line through my website: GeneDesrochers.com. If you liked this book enough to keep reading, please continue on below to read an excerpt from my forthcoming, as yet untitled, novel.

ACKNOWLEDGEMENTS

There are people, places, and other beings, who make my life as an author and this book in particular possible. My lifemate, Ms. Marvelous, a.k.a. Mindy. She reads to me, supports me, brightens the days, and shows belief when I have none left. My daughter, Miriam, inspires with her appreciation of her own special writing skills and support. My publishers, Acorn, Holly & Jessica, who gave me a shot and continue to let me keep shooting. My extraordinarily encouraging editor, Laura Taylor, who tirelessly poured over the pages until they were better. My writing ally, Elena Felix. To Ben, my son, who's long journey into manhood mirrors my own. To my parents for exposing me to so much sorrow and joy. To the islands, that still own my heart. To everyone who read early versions and shared your thoughts to help me craft a better tale: Shane Valentine, R.D. Kardon, and Tom Wing. Any faults with the story and research are entirely my own.

ABOUT THE AUTHOR

Photo © 2018 Miriam Sachs

Gene Desrochers lives and works in Los Angeles with his wife, kids, and cats. He is originally from St. Thomas. *Crime Paradise* is his third novel. He practices law when he isn't writing. If you ask he will regale you with his Caribbean accent and tennis prowess. Find out more about him – and the worlds he creates – at his website, GeneDesrochers.com.